ANATOPSIS

ANATOPSIS

Chris Abouzeid

DUTTON CHILDREN'S BOOKS

New York

DUTTON CHILDREN'S BOOKS
A division of Penguin Young Readers Group
Published by the Penguin Group
Penguin Group (USA) Inc., 375 Hudson Street, New York, New York 10014, U.S.A.
Penguin Group (Canada), 90 Eglinton Avenue East, Suite 700, Toronto, Ontario,
Canada M4P 2Y3 (a division of Pearson Penguin Canada Inc.)
Penguin Books Ltd, 80 Strand, London WC2R 0RL, England
Penguin Ireland, 25 St Stephen's Green, Dublin 2, Ireland
(a division of Penguin Books Ltd)
Penguin Group (Australia), 250 Camberwell Road, Camberwell, Victoria 3124, Australia
(a division of Pearson Australia Group Pty Ltd)
Penguin Books India Pvt Ltd, 11 Community Centre, Panchsheel Park,
New Delhi - 110 017, India
Penguin Group (NZ), Cnr Airborne and Rosedale Roads, Albany,
Auckland 1310, New Zealand (a division of Pearson New Zealand Ltd)
Penguin Books (South Africa) (Pty) Ltd, 24 Sturdee Avenue, Rosebank, Johannesburg 2196,
South Africa
Penguin Books Ltd, Registered Offices: 80 Strand, London WC2R 0RL, England

This book is a work of fiction. Names, characters, places, and incidents are either the product
of the author's imagination or are used fictitiously, and any resemblance to actual persons,
living or dead, business establishments, events, or locales is entirely coincidental.

CIP Data is available.

Published in the United States by Dutton Children's Books,
a division of Penguin Young Readers Group
345 Hudson Street, New York, New York 10014
www.penguin.com/youngreaders

Designed by Irene Vandervoort
Printed in USA   First Edition
ISBN 0-525-47583-4
10   9   8   7   6   5   4   3   2   1

For Kathy

Acknowledgments

Special thanks to Tatiana Wilcke, who inspired the original version of this story and suffered through its unsuccessful birth; to my mother and father, for their love and support over the years; to Mark and Pam and especially Mandy, for blessing me from the start with their enthusiasm and expertise; to my editor, Julie Strauss-Gabel, for recognizing the promise of this novel and making it so much better than it was; to Eliza McCormack and the Tuesday-night workshop, for their critiques and encouragement; to Susan Benett, for reviving my dreams of being a writer; and to all my friends who did not laugh when I told them I was writing a novel.

I am grateful to the following organizations for their support over the years: the Massachusetts Cultural Council, the Somerville Arts Council, and the St. Botolph Club Foundation. Thanks also to my friends at *SAIL*, Harris & Jeffries, rock.com, the law office of Andrew Cornell, and, of course, the great people at True Grounds and the Diesel Café for keeping me awake during the many months of rewriting.

Last but most important of all, I need to give endless thanks to my wife, Kathy, whose love and encouragement revived this book (and me) time and time again, and to Callie and Ben, who remind me every day why I love children and children's literature.

ANATOPSIS

Part I

Chapter 1

IN THE LATTER HALF of the Universe's most recent outward explosion, when things were slowing down a bit but not yet falling apart, when "alive" was still an exciting if not completely safe thing to be, there was a small planet with which you are familiar. In its youth, it had been bright blue, like a marble, but had since turned the color of badly mixed paint. And if you were to draw near it, you would in fact see that its waters were composed of a mishmash of pigments—rust, algae, methane, phosphorus—all whipped together by the tremendous waves and whirlpools that plagued this planet's surface. This was not a hospitable place, not the sort of world upon which one would expect to find life. And yet, there was one small spot of life left: a gaudy eye of land, its pupil grassy, its iris glinting with steel and glass, the lids speckled with castles and moats and lined with twin blue rivers.

On the southern lid of this island, in a magnificent castle atop the hill, there lived a princess named Anatopsis Solomon. Anatopsis— or Ana, as she preferred to be called—was the daughter of a witch, descended from a long line of witches, and there would be nothing especially unusual about this except that her mother, Queen Abigail Solomon, happened to be chairperson and president of Amalgamated Witchcraft Corporation (or AW, as it was more commonly called).

If you picture Ana's mother as the old-fashioned, cackling-but-colorful sort of witch one finds in fairy tales, you will be dangerously mistaken. She was a modern witch—shrewd, calculating, commanding to the last degree. She presided over a board of twelve witches and warlocks, directed thousands of employees, both magical and ordinary, and worked day and night to maintain her reputation as the most powerful woman in the Universe.

To the casual observer, Ana appeared to be a perfect copy of her mother. She was blessed with her mother's beauty—the long flaxen hair, moon-white skin, and green eyes so essential for beguiling friends and enemies. She had also inherited her mother's aptitude for all things magical. By the age of two, she had read her first Magic Primer; by three, she had mastered all of the Counting Spells; and by the age of five, she could set a cat to running in circles so tight it would explode with static electricity. In short, she was a prodigy.

The similarities between mother and daughter ended there, however. For whereas the Queen interchromafied her hair a necromantic black and kept it perfectly coiffed, Ana's hair resembled an unraveling rope. And whereas the Queen never behaved in any manner that did not suggest pride, dignity, and complete confidence, Ana was moody and unpredictable. One moment she might be shouting and flying about the castle with an old sword, whacking the heads off the gargoyles; the next she might be glowering and melancholy, a princess trapped in a windowless tower. And whereas the Queen believed there was no question that Ana would follow in her dear mother's footsteps, Ana had no interest at all in the family business.

"I want to be a knight-errant, like Father," she said, one morning a few days before her thirteenth birthday. She and her mother were seated at the long, polished witchadder table in the dining room. Ana had already managed to spill melonfish juice and crumbs of newt bread all over her ice-blue dress. "He gets to travel and meet lots of interesting people. He doesn't sit at a desk all day worrying about his net worth or which employees don't like him."

"Darling," the Queen replied, her back perfectly straight, her elbows tucked in, the skin of her melonfish removed in three deft movements of knife and fork, "if it weren't for my net worth, your father would be peddling used spells to half-witted hags. Or, more likely, hanging from a hook in a dragon's lair."

Ana scowled. Her father, Sir Christopher, was the best knight-errant in the Guild. He had traveled to nearly every corner of the Universe and brought back more relics and rare artifacts and disposed of more dragons than any knight-errant in history. Nevertheless, what her mother said was true: Without the Queen to support him, Sir Christopher would likely be a pauper by now.

And without her protection, he might have been eaten long ago, or worse.

"In any case, Anatopsis, I did not ask what sort of future you *want*," her mother went on. "I asked what sort of future you expect to have. You've missed two classes this month, and your tutor informs me that your performance has been abysmal."

"But it's so boring, Mother," Ana said. "I go to class all day. I do my homework at night, and then it's dinner and more homework and bed. I never get to go anywhere or see anyone or do anything. I hate it."

"Well, I took you into the city for your birthday just last year," the Queen said. "We went to a very nice restaurant, as I recall, and—"

"And then to your office, where you made me sit through that awful lecture about the new spellbinding system."

The Queen scowled. "I see," she said, stabbing at a fleshy cube of melonfish on her plate. "I had no idea you felt that way, Anatopsis. But since it was so awful for you, perhaps *this* birthday should be spent in class."

"You wouldn't!" Ana said, horrified at the thought of losing her holiday.

"Of course I would," the Queen said. "However, as it happens, Madame Mumm is gone. I dismissed her this morning."

Ana dropped her fork. Madame Mumm, the pinch-faced one-eyed crone who had been her tutor since she was three years old, was gone? Why? What had she done?

"Oh, don't look so surprised, Anatopsis," her mother said. "It is going to be your thirteenth birthday, after all. That means exactly one year from Friday, you will be taking your Bacchanalian examinations. Surely you didn't expect me to rely on a decrepit old thing like Madame Mumm to prepare you for the most important moment of your life?"

"Are . . . are you sending me away, then?" Ana asked, remembering all the times her mother had threatened to send her to Arctura 5, the remedial education planet.

"Oh, quite the contrary. I am giving you a little holiday until your new tutor arrives, and then I am chaining you to your desk," the Queen said, leaning back in her chair. "Mr. Pound will be here in a few days. I think you will find him quite . . . unique." She said this with an amused twist of the lips that did not bode well, Ana thought.

"In addition to a new tutor," the Queen continued, "I will be adding a new pupil to your class: Barnaby Georges."

"*Prince* Barnaby Georges?" Ana said, now completely bewildered. To be allowed to have a classmate—after all these years of begging and pleading—was a shock in and of itself. But Barnaby Georges, son of King Georges, the Queen's most hated competitor? Ana's mother could scarcely mention the King's name without turning twelve shades of purple. Why would she invite his son to share lessons with Ana?

"I—I don't understand. Why him? Why here?" Ana said.

"It's a tradition, darling," the Queen replied. "The heirs of the

Solomon and Georges families have always shared their final year of their education. Didn't you know?"

No, Ana had never heard of this tradition. And judging by the look of mock innocence on her mother's face, she had not been meant to know—until now.

"You see, darling," the Queen explained, "your new tutor, Mr. Pound, has prepared every Solomon witch and Georges warlock for the Bacchanalian exams since your great-great-grandmother was your age."

"But—but I've never even heard of him," Ana said. "And why does he teach the two families together? It doesn't make sense."

"I don't know why you have never heard of him. Perhaps if you listened more and complained less, Anatopsis," the Queen said. "As for teaching the two families together, it certainly would not be my preference. But it is a condition of his services, and, as you will shortly learn, one does not question Mr. Pound's conditions.

"Now then, when I was your age, I went to Georges Castle. When my mother was your age, Archibald Georges the Second came to our castle. It has been that way for generations now, and odd as it may seem to you, the arrangement is well worth the trouble. For without Mr. Pound's gifts, our glorious little clan would be nothing more than a mediocre family in a dreary, mass-produced castle along the river."

"I don't understand," Ana said.

"No, you don't. But you shall. In the meantime, consider this: You have the potential to be a great witch. In fact, you might become the greatest Solomon witch ever, if you listen to your dear mama. Prince Barnaby, on the other hand, has been through a dozen different tutors and still cannot remember which end of an asp to avoid. It's amazing King Georges hasn't obliterated him.

"Nevertheless, Mr. Pound is capable of miracles, and this boy will be your competitor one day. So I suggest you be on your guard and devote yourself completely to your studies, lest you find yourself working for him. Is that clear?"

Ana nodded.

"Good. Now, I'm going to have a guest room made up for him," the Queen continued. "He'll be free to return to Georges Castle on the weekends, but I doubt he will. His father has been much more temperamental than usual, of late."

"Aren't you worried he might spy on us?" Ana asked.

The Queen laughed. "Prince Barnaby is an incompetent nut-brained imbecile," she said. "I doubt he could discover how many flames there are on a candle, much less anything useful. Nevertheless, he will be monitored."

The Queen excused Ana from the table but stopped her as she reached the door.

"I want to be absolutely clear about one thing, Anatopsis," the Queen said. "Barnaby Georges is coming here because Mr. Pound demands it—no other reason. You will share classes with him, but beyond that, you are to keep your distance. He is not your friend. He is not a playmate. He is the enemy, and you will remember that at all times. Is that clear?"

Ana nodded. The Queen dismissed her again, and Ana walked out dazed and bewildered. How could her mother have kept this tradition—if that's what it truly was—a secret all these years? And the way she had smiled at the mention of Mr. Pound . . . what did that mean?

She went in search of her father, hoping he could shed light on these mysterious changes. She found him in the Subterranean Spell & Curse Casting Range (or SSCCR, as it was called)—an underground practice area that was little more than an enormous cavern hewn out of the rock beneath the castle. Its illusion-generating mechanism could reproduce anything from a single venomous vipermoth to an entire six-dimensional city, and there were only two such facilities in the entire Universe—one at Solomon Castle, the other at Georges Castle.

As Ana entered the chamber, a large slavering ogre with a terrible overbite was charging toward her father. Sir Christopher, a tall and gangly knight with comet white hair and a nose like a sword point, was standing in chain mail and tunic with sword drawn, ready to lop off the ogre's head. He did not notice, however, the Eonian saber-toothed slug darting toward him from the side. As Sir Christopher attacked the ogre, Ana fired a Salt Stream Spell at the slug, dissolving it into a puddle of ooze.

Sir Christopher commanded the SSCCR's mechanism to stop.

All traces of the slug and ogre disappeared, leaving only a dozen mice to scurry off into the darkness. There were always mice in the cavern—the SSCCR needed "living frames" for its illusions, and mice were far easier to house and care for than real trolls or saber-toothed slugs.

"Darling, I appreciate the assistance, but that was a bit cruel, don't you think?" Sir Christopher said, sheathing his sword.

"Sorry. It was the first spell that came to mind," Ana said.

While her father unbuckled his sword and began removing his greaves, she told him about her conversation with the Queen. At the mention of Mr. Pound, Sir Christopher suddenly looked very sheepish.

"Ahem. Yes, well—I suppose it's time, isn't it?" he said.

"You knew about him all along? And you didn't tell me?" Ana said.

"Your mother said she would banish me to the outer moons of Jupiter if I so much as whispered it in my sleep. But don't worry. Mr. Pound's an unpleasant fellow, but he has taught four generation of Solomons and Georges, and they've all come through without a scratch. Besides, I'll be here to protect you."

"I thought you were going off on another grail quest in a few days."

Sir Christopher blushed. "Yes, well, knight-erranting's not what it used to be, you know, and these grail quests are a frightful waste of resources. I thought perhaps I would stay home for a while."

Ana could not believe her ears. Her father had not stayed home for more than a month at a time since she was born. He had missed at least half her birthdays. And now he was going to be here every day?

"Oh, Father—that's wonderful!" she said, throwing her arms around him.

"I thought you'd like that," he said, grinning. "I just have to pop over to Guild Headquarters tomorrow to apply for a leave of absence."

"Tomorrow? But my birthday's in two days," Ana said.

"Oh, I'll be back in plenty of time." He gave Ana a kiss on the forehead, then went off to change his clothes.

As Ana climbed the eight flights from the deepest part of the castle to her bedroom, she wondered what her new tutor would be like. *Unpleasant fellow,* her father had said. What did that mean? She hoped it only referred to his appearance, but she was too excited by her father's news to care. Her father was going to stay! She could not wait to tell Clarissa.

Chapter 2

WHEN ANA REACHED HER BEDROOM, her best friend, Clarissa, was lying on one of the twin beds, reading a fat volume titled *Artimedius's Illustrated Guide to Olympus*. She was dressed in her chambermaid's uniform, her thick, copper hair tied into its usual braid, but she had clearly not ventured off the bed all morning except to borrow another book from the castle's library (a forbidden habit that the Queen often threatened to cure by turning her "grubby paws" into flowerpots).

"Don't you feel obliged to at least *pretend* you're my chambermaid?" Ana said, kicking aside the nightclothes and socks and underthings she had left strewn between the beds.

"And spoil you more than you already are? Certainly not," Clarissa said. "By the way, did you know that Hephaestus tried to make his own race of men? *Automatoi*, they were called—all forged out of metal. Probably rusted the first time it rained."

She held up a page with drawings of muscular metallic men,

all made of bronze. Ana hardly glanced at it, however, for she was not as enamored of books as Clarissa was, and in any case, she had suddenly noticed how thin and pale Clarissa looked. Two nights in the dungeons—for playing a loud game of Armor Bowling in the grand ballroom—would do that, of course. But her persistent patchwork of freckles had nearly faded away completely, and there were such dark bands pressed around her eyes, Ana could not help thinking of the tiny waif she had first laid eyes on years ago.

She could still remember how excited she had been, because her father—who had missed her two previous birthdays—was home and said he had a special gift for her. She begged and pleaded and fidgeted all through dinner until finally, once the Queen had excused herself, he summoned Benjamin, the butler.

She saw only Benjamin standing in the doorway, at first—no package in his arms, no telltale bulge under his coat. *Perhaps he's going to lead me to my present*, she thought, though she hoped not, for Benjamin was a walking needle of a man, with prickly gray hair and sullen eyes, and though he was mute and never so much as grunted at her, he somehow made it clear that he thought she was the most spoiled brat he had ever met.

Then a little shadow stepped out from behind Benjamin: a tiny, gaunt, mortal girl with hair the color of polished copper and spots all over her face. Someone had put her in a frilly new dress and new shoes and even tied a pink ribbon in her hair, but it was clear she felt no more at home in these things than she did in her new surroundings.

The girl stared at Ana. Her hazel eyes were aglow with confusion and excitement, but she did not look afraid—not much, at least. And this was unusual, for nearly all the mortals in the castle were afraid of Ana.

"Happy birthday, darling!" Ana's father said, beaming with pleasure. "Her name's Clarissa. She's to be your chambermaid: someone to tidy your room, brush your hair—all those things your mother holds so dear.

"Of course," he added, bending low to whisper in Ana's ear, "if she happens to keep you company as well, where's the harm in that?"

It was only then that Ana realized the girl was her present. A servant for a present? A mortal for a friend? Ana had tried playing with mortals before. It never ended well. They either got hurt or ran off screaming in terror, and this skinny thing looked as if she would snap in two if Ana so much as sneezed in her direction.

"She has dirt all over her face," Ana said.

The girl put a hand to her face, then laughed. "Those are freckles," she said. "Haven't you ever seen freckles before?"

No, Ana had never seen freckles before. Immortals did not have freckles. But for a mortal to correct her, let alone *laugh* at her—that was unthinkable.

"Send her back. I don't like her," Ana said.

But her father said there was no one to send her back to. "She has no family. And I don't like you being alone all the time," he said. "It's not healthy." And so Clarissa had stayed.

"Oh, bother the Greek gods," Ana said now, opening the closet and searching for a dress to replace the one she had stained during breakfast. She hated dresses—she was always tripping on the hems and tearing them, and when she flew about, the silly things flapped in her face or caught on doorknobs and gargoyles' horns. But her mother would not allow her to wear anything else. "I've got news."

She told Clarissa about Madame Mumm being dismissed, and her new tutor, and Prince Barnaby coming to Solomon Castle, and her father taking a leave of absence. A bit of color returned to Clarissa's cheeks.

"Perfect!" she said, an evil grin spreading across her face. "We can torment Prince Barnaby endlessly, and your father will tell your mother we're just 'high-spirited.' We should go out right now and find a moatmonster egg."

Ana smiled. A moatmonster egg in Prince Barnaby's bed would be the *perfect* way to welcome him to Solomon Castle. She hurried into her fresh clothes, wondering how a mere mortal with no magical powers of her own could be so brilliant at devising magical pranks. Making the food talk back to the chef; bewitching the dining-room chairs so that they scurried away whenever anyone tried to sit; causing ball lightning to shoot out of the toilets—these had all been Clarissa's ideas. And though it was always Ana who had to cast the spells, everyone in the castle knew who supplied the imagination. In fact, the Queen had taken to punishing them both for *any* questionable activity that occurred in the castle, giving Clarissa a few days in the dungeons and Ana an equal number of days under room arrest. But it was all worth it, as far as Ana was concerned.

Ana slipped into an old jumper and pulled her hair back into a long ponytail. Then she and Clarissa raced outside to search the banks of the moat for eggs. They found only broken ones for the moatmonsters—pink blubbery things, like manatees with bad skin and razor-sharp teeth—were always eating one another's eggs. There were, however, hundreds of masses of frog eggs floating in the water, and this gave Clarissa an idea.

"Let's fill some buckets with frog eggs and hang them from the portcullis," she said. "When Prince Nutbrain passes beneath—"

"He won't be here for days," Ana said.

"Right. Think what a stinking mess they'll be by then," Clarissa said.

So Ana conjured up some buckets. Of course, in conjuring up the buckets and using a Scooping Spell to gather the eggs, she spattered the banks of the moat with bits of athen, a dull, steely-looking metal that appeared whenever and wherever magic was employed. Athen was a terrible nuisance to everyone, and as it could not be melted, cut, or destroyed by any means known to anyone, the servants were constantly having to cart it away.

"Ridiculous," Clarissa said, stepping over several lumps of athen. "If you Immortals didn't have us to clean up after you, you'd be buried in your own wastes by now."

Ana rolled her eyes. Clarissa was always criticizing one thing or another about Immortals. "Since it bothers you so much, you can carry *your* bucket up the stairs," she said, and sent her own bucket floating up to the ramparts of the castle.

The bucket was heavy, and Clarissa grumbled all the way up the steep, stony steps. When they emerged onto the parapets, she set the bucket down and peered through the crenellations.

"Look at that," she said, pointing to something in the distance.

Ana looked out. There was nothing but the usual patchwork of estates clinging to the hillside below them—castles and moats and enchanted gardens of every size and shape. And, of course, on the far side of the river stood the city, its towers bristling like glassy spears.

"Over there," Clarissa said, pointing eastward.

Ana gazed at a misty brown smudge in the distance: the ghetto. She had seen it many times from the parapets and from the window of her mother's office—a crumbling, soot-stained cake perched on the very edge of the harbor and bathed in a mustard-like haze. This was where most of the mortals lived, when they were not at the castles or offices; this was where Clarissa had been born.

Clarissa was not pointing to the ghetto, however, but to the giant whirlpool in the harbor—the Maelstrom. It swirled and smoked and sprayed, but there was nothing unusual in this. The Maelstrom had been doing that as long as anyone could remember. No, what was new was the glow emanating from the Maelstrom's mouth, a faint reddish cast, like a watery volcano waking.

"That's odd," Ana said. "Do you think Mother or King Georges flushed something particularly noxious today?" The two monarchs' companies were always flushing their wastes into the oceans. Spell residues and curse by-products, discarded potions, fragmented charms, and floating bits of necromancy—all of these found their way into the oceans, and for this reason the waters of Earth had long ago ceased to be anything but burning miasmas of magic.

"Perhaps," Clarissa said. But she did not look convinced. In fact, she looked worried.

Ana, watching Clarissa stare out at the glowing Maelstrom, was reminded again of Clarissa's arrival at Solomon Castle. In the first few weeks, Ana had done everything possible to get rid of the girl, but every morning when she woke up, Clarissa had been standing there in her room, ready to play chambermaid. And then one day, when Ana had actually needed the girl, she was gone. Ana had searched everywhere and finally found Clarissa on the parapets, where she had no business being.

"Didn't you hear me calling you?" Ana said, annoyed.

Clarissa did not even bother to turn around. Ana drew closer to see what the girl was staring at and saw only the misty brown smudge near the harbor, where the Solomon River and the Georges River crashed together.

"The ghetto? You're pining for the ghetto?" Ana said. She could not imagine anyone being homesick for such a cesspool.

"Yes, the *ghetto*," Clarissa snapped, turning around. "Why? Do you think it's so wonderful here? Do you think I should feel lucky just to be your stupid maidservant? I wish I'd never come here!"

Ana was on the verge of turning her into a legless, overturned turtle when she noticed the wet, splotchy trails on Clarissa's face. Mortals cried a lot, especially when faced with punishment. In fact, they tended to grovel and sob and do all sorts of other irritating things. But Clarissa's tears seemed different to Ana.

"Do you know what Benjamin wrote on his little notepad when I came here?" Clarissa sniffed, wiping at her nose. "He wrote that you and I were about as likely to become friends as a cat and a mouse. I didn't believe him. But now . . ."

Ana scowled. "It's not my fault you mortals are so fragile," she said.

Clarissa's face flushed bright red. "And it's not my fault I'm a mortal!" she snapped. "Besides, you have mortal blood, too."

Ana flinched. "What are you talking about?" she said.

"You're a *slag*!" Clarissa said. "Your father's part mortal, so that makes *you* part mortal, and that means you're a *slag*."

Ana could have obliterated Clarissa for such an insult, but she was too shocked. How did Clarissa know? Had Ana's father told her? No. The Queen would tie his head to a passing comet if he so much as mentioned it to anyone.

"You don't know anything," Ana whispered, suddenly aware that the castle's Monitoring Spells could be reporting the entire conversation to her mother.

"I do. You're half-mortal. Everyone knows it."

"A quarter!" Ana hissed. "My father's half-mortal, and that makes me only one-quarter. But if you don't want to be torn to pieces when Mother comes home, you'll shut your mouth right now."

Clarissa shrugged. "I'm not afraid of her," she said. "You are, though. Good little Anatopsis—apple of her mother's eye."

"At least I have a mother!" Ana spat. She turned away, convinced she had been as patient as possible with this awful girl. Suddenly Clarissa jumped on her and knocked her to the ground.

"Take that back!" Clarissa shouted, sitting on top of Ana. She flailed and scratched and punched at Ana, and though Ana had more than enough power to stop her, she was far too bewildered to think what to do, for she had never fought anyone in this way.

Fortunately, the castle's Monitoring Spells had done their work. Just as Clarissa delivered a sharp blow to Ana's nose, the Queen materialized beside them.

"Disgusting little vermin!" the Queen shouted, snatching Clarissa up with a Rat Catching Spell and slamming her into the battlement wall. "How dare you!"

Ana sat up, gasping for breath. An alarming amount of blood

was dripping from her nose. She found it a bit fascinating, for she had never had a bloody nose before. But her mother was about to unleash a Vaporization Curse, and however angry Ana was, she did not want her mother interfering.

"Don't!" Ana said, stumbling to her feet. "She didn't do anything,"

"She assaulted you, Anatopsis!" the Queen said. "I saw her!"

"I . . . I asked her to do it," Ana lied. "I wanted to practice my Self-Defense Spells on a real person."

"She's not a person, Anatopsis. She's an animal. And look at you—she bloodied your nose! She has to be put down."

"No! She's mine—not yours. I'll decide what to do with her."

The Queen eyed Ana. "I don't have time for this nonsense, Anatopsis," she said. "The Monitoring Spells told me you were in danger, and like a good mother, I flew to your aid. Now you tell me you were deliberately rolling about on the battlements with a filthy-faced mortal? I'm tempted to throw you both in the dungeons." She gave Ana one last disgusted look, then vanished.

Clarissa stared at Ana. For a moment, neither of them said a word, as if they feared the Queen would return at the first sound. Then Clarissa sat up, rubbing the lump on the back of her head.

"I thought you wanted me gone," she said.

Ana scowled. "I don't like Mother interfering," she said.

Clarissa nodded. "Well, thanks," she said, struggling to her feet. "I suppose I'll have to leave you alone now."

Ana shrugged. Only a few minutes ago, she would have welcomed this offer. Now she felt strangely disappointed. A mortal who wasn't afraid of her, a mortal who dared to attack her, to hurt her . . . She knew she shouldn't tolerate such behavior. And yet, she felt more curious than angry.

Another drop of blood fell onto her hand. She studied it as if it had fallen from the sky. "Does this stop by itself?" she asked. "Or do I have to do something?"

"Why don't you just use a spell?" Clarissa said.

"Mother won't let me do spells on myself. She's afraid I'll get disfigured," Ana said. "But when I'm of age, I'm going to interchromafy my hair and make my legs longer and my arms stronger."

Clarissa rolled her eyes and untied her apron. "Hold this against your nose," she said, handing the apron to Ana. "It'll stop in a minute."

Ana pressed the apron to her face. Soon they were walking down the stairs together, Ana trying not to stumble as she walked with her head back.

"You know, you Immortals are useless," Clarissa said. "You have all this magic, and you don't do anything with it."

"Like what?" Ana asked, expecting Clarissa to say something horribly mortalish, like *Free the mortals* or *Clean up the ghetto*.

Instead, Clarissa pointed out one of the arrow slits and said, "Do you see that drawbridge? If I had your power, I'd put a spell on the bridge so it snapped shut every time your mother came

home. Or I'd turn the floors of the castle to ice and skate everywhere. I'd make all the meals uncook themselves just as they
were put on the table—"

"You wouldn't dare," Ana said.

Clarissa grinned. "*You* wouldn't dare," she said.

Ana threw the apron at her. They raced down the stairs and
within minutes were skating through the castle. By nightfall, they
had destroyed three doors and half the gargoyles in the castle, and
by the next day they were receiving their first punishments.

Now, as Ana snapped out of her trance and helped Clarissa
hook the buckets to the top of the portcullis, she began to worry.
What if Barnaby treated Clarissa like a servant? What if he had
no sense of humor? What if he truly was a nut-brained imbecile?

Chapter 3

ON THE NORTHERN LID OF THE ISLAND, in a dark, foreboding castle atop a hill, lived Prince Barnaby Georges. His father, King Archibald Georges the Third, was chairperson and president of Consolidated Necromantic Industries (or CNI, as it was more commonly called) and as shrewd and calculating a ruler as his nemesis, Queen Solomon. But unlike Anatopsis, Barnaby was no more a copy of *his* parent than a cat is a copy of a lion. Where King Georges was massive and menacing, Barnaby was slight and scatterbrained. Where King Georges had bushy eyebrows and a shining bald head, Barnaby had thin, fair eyebrows and a mop of blond unkempt hair. And while his father could turn a thousand witches and warlocks into bat soup with a flick of his fingers, Barnaby, even by his thirteenth birthday, could not so much as pass himself the sugar bowl without setting the napkins on fire.

"You're a disgrace!" his father would bellow whenever Barnaby's spells went awry—which was nearly all the time. His Invisibility Spells made everyone else invisible. His Levitation Spells came out as Levity Spells, causing the satyrs in the court to literally explode with laughter. And he once turned his tutor into a moth— a harmless mistake if not for the hordes of bats in the castle.

Now, on the evening of Ana's birthday, which is to say two days after she and Clarissa had arranged the buckets of frog eggs for his arrival, Barnaby was lying on his bed in a dark, stony room, unwinding the copper wire from a small electric motor.

Suddenly the door to his room exploded. In stepped the King, lightning bolts crackling from his fingers. Spells shot this way and that, melting the stones out of the walls and sending the gargoyles fleeing from the room.

"Is this what you do behind my back?!" the King bellowed, his eyes swirling from red to violent purple at the sight of the motor in Barnaby's hands. "Is this what you do?!" He caught Barnaby in a Fist of Fate Spell and sent him spinning like a beach ball into the air. "Give me one good reason why I shouldn't just throw you into the Maelstrom!"

Barnaby, falling hard onto the floor beside his bed, could not think of a reason, though he wished he could. There was no greater threat than to be thrown into the Maelstrom. It was saturated with magical wastes, and any Immortal thrown into it, even one as powerful as King Georges, would be battered and cursed for eternity by the hodge-podge of sorcery in its waters.

"I—I'm sorry! It won't happen again!" Barnaby cried.

"No, it won't!" the King said, snapping his fingers.

Two Security Trolls—massive pink columns of fur with claws and teeth and a vocabulary consisting entirely of grunts, growls, and whistles—entered carrying a dwarf dressed in red-and-black coveralls. Immortal dwarves were as common as athen, but this particular dwarf was a mortal—one of the castle's workmen, to be exact, charged with fixing the thousand and one things the King and other Immortals could not be bothered to waste their magical powers upon. He was much slighter and shorter than his Immortal counterparts, with limbs oddly out of proportion to his body, and whereas Immortal dwarves tended to be vicious and greedy, this dwarf had never been anything but kind to Barnaby.

"Alexander!" Barnaby cried at the sight of his friend dangling between the two trolls. "Let him go! He didn't do anything!"

"Didn't do anything?" the King said. He pointed a finger at Barnaby's dresser. The bloodwood drawers flew across the room. As they struck the wall, they smashed open, showering Barnaby with bits of metal. Wires and wheels, small motors, metal plates and hinges and screws of every size scattered everywhere. Interspersed within this bric-a-brac lay all sorts of half-finished devices—amalgamations of parts that looked as if they had been pasted together by a half-witted inventor.

"In all my one thousand years, I've never seen anything more disgusting!" the King shouted. "Is this what you do in your spare time? Play servant? Is this what that little beast has been teaching you?"

It was true—Alexander had been teaching Barnaby how to

build things. He was the castle's blacksmith, and Barnaby had stood in the doorway and watched him make a set of door hinges once. The conversion of unformed metal into useful, beautiful objects had fascinated Barnaby. To piece things together like that, to manipulate matter and connect the forces of nature with his own hands, had seemed more magical to him than any magic he had ever learned. He could not cast a spell to save his life, yet he was certain he could do this. So he had asked the dwarf to teach him, and the dwarf, to Barnaby's surprise, had agreed.

But now it was all going to be taken away from him: years' worth of work, collecting and building, piecing things together bit by bit. His father would never allow him to touch so much as a hammer again. And Alexander . . . Barnaby did not want to think what would happen to him.

"It was my fault," Barnaby said. "He didn't want to teach me, but I told him I would turn him into a frog if he didn't, and if you're going to punish anyone, it should be me, because he's only a mortal and—"

"Quiet!" the King barked. Barnaby had an unfortunate tendency to blather on whenever he was frightened or nervous—a habit that only infuriated his father more. The King turned to the Security Trolls.

"Take that dwarf to the dungeons," he ordered. "I want him on the rack and stretched to normal height before morning."

"No!" Barnaby cried. He cast a fireball at the trolls—they

were dreadfully afraid of fire—but it fell to the floor and sputtered out, and the trolls left with their prisoner.

"Is that the best you can do?" The King sneered. "A dozen tutors and you can't throw a simple fireball? I should blast you
right now and be done with it."

Barnaby, seeing the hate and bitterness in his father's blood-
shot eyes, braced himself. The King let fly a Vaporization Curse.
But it struck the scattered parts and bric-a-brac, not Barnaby. And
as the last piece vanished, the King turned on his heel and
stormed out.

Barnaby sat beside his bed, trembling and crying. He wished
he were anywhere but Georges Castle, anyone but the son of
King Georges.

He soon heard the *click-click* of claws on the floor.

"Botched your homework again?" a voice said.

Barnaby peered over the bed to see Uno, his Saint Bernard dog,
standing in the doorway, a small, forked bone clenched between
his teeth. Uno had been with Barnaby as long as either of them
could remember, and this was unusual for two reasons. First, he
was the only dog anyone in the castle had ever seen. Second, the
King—who hated all things mortal, including dogs—had allowed
Barnaby to keep him. Perhaps the strangeness of the Saint Bernard
breed—with its enormous head and droopy eyes, the powerful
jaws capable of taking a centaur's leg off, and the masses of fur—
appealed to the King. But most likely he simply thought Bar-

naby's attachment to Uno would make the dog useful should Barnaby ever need "motivation."

"Where have you been?" Barnaby said, wiping the tears from his face.

"In the kitchen, getting you another wishbone," Uno replied. Ever since Barnaby had heard about the magical properties of wishbones, he had been collecting and breaking them. As far as Uno was concerned, the only things they reliably delivered were splinters between one's teeth. But they seemed to lift Barnaby's spirits, so Uno indulged him now and then.

He stepped carefully around the puddles and came to sit beside Barnaby. "Daddy Dear throw another tantrum?" he said.

Barnaby told him everything. "He hates me," he said, once he had finished his story. "I wish he would just send me off somewhere."

"He never will," Uno said, settling down to gnaw on his bone. "You're the heir, the princeling, the future of the Georges family. And it's not you he hates, in any case. It's your mother."

"Why do you always say that? You've never even met her."

Uno licked his chops. "I hear things now and then. If your species had evolved beyond the auditory shellfish stage, you might, too. But since you've only got those useless oysters on the sides of your head, you'll have to take my word for it. Your father hates your mother."

"That's silly," Barnaby said. "It's been thirteen years since she left. And he has dozens of attendants in the palace. Why would he still care about one mortal servant who left him?"

"*Because* she left him, obviously," Uno said. "I'm not an expert on human nature. It's one of those contradictory subjects, like 'business ethics,' which I prefer to avoid. But it doesn't take a genius to see he's never forgiven her for whatever it was she did. Why do you think there are no mortal women in this castle?"

Barnaby sighed. He didn't like to discuss his mother. In fact, whenever the subject arose, he felt as if someone were pouring a bag of sand into his chest. He had never met his mother, had never seen a picture of her. He did not know her name or what color eyes or hair she had had, did not know if she had loved him or even cared about him. The only thing he knew was that she had betrayed his father and she was dead. His father had been sure to tell him that—many, many times. In fact, that was the only thing he would tell him.

"Honestly, I don't care who he hates," Barnaby said, rising. "Right now, all I care about is Alexander. Do you think the torture master's put him on the rack yet?"

"I doubt it," Uno said. "He usually leaves early on Fridays."

"Then let's go," Barnaby said. He pressed a button in the dark panels behind his bed. A door slid open to reveal a narrow passageway. It was not a *secret* passageway, since the King knew of it, but it was still the best means of reaching the dungeons unseen. And Barnaby liked to go to the dungeons. It was quiet and safe there, and he was so familiar with every nook and cranny that even the King would have been hard-pressed to find him.

They descended the stairs quickly and began going from cell to cell, peering through the bars and asking all the prisoners if they had seen Alexander and the Security Trolls go by. Howard, Katrina, and Flora—the three heads of a Hydra in cell 53—said they had heard something unusual. But they had fought about whose turn it was to look through the grate, so none of them could say where the trolls had gone. A few of the other prisoners said they had seen the trolls.

Finally, one of Barnaby's old tutors, in cell 433, said he was sure he had heard someone being put in the cell at the end of the corridor. Sure enough, when Barnaby and Uno reached the very last cell, they found Alexander. He was too short to reach the viewport, so Barnaby had to speak to him through the narrow food hatch at the bottom.

"I'm sorry. I really am," Barnaby said. "I didn't mean for this to happen."

"It's all right. I'm not dead yet," the dwarf said. "Besides, warlocks don't apologize. Remember?" Then, seeing Barnaby near tears, he said, "Look, getting upset's not going to help. How about we concentrate on getting me out of here instead?"

"How do you propose we do that? Ask the King for the keys?" Uno growled.

"Almost," Alexander said. "Barnaby, did your father take the tools I gave you?"

Barnaby's face brightened. His father hadn't destroyed the tools! He told Uno to stand guard, then rushed back to his room. The heavy canvas roll was still safely hidden beneath his mattress. He pulled it out, tucked it under his shirt, then raced back to Alexander's cell.

"What do I do?" Barnaby said, unrolling the tool kit. Hammer, chisels, screwdrivers and wrenches, a try square, a pair of wire cutters—they were all there.

Alexander gave him directions. It was not an easy job, but after ten minutes of prying and twisting and banging, the lock gave way. Luckily, the trolls never bothered to put magical locks on mortal prisoners' cells.

"I did it! I can't believe it!" Barnaby said as the door swung open.

"I told you—you're a born craftsman," Alexander said, stepping into the corridor. "Or at least a born locksmith."

"But how will you get out of the castle?" Barnaby said. "There are alarms everywhere."

"I have a way."

"Then take us with you! Father will be furious when he finds out you're gone, and I—"

Alexander shook his head. "I can't. I'm sorry."

"Please," Barnaby begged. "We won't be any trouble. Uno could carry you, if it's far—"

"Me? I'm not a sedan chair!" Uno barked.

Alexander smiled. "Your father would tear the planet apart

looking for you," he said. "But don't look so glum. You'll be leaving, too, in a few days."

"What do you mean?" Barnaby said.

"You're going to Solomon Castle. Didn't your father tell you?"

No, his father hadn't said a word about going to Solomon Castle. And as Barnaby stared, dumbfounded, the dwarf raced away, his too-large head disappearing into the depths of Georges Castle before Barnaby could even say good-bye.

Chapter 4

EVERYTHING WAS GOING WRONG. The buckets of frog eggs had come loose on Ana's birthday, spattering the Queen with slime just as she was going off to work. Clarissa had been sent back to the dungeons for a night. Ana had spent her birthday confined to her room, and not only was there was no quantum-foam cake with comet-tail frosting for dessert, there was no celebration at all. Worse yet, her father had missed her birthday—again. He had not even bothered to call her on the crystal ball or send a card or letter.

Now it was Monday morning, and Ana, having just peeked in the door of her classroom at the top of the easternmost turret, could see that Barnaby Georges *was* an incompetent nut-brained imbecile. For he was already at his desk, hands folded neatly in front of him, paying very close attention to whatever was going on at the front of the class, and though this would have been too prim and proper for Ana under most circumstances, it was dou-

bly troubling to her now. For there was nothing going on at the front of the class. The teacher had not arrived yet.

Ana, taking a deep breath, went in and began to introduce herself. She had gotten no further than "You must be Prince Barnaby," however, when something huge and furry shot out from under the desk and knocked her over.

"Uno! Stop!" Barnaby shouted.

It was too late. Ana already lay flat on her back, pinned beneath the largest, mustiest, most threatening animal she had ever seen. The word *dog* never entered her mind, for she had never seen one. All she knew was that whatever was sitting on her was very heavy and smelly and was about to drown her in what she hoped was not poisonous drool.

"Get off!" Barnaby shouted, tugging at Uno's collar.

"She's a witch!" Uno snarled.

"Of course she's a witch," Barnaby said. "What did you expect to find here—neutrino monkeys? Now get off of her."

"What's she doing here?" the dog growled.

"She's the Princess. It's her castle, remember?" Barnaby said. "But if you don't get off of her, she's liable to turn you into a bowl of pickled newt legs."

"I'd like to see her try," Uno grunted. But he allowed Barnaby to pull him away.

Ana struggled to her feet. As she brushed herself off, Barnaby apologized over and over again, saying that Uno was just a bit overprotective, being a dog and all, and he hoped she wouldn't take it personally.

"It's all right," she said. "I'm not hurt." She stared at Uno, fascinated and repulsed at the same time. Clarissa had mentioned dogs many times, but in her stories they had always sounded cute and endearing. There was nothing endearing about this one, however. He smelled like a moldy mop and had droopy eyes, and he did not seem able to stop panting and drooling.

"Is that his name—Uno?" Ana asked, glancing at the small brass name tag dangling from the dog's collar.

Barnaby nodded. "It means 'one,'" he said. "Because he's the only one, you see?"

"Of course," Ana said, though she had not the slightest idea what Barnaby was talking about.

"He's a bit distrustful," Barnaby said. "But he's a wonderful dog and a good protector. He can bring you brandy in a snowstorm, you know, if you happen to get caught in one. Though we don't get many snowstorms, do we? And we don't have any brandy, either. But if we did . . ."

Barnaby began a long, nervous digression on dogs and snowstorms and brandy. Finally, Ana had to cut him off.

"Do you always talk like this?" she asked.

Barnaby blushed. "No. Not *always*, that is. I'm sorry."

"That's all right. But it does make you sound a bit . . . um, out of your mind, if you don't mind my saying so."

Barnaby smiled. "I wouldn't be at all surprised. Uno and I don't get out much, and we hardly ever talk to anyone—except the servants, but they don't say much, because of being afraid, you know. But still, I have an idea that when one is out of one's mind, one feels it. Life suddenly becomes much more pleasant or one's hat no longer fits, something of that sort . . ."

Barnaby would have gone on much longer about the relation-ship between sanity and hat sizes, but he and Ana and Uno were suddenly struck dumb by a terrible chill—a feeling of cold so ab-solute and penetrating that Ana thought her heart would go numb.

A stocky, barrel-chested man with gray face and bluish hands had materialized at the front of the room. He was dressed in a short black coat and a derby hat, and the collar of his shirt was so stiff it could have been made of marble.

"I am Mr. Pound," the man said. His voice was deep and reso-nant, as if it emanated from some enormous cave inside him, but there was no inflection to his words, no expression on his face, only a vague haughtiness in the way he surveyed his pupils.

Ana wished her father had been home so she could ask him more about Mr. Pound. Her mother had offered nothing more than mysterious smiles, and though Ana had managed to find a mention or two of Mr. Pound in Patterson's Field Guide to Deities, there was little factual information, only a smattering of legends and rumors.

The one thing all the sources agreed on was that Mr. Pound was a demigod. This in itself was surprising, for according to

Madame Mumm, the gods had all vanished thousands of years ago. But the guide speculated that Mr. Pound's father might have been the last one, and that he had deliberately planted his seed in a human to preserve his kind. The plan must have gone awry, however, for the victim died before giving birth, and what emerged from her remains was neither god nor human, neither alive nor dead, but only a portion of each. At least, that was the author's theory. But now, seeing Mr. Pound in the flesh, Ana thought he looked at least three-quarters dead.

Mr. Pound commanded Barnaby and Ana to sit. Then, without preface or introduction, he began a lengthy review of basic spell-casting theory. Ana sighed, bracing herself for hours of utter boredom. She soon discovered, however, that her interest or lack thereof was irrelevant. Her ears listened whether she willed them to or not. Her eyes remained fixed upon Mr. Pound no matter how hard she struggled to move them. And though she was sure she could not repeat a word of his lesson, she felt his knowledge pouring into her, as if he had removed the top of her head and inserted a garden hose.

Throughout the lecture, Mr. Pound's gaze shifted back and forth between Ana and Barnaby. His gray, lifeless eyes seemed to probe and prod them, as if he were trying to determine which of them, if either, was worth his time. Ana sensed that he would have preferred to cut them open, but something prevented him.

Perhaps he's not as powerful as he pretends, Ana thought, watching how stiff and clumsy his movements were, as if his limbs weighed hundreds of pounds. But Mr. Pound quickly disabused her of this notion. At the conclusion of the morning lessons, he summoned one of the prisoners from the dungeons—an elderly mortal woman—and performed a Dissolution Spell on her. The woman melted into a puddle on the floor, and even after Mr. Pound had excused Ana and Barnaby for lunch, Ana could still see the terror in the poor woman's eyes.

After lunch, Mr. Pound brought Ana and Barnaby to the Subterranean Spell & Curse Casting Range to test their skills. Ana, nervous under Mr. Pound's unblinking gaze, miscast half her spells, including a simple Muffling Spell, which, instead of silencing a screaming Harpy, squashed it flat.

Barnaby fared even worse. His Muffling Spell silenced the Harpy, but only by producing a thick neck scarf that accidentally strangled it. His Dehydration Spell created a small rain cloud in the cavern, and his attempt at spotshifting—a means of teleporting from one place to another—left him half-embedded in the cavern's ceiling, a predicament from which Mr. Pound rescued him, but only after fifteen minutes of extreme discomfort.

If Mr. Pound was displeased by their efforts, he did not show it. At least, his haughty expression did not change, and he made no comments or criticisms.

When he finally dismissed them, Barnaby and Uno hurried away as fast they could. Ana trudged alone up the stairs. As she was passing through the entrance hall, a letter leaped out of the mail cauldron and into her hands. She recognized the Knights-Errant Guild's crest and tore the letter open. But there was only a short note inside:

Dearest Anatopsis,

I have missed your birthday again. I am terribly sorry. I thought I would be back in time, but the client insisted it was an emergency quest. I was not even allowed time to retrieve my armor.

I hope to be back in a few months, but, of course, these quests are very unpredictable. In the meantime, study hard and remember that I want only the best for you.

With affection,

Your Father

An emergency quest? Ana had never heard of such a thing. She studied the letter again. "Dearest Anatopsis"? Her father never used her full name. "Study hard"? "With affection"? These weren't the sorts of phrases he would use. They sounded more like . . .

"Mother!" Ana said, crumpling the letter in her hand. She stormed into her mother's study, kicking the door open with such force that the carved snakes in the Queen's desk recoiled.

"You did this, didn't you?" Ana said, throwing the letter on the Queen's desk. "You arranged the whole thing!"

The Queen, who had only just returned from AW, was perusing her own mail.

"Your father's a knight-errant, darling," she said, without looking up from her stack of envelopes. "Quests are what knights-errant do. I'm sure he'll return once he's found whatever it is he's questing for."

"He's not on a real quest, and you know it," Ana said.

The Queen set her mail down. "There are all sorts of quests, Anatopsis—voluntary ones and involuntary ones," she said. "Since your father cannot be trusted to let Mr. Pound perform his duties, I thought it best he depart on an extended tour of the Universe. And I warned him that if he insisted on returning to Solomon Castle, he would find the consequences very uncomfortable."

Consequences. Ana could guess what that meant: the dungeons—an especially daunting prospect for an adventurer like her father. Furious, she fired a Scattering Spell at her mother's mail and sent it flying in a dozen different directions. But the Queen cast a counterspell, and the mail stacked itself neatly upon her desk again.

"Don't try my patience, Anatopsis. Everything I do is for your own good. You should know that by now," the Queen said. "Now please just do your work, and if you pass your Bacchanalian examinations, I promise I'll allow your father to return—assuming he hasn't been eaten by a jabberwock by then."

"But that's a year from now!" Ana said.

"Yes, it is, isn't it? But I could banish him forever, if you prefer. Now please go."

Ana ran out the door, fighting back her tears. At the bottom of the staircase, she ran into Clarissa.

"What's happened? What's wrong?" Clarissa said, stopping

her. Ana told her of her mother's treachery. "Why would she do that? It makes no sense," Clarissa said. "Of course, nothing your mother does makes sense. Come on—I've got something to show you."

She led Ana into the castle's library—a dark, vaulted rotunda with marble floors and shelf upon shelf of dusty old books, some of them the size of bed mattresses. Half a dozen of the Solomon family's albums, leather-bound tomes bulging with mementos and spirit projections, lay spread out on one of the gleaming bloodwood tables.

"Why were you looking at those?" Ana asked.

"I was trying to find more information on Mr. Pound," Clarissa said. "If he's been tutoring Solomons for thousands of years, there should be something in these books, shouldn't there? But there isn't."

"Nothing?" Ana said. "Are you sure?"

"I went through every album. But there's something else. Look." Clarissa flipped open one of the thick, leather-bound albums.

"There's nothing in that one. I've looked before," Ana said.

"Well, it's full now," Clarissa said. And, in fact, it was—page after page of noisy, busy images, three-dimensional recordings of various Solomon and Georges ancestors sharing lessons together. There were spirit projections of Ana's grandmother trying to learn shape-changing spells while Barnaby's grandfather flicked newt eyes at her. There were projections of Ana's mother— hundreds of years younger, her hair immaculately brushed but not yet dyed necromantic black—and King Georges—sporting a full head of hair and looking much more mischievous than cruel—sitting together in the library at Georges Castle, teasing each other about who was the best transmogrifier.

None of the scenes had been there before—Ana was sure of it. Or at least, none of them had been visible before.

"Mother must have been hiding them. But why?" Ana said.

"Perhaps because she didn't want you to know about the shared lessons until now," Clarissa said.

Ana and Clarissa pored through the rest of the album. There were spirit projections of her mother and King Georges in the SSCCR, at the dinner table, even struggling through examinations. But there was not a single record of Mr. Pound—not an image, not a record, not even an old-fashioned hologram. It was as if he had never been there.

Chapter 5

BARNABY'S FIRST FEW WEEKS at Solomon Castle were not the worst he had ever suffered, but they were torturous nonetheless. Ana and Clarissa, having decided he was more suitable as entertainment than as a friend, quickly set about tormenting him. They put hair-weaving spiders in his pillow. They filled his closet with invisible shriekbats. They cast an Attractor Spell on his clothes so that anything he brushed up against would stick to him. And they were always giggling whenever he passed by.

He had not expected them to like him, of course. He had learned a few things in his years at Georges Castle, and one of them was that people—Immortals especially—did not take to him very well. The reasons were always different: He was the son of the most powerful warlock in the Universe; he was heir to the Georges throne; he was incompetent; he was fearful; he was forgetful; he talked too much when he was anxious. But the result was always the same—scathing looks from his father; sneers from members of the court; lots of eye rolling and laughter behind his back, not to mention the occasional Tripping Spell or Sneezing Charm or a horde of ravens suddenly appearing out of nowhere and showering him with their droppings.

Nevertheless, he had been hopeful. For when he had arrived at Solomon Castle that first night, he had not been greeted by the Queen or the Princess (much to his relief), but by the most fascinating servant he had ever seen: a girl—a *mortal* girl.

"Ana's not allowed to see you," the girl—Clarissa—had explained as she led him and Uno up the stairs to his room. But Barnaby hardly heard her. He was staring at her braid and hands and the skinny backs of her legs. *Do they all have hair that color?* he wondered. *Like Martian sand? Do they all have spots on their faces?* Could his mother have looked like that? It was difficult to imagine, for this girl seemed rather ordinary-looking, and he could not think of his mother as having been anything but extraordinary.

Clarissa opened the door to the guest room. Barnaby was amazed at how much lighter and airier it was than his chamber at Georges Castle. There were actual windows along one wall! Uno began sniffing through all the corners, sure that the Queen must have laid spells and spy charms everywhere.

"I hope he's house-trained," Clarissa said as she fetched sheets and towels and pillowcases from the linen closet. "The Queen won't tolerate any messes."

"Messes?" Uno growled. "Why you little . . ."

"He's—he's all right," Barnaby stammered. "He can take care of himself."

Clarissa tossed the linens on the unmade bed, then, much to Barnaby's surprise, sat down. She explained about laundry and mealtimes and which parts of the castle to avoid if one did not want to be arrested by the Queen's Security Trolls. As she spoke, Barnaby began to see she was not so ordinary after all. Her eyes gleamed with a sparkling, nutty hue, like a potter's glaze, and there was a sharpness to her pupils, a challenge, as if she dared anyone to suggest she was merely a servant. Barnaby began to see how his father might have been attracted to someone like this. For his father loved all things dangerous.

Two servants entered carrying Barnaby's suitcases. They dropped them by the bed, and Barnaby cringed as the last suitcase emitted a distinct clanking noise.

"What's that?" Clarissa asked.

Barnaby blushed. His tools were in the bag, as well as a few odds and ends the King had not destroyed. But he was not about to tell Clarissa, for fear she would tell the Queen.

"Shackles for nosy mortals," Uno growled. "Want to try them on?"

"Don't, Uno," Barnaby said.

"It's all right," Clarissa said, getting to her feet. "I'm only a servant, after all. But it'd be a shame if you needed to know something and the stupid chambermaid forgot to tell you, wouldn't it?

"For example," she said, reaching for the doorknob, "the sales dwarves come once a month for dinner. There's nothing they'd like better than a nice fat dog, and—"

"And there's nothing I like better than a nice, fat mortal leg," Uno replied. But Clarissa only smiled and left.

Long after she had vanished, Barnaby was still staring at the door.

"Hello!" Uno said, butting him in the leg. "Our little fairy gadfly is gone. And before you go getting yourself entranced by Miss Snaps-a-Lot, remember: 'A servant bites with its master's teeth.'"

"What's that mean?" Barnaby asked, shaking himself out of his trance.

"It means your future classmate's not likely to be any friendlier," Uno said.

Uno proved quite right, unfortunately. Ana was not as rude to Barnaby as Clarissa had been. In fact, she was almost friendly during classes. But as soon as Mr. Pound dismissed them, she would go off in search of Clarissa, and the two of them would then set about plotting new ways to make him feel foolish.

Were they expecting him to break down and leave? If so, they would be sorely disappointed. For despite their constant tormenting of him, he had never felt safer or calmer or enjoyed so much privacy. And however dreadful Mr. Pound's lessons might be, when evening arrived, he and Uno could go to their room and no one would bother them. There were no loud, endless parties in the main hall. Ghosts and sprites and drunken trolls and dwarves did not barge into their room in the middle of the night and insist Barnaby sing bawdy songs with them. Most of all,

Barnaby did not have to endure the nightly terror of demonstrating to his father whatever he had learned (or not learned, as was most often the case). And nothing Ana or Clarissa or the Queen or even Mr. Pound did could ever match what the King would do if Barnaby returned to Georges Castle before the Bacchanalians.

As the weeks progressed, Barnaby found ways to protect himself. He changed the lock on his door. He ignored any and all requests from Ana or Clarissa. (They liked to send him off on ridiculous missions, always claiming it was vitally important and he would be doing them an *enormous, enormous* favor—usually said with wide, batting eyes and innocent smiles.) Then, to escape his tormentors further, he resorted to a time-tested strategy: He hid in the dungeons.

Evenings and weekends, when Barnaby and Uno had little else to do, they would wander through the various levels of the dungeons, peeking into this cell and that to see who was imprisoned. The subterranean world of Solomon Castle was surprisingly similar to that of Georges Castle, they found—dark and dank, with only a few glow lamps here and there and lots of moanings and groanings from the prisoners. There was one substantial difference, however: The dungeons of Solomon Castle were mobile. The cells shuffled themselves about every hour or so, and a cell that might have been in the middle of the first floor one moment could be at the end of the fourth floor the next. This confused Barnaby and Uno no end, but thanks to

Uno's keen sense of smell, they were able to avoid getting lost altogether.

They soon made friends with several of the prisoners: Mrs. Sonyanova, a very nice if often despondent hag who had been imprisoned for telling the Queen her daughter was a brat; Tendine Ixlix, a traveling beauty-products salesman whose Anti-Wrinkle Potion had given the Queen a blemish; Sir Plimsole, a knight who had inadvertently slain one of the Queen's demon couriers; and several others, both mortal and Immortal.

The one aspect of the dungeons Barnaby and Uno did not like was running into Benjamin. The lanky, needle-haired butler seemed to spend a fair amount of time skulking about the corridors, and though he never said (or wrote) a word to them, his scowls and general air of menace made Barnaby very uncomfortable.

"What do you suppose he does down here?" Barnaby asked one day, after seeing Benjamin hurry out of one of the oubliettes—a false corridor that led to a long and deadly plunge into the sewers.

"Who knows? These mortals are all a sneaky lot," Uno said.

Barnaby was not sure he agreed, but he could not think of any duties the butler might have down here. *Perhaps I should tell Ana,* he thought. But she and Clarissa had done nothing but make fun of him since his arrival. And what if Benjamin had only been visiting friends? No, Barnaby would not tell Ana. She would only laugh at him.

Chapter 6

As THE WEEKS PASSED, classes became slightly more bearable. Both Ana and Barnaby learned to dress warmly for their lessons, and Mr. Pound no longer subjected them to his lengthy exploratory gazes, perhaps because he had concluded there was nothing to be found. Still, he made Ana nervous. She wrote to her father—care of the Knights-Errant Guild—and asked him to see if the Guild had any information on Mr. Pound. But he did not reply.

After three months of review, Barnaby and Ana were ready to begin the study of curses. This was a momentous occasion in any witch's or warlock's education, for though spells were useful for controlling the lesser beings, they contributed no more to an Immortal's status than fur does to a bear's. It was curses and curses alone that determined an Immortal's standing in the community.

"The First Law of Curses," Mr. Pound explained one morning, "is that a curse, once cast, can neither be removed nor reversed—*except by its caster*. Should someone transform you into a saber-toothed slug marooned on a planet of salt, you would remain in that agonizing state for eternity—unless your attacker took pity on you. This is what differentiates a curse from a spell, and what gives a witch or warlock true power."

Mr. Pound went on for quite some time about the history of curses and the "Cursery System," a fancy term that only meant everything in the Immortal economy revolved around curses. He spoke about an ancient warlock who had discovered a means of recording curses, and some musty old witch or other who had invented a way of packaging them, and how the corporations now controlled the production and distribution of all curses, licensing them to individuals according to strict rules concerning one's net worth, power quotient, and production history.

It was all basic sorcero-economics, as far as Ana was concerned, and as boring a subject as she could imagine. She prayed he would move on to something more practical, such as how to curse demigods out of existence.

At last, Mr. Pound handed out their first curses. They were nothing more than scrolls packed within intricately protected cardboard tubes with all sorts of disclaimers and licensing information printed on them. Ana and Barnaby tore open the tubes, slipped the scrolls out of their plastic sleeves, broke the seals, untied the ribbons, unrolled the stiff parchment, and finally cast their eyes on their first words of power.

It was a very disappointing moment, all in all. The long, serpentine lines of script looked as if they had been inked by a madman, and the curses themselves were as minor as curses can be.

"I got a Wart Curse," Ana whispered. "What did you get?"

"A Foot Fungus, I think—or Hoof-and-Mouth Disease. I'm not sure," Barnaby said, squinting at the eerie, shimmering lines.

They had to memorize the curses quickly, before the scrolls self-destructed. Then Mr. Pound handed out six more sets of curses. By the time he dismissed them for lunch, the room looked as if it had been attacked by paper fairies.

After lunch, they met in the SSCCR to practice their new curses. Barnaby's attempts failed altogether, of course, as he could barely remember, much less recite, the words on his scrolls. Ana fared little better, however. The curses seemed to have a mind of their own, often firing off in directions she had not intended. And when she did finally manage to strike down a quartet of ogres, the Anxiety Curse turned them into a puddle of slime rather than the huddled mass of nervous, tearful monsters she had expected.

"I don't understand it," Ana said, feeling discouraged. "I'm sure I said it right."

"It is not just a matter of speaking the words, Princess . . ." Mr. Pound began. But a sudden flipping noise from the puddle distracted him. Some tiny creature was writhing or swimming about in there. A worm? A tadpole or minnow? Ana could not tell and did not care. She only wanted to try the curse again. But Mr. Pound kept staring at the puddle, as if he expected some magical beast to rise out of it.

———

A few days later, Mr. Pound announced a surprise field trip. Ana and Barnaby groaned, for they had been on a few field trips already with Mr. Pound, and the excursions invariably involved lengthy, difficult spotshifts followed by at least an hour of blasting, liquefying, and transmogrifying the local inhabitants. But Mr. Pound promised that this destination was neither distant nor populated.

"Mount Olympus," he announced as they emerged from their spotshifting into an elaborate, open-air temple high above the clouds.

Ana and Barnaby, astounded to find themselves in such a historic place, gaped at the marble courtyard, the dais inlaid with gold, the curving line of thrones, each intricately carved with the signs and symbols of its god, and the gargantuan columns standing like guards behind them. This was not one of Olympus's many shadows—the earthly peak near Thessalonica, or the Acropolis, that man-made collection of crumbled statues and dangerously unstable columns. No, this was the *true* Mount Olympus, home of the Hellenic gods so glorified in myth and legend and so obsessively studied by mortal and Immortal historians. It was a destination no mortal or Immortal could visit without the aid of a god—or demigod, in this case.

Ana could not contain her excitement. The Hellenic gods were her favorites: Zeus, Hera, Athena, Apollo—there were so many of them, and she loved them all. But as she turned this way and that, trying to take in every glorious detail, her excitement quickly turned to disappointment. For though the house of the gods was even more stunning than she had imagined—sylvan pools running through the courtyard, marble busts and statues everywhere, the roof decorated with elaborate friezes and the columns leafed in golden rays from the sun—it was clear no one had lived there in eons. Zeus's lightning bolts lay scattered across the dais, as if he had thrown them down in disgust and walked away. Athena's shield and helmet had been tossed in a corner; her spear was broken in two. And Apollo's chariot was missing not only its horses but its wheels as well.

"What happened to them?" Ana asked, blowing a mound of dust off one of the thrones.

"They were murdered," Mr. Pound replied, the bitterness of his tone surprising Ana. She had never heard any emotion from him before, other than disdain.

"What do you mean? How can gods be murdered?" she asked.

"They were alive, were they not?" Mr. Pound said. "Therefore they could be destroyed. Prometheus, the Titan, stole their power and broke it. In that moment, all of Creation was split: Life gave birth to Death; Hope struggled against Despair; creatures great and small began to prey upon one another. Even magic .gained its opposite: athen. And with such opposition arose imperfection, for what had been a unity was now nothing more than a war of fragments."

Ana blinked in surprise. She had never heard before that magic and athen were opposites. It made sense, of course: One was a force that transformed matter; the other was matter no force could transform. But why had no one ever pointed it out to her?

"The gods were not able to retrieve what Prometheus had stolen," Mr. Pound continued. "They lost control over their own creations, over themselves, and, in time, faded into oblivion."

A strange white glow had appeared in Mr. Pound's eyes, as if his pupils had cracked and whatever lay behind them were struggling to get out. Ana felt a strange prickling on her face, fiery threads burning against her cheeks. *He's angry,* she realized, and it frightened her. She walked away, pretending a sudden interest in Athena's shield.

Meanwhile, Barnaby, who did not much care for Mount Olympus or the gods, had been wandering through the courtyard. He noticed that behind the columns ran an enormous curved wall of rock, and there were steps on either side of this wall, leading to a flattened top a hundred or so feet above the temple. In the very center of the wall, just below the top, was a decoration of some sort, a groove shaped like a giant wishbone with a hollow at its base:

It was lopsided and crude, and the little round hollow was actually a hole through which Barnaby could see clouds—not the sort of workmanship all-powerful beings tend to flavor. *Some visitor must have carved it,* he thought.

He climbed up the steps. From the top, he could see the entire Earth below him: oceans, continents, poles, even the tiny green island of the city, all joined together into a broad disk around the base of Mount Olympus. This strange, panoramic perspective was made possible by the mountain itself, which was not connected to the Earth, but existed on a different plane altogether.

The view must have been heavenly once, Barnaby thought. But now it was nothing short of a nightmare: sulfurous clouds roiling and boiling and eating away at the mountaintops; brown, tarry seas pierced by whirlpools and phosphorescent geysers; and land so saturated with magic it burned or devoured everything it touched.

The sight made Barnaby dizzy. He turned to climb back down the steps, then suddenly spied something swinging far below: a set of giant black chains rattling against a rock.

"What's that?" Barnaby said to Mr. Pound, who had suddenly appeared on the mountaintop with him, Ana close behind.

"The rock to which Prometheus was bound," Mr. Pound replied. "Zeus had him chained there for bringing fire to mankind. Every day an eagle came and tore out his liver."

"Ugh," Barnaby said. "All because of a few flaming sticks of wood?"

"*Fire* is metaphorical," Mr. Pound said. "What Prometheus brought the humans was not the secret of combustion, but the power of the gods."

"But you said he broke it," Ana said, leaning out to look at the chains.

"He did. And then he bestowed the fragments on the humans, Princess," Mr. Pound said. He paused. "Have you never wondered why there are mortals and Immortals? They were one race, once. But when Prometheus brought his gifts, those who received one part gained Life and Power, whereas those who received the other part gained Death. The former became the Immortals, the latter the mortals."

Ana stared harder at the chains. Her Immortal history books had never mentioned a shared genealogy between mortals and Immortals.

"Why did the mortals get Death and the Immortals get everything else? That hardly seems fair," Barnaby said.

"Not only Death. The mortals received other gifts as well— Knowledge and Imagination, Craft, Invention. The Immortals inherited none of these things."

"But that can't be true. Immortals invent all sorts of things," Ana said. "We have books and pictures and architecture and industry—"

"Your books are unrefined histories, Princess," Mr. Pound said. "Your pictures are spirit projections and holographs. Your architecture is nothing more than a panoply of designs stolen from various mortal cultures. Even your castles are copies of dwellings invented by mortals eons ago. To put it bluntly, your race mimics well, but it creates nothing new. As for industry, your parents' companies have never created anything new. They package curses, but they do not create them."

The contempt in Mr. Pound's voice was unmistakable, and once again Ana felt the heat of his anger. *I've had enough of these gods,* she thought. She hoped Mr. Pound would take them back to the castle now, but instead, he spotshifted them to a narrow ledge at the base of Prometheus's rock.

The rock was enormous, a massive cliff split in two, the chains set in such a way that Prometheus would have been held spread-eagled in the cleft between them. Lines of blood coated each side of the rock.

Ana shuddered at the thought of the eagle diving down upon Prometheus every day and tearing out his liver. But then she noticed how regular the lines were, as if they had been scrawled by someone. Words, she realized—Ancient Greek, though perhaps any language scrawled in blood on the side of a rock looked like Ancient Greek.

"What—what does that say?" she asked, pointing to the lines.

"It is a prophecy—Prometheus's last words," Mr. Pound said, his voice flat and more disdainful than ever. He recited:

Half and half now torn away
Could yet be whole again one day,

When a dead heart seeks and a dead eye finds
Two of mortal and Immortal kind.
In ice from a sword, flames from a shield,
Two enemies united, one bearer revealed.
Then let fear meld creation, desire,
Hate stoke the hottest of fires
Enough to crack sword, shield, and stone,
Enough to melt athen, turn spirit to bone.
In the forge of Hephaestus let Man's heart meet
The white-hot fire of despair and defeat,
And if it melts, the gods shall reign,
And Mankind never dream again.

Ana blinked. "'Never dream again'? What does that mean?" she asked.

But before Mr. Pound could reply, an odd thing happened: The words began to shimmer, then glow. Then suddenly they burst into flame and vanished, leaving no trace but the scent of smoke and brimstone.

Chapter 7

ANA RETURNED from the field trip exhausted and bewildered. Seeing Prometheus's rock and the bloody lines on it had been disturbing enough. But the way Mr. Pound's eyes had seemed to crack open when the lines had burst into flame, the way he had held her and Barnaby paralyzed in his gaze, probing and measuring, burrowing deeper and deeper, as if he were sure one of them must be hiding something, as if it were their fault the lines had vanished . . . It made her skin crawl just to think of it.

She wanted to vanish into her room and forget the entire trip. But as she was passing through the foyer of the castle, a letter leaped out of the mail cauldron and landed in her hands. At first she thought it was junk mail, for the envelope had a fourth-rate Bulk Mail Stamp Spell on it, and the return address said only:

School of Engineering
UCSB
Alpha Centauri
Galaxy 12, Septant 3, Chrono-Variance ±0

But each time she tried to throw it away, the letter would leap back into her hands. So finally she took it to her room and opened it.

Dearest Ana, it said.

I received the letters you sent to the Knights-Errant Guild and sent five of my own to you, but they were all returned marked UNWANTED. My current host, an old friend from the Guild, kindly offered his school's mail services to send this one. I hope it works.

You were, I am sorry to say, quite correct in your suspicions concerning my quest. I went off to Guild Headquarters fully intending to submit my request for a leave of absence and return in time for your birthday. Your mother intercepted me at Guild Headquarters, however. She made quite a scene, accusing me of interfering in your education and being a bad influence. Since she did not trust me to allow Mr. Pound to perform his duties, she thought it best if I do not return to Solomon Castle for the next few months. Naturally, I protested, but your mother can be a bit of a despot, as you know. She said it is only a temporary injunction—just until you complete your Bacchanalians—but she made it quite clear what my fate will be should I come within a mile of Solomon Castle before then. So I am afraid I will have to bow to her will for the time being.

On a happier note, my friend here wants me to attend the UCSB school and become an engineer. It sounds intriguing, especially as the knight-erranting business has fallen on hard times. (By the time you complete your schooling, I doubt it will even be a viable profession anymore.) But I am not sure whether I can accustom myself to carrying hard hat and clipboard instead of helmet and sword.

In any case, I am glad to hear you and Clarissa are well, and I hope the two of you will be kinder to Prince Barnaby. Your father is part mortal, too, don't forget.

Stay well and write soon so that I know you have received this letter.

With much love,

Your Father

P.S. I have made some inquiries about Mr. Pound, as you asked. No one seems to know much, but I really wouldn't worry if I were you. Your mother, for all her faults, would turn him into a dragon snack if he tried to harm you.

Ana refolded the letter and handed it to the envelope, which quickly restuffed itself. *No wonder I haven't heard from father,* she said to herself. *Mother's put a Mail Filtering Spell on the castle.*

She hid the letter in the top drawer of her dresser, then sat down at her desk to begin her homework. But she could not concentrate. She would not be seeing her father until after the Bacchanalians. That was still nearly nine months away. And he would not be a knight-errant anymore. UCSB—what was that? She had never heard of it. The thought of her father becoming an engineer disturbed her. It sounded like a mortal sort of occupation.

Does this mean I can't be a knight-errant? she wondered. Would she be forced to follow in her mother's footsteps? It was all too horrible to contemplate.

Suddenly Clarissa entered, her braid half-undone and her apron streaked with dirt. "What's the matter with you?" she asked.

Ana told her about the letter and her mother banishing her father. Clarissa was not surprised.

"But I've got just the thing to cheer you up," she said, pulling Ana off the bed. "Come on."

"Where are we going?" Ana asked as she followed Clarissa down the corridor. The answer was soon all too clear: Barnaby's room.

"He and Uno have gone down to the dungeons," Clarissa said, stopping in front of Barnaby's door. "They're always down there. In fact, if your mother put them in a cell, I don't think they'd notice."

"So why are we here?" Ana said.

Clarissa grinned and removed a key from her pocket.

"Oh, I don't know if that's a good idea," Ana said, remembering her father's request that she be nicer to Barnaby. "What if he comes back?"

"He won't," Clarissa said. "And if he does, it's his own fault for being so secretive. He changed the lock on the door himself; did you know that? And he never lets anyone in, not even to clean or collect his laundry. He puts his dirty things out in the hallway, and then takes them in again when they're clean."

"Well, we did put hair-weaving spiders in his pillow, remember?" Ana said. "And if he changed the lock, how did you get the key?"

"It fell out of his trousers when I was collecting the wash yesterday. So I made a copy," Clarissa said, unlocking the door and pushing it open. "Now let's see what Prince Nutbrain's been up to since we were last here."

Ana stepped over the threshold. She was immediately assaulted by the state of the room. It was not a simple matter of untidiness or the fact that no one had cleaned in weeks. No, it was *complete* disorder. From one wall to another, the room was littered with pieces of wood, strange metallic devices and trinkets, wooden toys, masses of wire, gears, springs, nuts, bolts, nails. A collection of small motors rested on top of Barnaby's dresser. Two drawers, hanging open, were filled with assorted screws and washers, rivets, and various metal plates.

"What is all this?" Ana asked, picking up what looked like a miniature spinning wheel with wire teeth. She held it gingerly between thumb and finger, as if it had been dipped in magical waste. Being an Immortal, she was not used to touching mechanical things.

Suddenly the door banged open. There stood Barnaby, out of breath. At the sight of Ana and Clarissa, his face turned the color of blood.

"What—what do you think you're doing?" he said.

He looked as if he might tear the doorknob off, and in that moment, Ana realized she and Clarissa had gone too far. Harmless pranks were one thing. But to invade his privacy like this . . . Ana's stomach fluttered. She started to apologize, but

Barnaby crossed the room and snatched the miniature wheel out of her hands.

"I can't believe you would just break in like this!" he said. "If Uno were here, he'd bite your fingers off."

Clarissa seemed a bit embarrassed, too, but she was not one to admit such a thing. "We only came in to clean," she said. "You never let anyone in your room, and it's filthy."

"What do you care what my room looks like?" Barnaby snapped. "Get out!"

Clarissa shrugged and started for the door. Ana, however, remembering her father's letter, thought she should say something.

"We *are* sorry, Barnaby," she said.

"No, you're not. At least, she's not," he said, pointing to Clarissa, who looked more defiant than apologetic.

"Well, *I* am," Ana said. "It was a terrible thing to do, and we won't do it again. But if you don't mind my asking, what is all this?"

"None of your business," Barnaby said.

She pointed at the little spinning wheel in his hand. "Did you make that? Is it a sculpture? Mother says modern art is rubbish, but I rather like it."

"It's not art!" Barnaby snapped. "It's for combing Uno's fur. He gets lots of knots and tangles, and it's tiring brushing them out. So I use this. The wheel goes round and round and drags the combs through his fur. He loves it."

"And that?" Ana asked, pointing to a pair of arms attached to his bed. They had pincers and were connected together by a complicated series of screws and wheels and pulleys.

"That makes the bed," Barnaby said. He pointed to a basket on wheels, with similar arms and pincers and screws. "And that one gathers and puts away the laundry."

"But how did you build all this?" Ana asked.

"There was a mortal in Father's castle. He saw I was interested in fixing things, so he showed me how to do it," Barnaby said. "He even gave me some tools."

Clarissa, standing by the door, suddenly became interested. "What kind of tools?" she asked.

Barnaby was not about to show them, however—not after all they had done to him. "Just ordinary tools," he said. "Pliers and chisels and hammers and things."

"Can you make anything you want with them?" Ana asked.

"No," Barnaby said. "In fact, compared to most mortals, I'm not very good at all. But it's easier than casting spells, and much more predictable—at least for me. Now, if you don't mind, Uno's waiting for me." He pulled open a drawer and removed a crude wooden box with antennae and knobs and a numbered keypad on it.

"What's that?" Ana asked.

Barnaby hesitated. "It's to find prisoners, if you must know," he said. "You enter the number of the cell, and it beeps when you're pointed in the right direction. Whoever designed the dungeons botched the Randomizing Spell, you see, so the cells repeat the same pattern every few days and . . ."

Both Ana and Clarissa looked at him in surprise. *Perhaps he isn't such a nutbrain after all,* Ana thought.

Suddenly Uno came bounding into the room, looking for all the world as if he were being chased by a flock of hippogriffs.

"Someone's broken Mrs. Sonyanova in two!" he barked, his fur standing on end.

"What do you mean, 'broken in two'?" Barnaby asked.

"I mean she's in two pieces now instead of one. What do you think I mean?"

They all looked at one another, then raced down to the dungeons.

Chapter 8

TO ANA AND CLARISSA'S AMAZEMENT, Barnaby's device located Mrs. Sonyanova's cell in no time at all. The three of them crowded around the small barred viewport while Uno peered through the food hatch below. Ana braced herself for a gory sight, but, in fact, Mrs. Sonyanova's demise could not have been any cleaner. She had been split from head to toe, and the separate halves not only lay on opposite sides of the cell, but they were completely hollow—like pieces of a sarcophagus. No blood, no bones or internal organs, nothing but empty space surrounded by petrified skin and clothes.

"It can't be her," Clarissa whispered. "It must be a mannequin. She's escaped."

Ana did not think that likely. Hags had minuscule sorcerological powers. Mrs. Sonyanova could not have even undone the Locking Spell, much less escaped from Solomon Castle undetected.

"Do—do you think she did it herself?" Barnaby asked. "She was very despondent the other day. She kept saying she wished he would come back, that she was so tired—"

"Who would come back?" Ana asked.

Barnaby shrugged. "She didn't say."

"Well, before you go on shedding such brilliant light on the case," Uno said, "come see the others."

"Others?" Ana and Barnaby and Clarissa asked together.

He led them farther down the corridor. In at least a dozen cells, they found mortals and Immortals who had suffered the same fate as Mrs. Sonyanova—each of them split in two and emptied, their hollow remains tossed aside like eggshells. They must have been awake during the attack, too, for all had the same strange expressions on their faces: peace on one side, despair on the other.

"Does your mother clean house now and then?" Barnaby asked.

Ana shook her head. With the exception of those receiving short-term punishments, her mother tended to forget about her prisoners.

"It's probably that Benjamin," Uno said. "We see him skulking about all the time down here."

Clarissa glared at him. "Benjamin wouldn't hurt a fly," she said.

Uno snorted. "You obviously don't spend time in the kitchen," he said.

"Benjamin certainly couldn't split anyone in half. It has to be Mr. Pound," Ana said.

Barnaby shivered. "But why?" he asked.

"Probably wanted a snack," Uno said. "I mean, someone who melts, incinerates, and transmogrifies people for educational purposes isn't likely to eat sandwiches, is he?"

Clarissa suddenly looked a bit sick. "Just like in the story," she muttered.

Everyone stared at her. "What are you talking about?" Ana asked. "What story?"

"That old mortal legend. I've told you about it," Clarissa said. "There's this creature that lives at the bottom of the Maelstrom. Every thousand years, he comes out to feed on mortals. He cuts them open with his fiery eyes and devours everything inside. Then he disappears again."

"You're not serious?" Ana said. "You think Mr. Pound lives in the Maelstrom?"

"I'm not saying he is the monster. I just mean this is all frighteningly similar. Perhaps we should tell your mother," Clarissa said.

Ana's eyes widened. She could not remember Clarissa ever suggesting telling her mother *anything*. "She'll think we're only trying to get rid of him," she said. "We have to have proof."

"Fine. Then let's get it," Clarissa said. "He can't devour a dozen people without leaving some sort of evidence, can he?"

Ana liked that idea. They would go back through the cells and gather clues, and then they would force Mr. Pound to confess— just like in those old mortal books she sometimes read with Clarissa. Better yet, it would be a kind of quest: hunting for hidden things, defeating the evil giant.

They started in Mrs. Sonyanova's cell, searching for footprints and fingerprints, spell residues and curse trails. Ana examined the energy field for auras, traces of which should have been everywhere, since all living creatures have auras. But there was nothing—not even a *hint* of Mrs. Sonyanova's aura. And the other cells were equally devoid of clues.

Clarissa and Barnaby spoke to the other prisoners. Some acknowledged hearing whimpers or pleas, but such sounds were common in a dungeon. One or two had also noticed mysterious flashes of light, but what this could mean, no one knew.

When the foursome had finished their investigation, they had nothing to show for it. The perpetrator had left no evidence other than the bodies. But this only convinced them that Mr. Pound must be the culprit. For who else could wipe away the victims' auras?

"We'll have to catch him in the act," Ana said as they climbed back up the stairs to the first level of the dungeons.

Uno, trotting along beside Barnaby, snorted. "Spying on a demigod. What a delightful idea. I'm sure he won't notice."

"Do you have a better suggestion?" Clarissa asked.

She still looked oddly pale and preoccupied, Ana thought. Of course, most of the victims had been mortals, and she had grown up with the tale of the monster, so perhaps it meant more to her than it did to Ana and Barnaby. Still, Ana was not used to seeing Clarissa this way. Was there something else bothering her?

"Do nothing," Uno said. "I've found that's usually the best course when dealing with beings more powerful than oneself."

"I thought dogs were supposed to be brave and noble," Clarissa said.

"Really? I thought mortals were supposed to be seen and not heard," Uno replied.

"Stop it," Ana said. She paused near the bottom of the stairs to the ground floor. There was an oubliette to her left, and across from it was the utility closet where the torture master stored his various implements—pincers, flaying knives, masks lined with nettles or spikes, tubs full of special caustic gels, truth potions.

"We could take turns hiding in there," Ana said. "When Mr. Pound passes by on his way to the dungeons, we can follow him. What do you think?"

"I think I would rather twist my head up like a dishrag and shove it into a bottle—assuming Mr. Pound doesn't do it for me," Barnaby said. "What makes you think he won't know we're there?"

"We can pretend we're looking for bone crushers or fingernail peelers," Ana said.

No one else liked her plan. Uno thought it was a shortcut to annihilation. Barnaby doubted they could catch Mr. Pound in the act, and if they did, what then? The Queen would sack him, and then what reason would Barnaby and Uno have to remain at Solomon Castle?

Clarissa did not object to the plan itself, but she did not like the hiding place. "Why does it have to be in that closet?" she said. "Why not farther down?"

"Because the dungeons are mobile beyond this level," Ana replied.

"Yes, but . . . sitting in the dark with all those hideous things . . ." Clarissa said.

"They're not *alive*," Ana said, annoyed by Clarissa's sudden squeamishness. They had been in that closet at least a hundred times before, and Clarissa had never said a word. In fact, years ago, Clarissa had had the brilliant idea of putting a Reflecting Spell on the implements so that all the pain the torture master caused his victims would be transferred to him instead. Ana could not understand why she was nervous now.

After much argument, Ana finally prevailed, and they agreed to take turns hiding in the utility closet. They would do it only at night, however, for between Mr. Pound's teaching responsibilities and his frequent consultations with the Queen, they doubted he had many opportunities to attack prisoners during the day. Ana and Clarissa would watch from ten until one in the morning, Barnaby and Uno from one until four.

Only Ana was excited about the plan. The others climbed the stairs as if they were going to the gallows.

It really is like a quest, Ana thought—*four brave knights trapping an evil demigod.* But Clarissa remained silent and gloomy all the way back to their room. *Is she really afraid?* Ana wondered. *No, there must be something else bothering her.* But Ana could not guess what it might be.

Chapter 9

SITTING IN THE CRAMPED, dusty utility closet for hours on end was the most uncomfortable and tedious task Ana had ever undertaken. She had hoped they would catch Mr. Pound within a night or two, but three nights passed, and no one saw him coming or going. Yet the number of victims continued to grow—by at least one or two a day.

"Can't we stop this now?" Clarissa said to Ana on the fourth night. "He's obviously not *walking* down here, and I'm exhausted."

"You're right," Ana said, yawning. It was the end of their watch anyway. And if the circles under Clarissa's eyes grew any darker, people would mistake her for a zombie. "You go. I'll stay just long enough to tell Barnaby and Uno we've called it quits."

Clarissa nodded and left.

Perhaps it isn't Mr. Pound after all, Ana thought, sitting alone in the rusty-smelling closet. *Perhaps it's a poltergeist or a pack of goblins.* But the exorcist had been to the castle only last week.

She waited and waited. Long after Barnaby and Uno were sup-posed to relieve her, they had still not appeared, and she was growing very angry. But finally the door popped open.

"Sorry, sorry, sorry," Barnaby said, closing the door and tak-ing a seat beside Ana. "I stopped in the kitchen for a snack. Uno's coming as soon he finishes his scraps. Here—I brought you this." He reached into his shirt pocket and pulled out a wishbone.

Ana laughed. This was at least the twelfth or thirteenth wish-bone Barnaby had collected since coming to Solomon Castle.

"Why are you so infatuated with those things?" she said. "They never work."

"One of them might," Barnaby said. "Besides, they're the only form of magic that doesn't require skill."

"And what do you wish for? More springs and screws? A chest to put them in?"

Barnaby blushed. "A planet of my own, actually. I'd outlaw sorcery, and anyone who cast a spell or curse would be pelted with hailstones and driven out into space."

"Wouldn't that get a bit dull?" Ana said.

Barnaby shrugged. "Better than going back to Georges Castle or staying here," he said. "I mean, wouldn't you leave, too, if you had half a chance?"

"Yes, but I wouldn't wish myself onto a desert planet. I'd travel, be a knight-errant, and fight ogres and cyclopes and that sort of thing."

"Well, all that sounds a bit exhausting to me—and dangerous," Barnaby said. "But I suppose if I had your skill, I wouldn't mind it."

"I don't have any skill," Ana said. "I'm barely able to keep up with the lessons."

"But you're going to pass the Bacchanalians. Whereas I'll be lucky to cast a single spell correctly. And then you know what will happen."

Ana nodded. "Your father will be upset."

"He'll toss me into the Maelstrom. And even if he doesn't . . . Well, slags don't usually last very long on their own, do they?"

He twirled the wishbone in his hand. "So these things are my best chance. Either they grant me my wish and Uno and I find a planet with no other inhabitants, or . . ." He held the wishbone out to Ana. "I can never remember whether it's the larger piece that gets the wish or the smaller one," he said.

"It doesn't work that way," Ana was about to say, but suddenly she heard footsteps. They were too heavy to be Uno's and too light to be Mr. Pound's. She peered through a crack in the doorjamb. Benjamin! It was too late to escape. She cast an Invisibility Spell over herself and Barnaby, hoping the two or three grains of athen she produced would go unnoticed, and held her breath.

The latch lifted. Benjamin entered, carrying a glowing crystal in one hand. He looked this way and that, his long, hatchet nose twitching as if he could sniff out any Immortal hiding there. He swiped at the air with his hands, narrowly missing Barnaby's face, but finally seemed satisfied that no one was there.

How strange, Ana thought as Benjamin closed the door. *It's as if he knew we might be here.* Had Clarissa told him? Why would she do that?

Ana slid to the door. Through the crack in the doorjamb, she could see Benjamin pushing one of the castle's waste carts into the oubliette across the way. "What's he doing?" she whispered.

Barnaby did not know and did not care. He suggested they leave, but Ana was too curious. She waited a minute or two, then, still invisible, tiptoed down the passageway. Barnaby, not knowing what else to do, ran after her, latching a hand onto her shoulder.

Together, they crept farther into the oubliette, a long, stony tunnel with no purpose other than to confuse invading enemies. It ended at a hundred-foot plunge into the castle's sewers, and since the water in the sewer burned with gallons of magical wastes— spell fragments, curse reagents, and various other kinds of discarded sorcery—there was a flickering red glow everywhere, making the tunnel look remarkably like the entrance to a volcano.

As Ana and Barnaby drew close to the end of the tunnel, the scent of smoke and brimstone and a wet, froggy odor, like swamp ooze, grew stronger. They stopped a few feet away from Benjamin. He had his back to them and was standing at the very edge of the drop, slowly paying out a length of rope.

Ana silently cast Levitation Spells on herself and Barnaby. They floated as near as they dared to the place where Benjamin stood, but there was not sufficient space to pass between Benjamin's head and the roof of the tunnel, so they could not see what lay at the end of the rope.

A jangling crash came from below. A moment later, someone hissed, "The knot's stuck!"

That there could be someone in the sewers was startling enough. No one could survive in that muck. But far more startling was Benjamin's reply.

"Hurry up! This isn't a fishing party!" he hissed, leaning out over the ledge.

Ana was so shocked she banged her head against the ceiling. Poor Barnaby lost all concentration on his levitation and went down when he meant to go up. He struck the ground with a thick and extremely audible bump, and though he managed to maintain his invisibility, it did him little good, for Benjamin had clearly heard him.

"Hang on," Benjamin said, setting down the rope. He drew a long knife from under his coat and slowly advanced toward the spot where Barnaby was sitting.

Do something, Ana silently begged. But Barnaby was too frightened to move. Desperate, Ana cast the first spell she could think of. It should have turned Barnaby into a mouse, but the spell went awry somehow, as many of her spells did these days, and instead of transforming Barnaby, it conjured up a small white mouse with a very pink nose. The mouse squeaked at the sight of Benjamin, scurried between his legs, and disappeared into a crevice in the stones.

"Bah! Another miserable rodent," Benjamin spat. Just to be certain, he kicked his foot this way and that in the spot where Barnaby had been. But Barnaby had finally managed to levitate out of reach.

Benjamin returned to his post. He pulled the rope back up. An empty canvas sack dangled from the end. He reached into his cart for another load, and when Ana saw what he was stealing, she nearly bumped her head again. It was not jewelry or clothes or the family silver, but books—a dozen or more. *What could he possibly want with those?* she wondered.

He slipped the books into the sack, wrapped and tied the sack carefully, then lowered it to his accomplice below. After a few minutes, he pulled the rope back up, minus its sack, and coiled it up.

"Right. I'll see you in a few days," the accomplice called from below.

"Unless those brats decide to play hide-and-seek again," Benjamin replied, hiding the rope under a loose stone. "Three nights wasted! As if it's not taking us long enough to get all these books out."

He knew we were there! Ana thought with a start. *How? Clarissa must have told him. But why? To warn him away?* That meant Clarissa knew about Benjamin's activities. *Of course,* Ana thought, *that's why she made such a fuss about hiding in the closet.*

Ana was furious now. She had no time to dwell on Clarissa's deceit, however. Benjamin was hurrying out of the oubliette, and she and Barnaby had to retreat quickly to the opening in order not to bump against him.

Once Benjamin was gone, Ana wanted to see who was in the sewers. She flew back down the corridor, and Barnaby—who was not curious at all but did not want to be left behind—followed closely after her.

The shaft leading down to the sewer was much larger than Ana had expected, a cavernous space with vaulted brick ceilings. Three enormous tunnels led into it, and in the center lay a wide, bubbling pool of waste. The stuff might have been lava, it was so hot and gave off so much smoke, but Benjamin's accomplice seemed unaffected by it. He stood up to his knees in the muck, protected (much to Ana's surprise) by a pair of thigh-high, silvery boots and blue-and-white Amalgamated Witchcraft coveralls and thick glasses.

That these items offered any protection at all from the deadly water was surprising. Far more surprising was the fact that the intruder was a dwarf. Ana had met many Immortal dwarves, but this one appeared to be shorter and thinner and the proportions of his limbs did not look quite right. *He must be a mortal dwarf,* Ana thought, and this realization excited her even more, for she had never seen a mortal dwarf before.

Barnaby, for his part, was surprised, but not for the same reasons. *Alexander?* he thought, staring at their visitor. The intruder looked the right size and shape, but his head was wrapped in too many layers of dirty brown cloth for Barnaby to make out his face.

A small, metallic dinghy floated behind the dwarf, chained to his waist. The sack of books lay strapped on top, and underneath was a mound of what Ana and Barnaby at first mistook for rubble. On closer examination, however, they realized it was athen—dozens of lumps of athen. What a mortal could want with athen, and why he would bother to sneak it out when he could have as much as he liked, Ana and Barnaby could not begin to guess.

The dwarf adjusted the chain around his waist. Then he set off on his journey back through the sewers, the dinghy trailing heavily behind him.

"Is he going to the ghetto, do you think?" Ana whispered to Barnaby, once the dwarf was out of sight.

"I don't see how. It's miles away," Barnaby replied, breathing heavily from the smoke and heat and the inherent difficulties of maneuvering in midair. "I'm more interested in why he's taking those books and all that athen."

"A good question," Ana said, floating back up to the oubliette.

Barnaby was about to follow when he suddenly noticed something protruding from the muck below him—a thick, gleaming stick. He reached down and pulled at it, and what popped out of the mire was a small steel hammer.

The mortal must have dropped it, he thought. He flicked the hammer to get the last bits of waste off, then slipped it under his shirt. And he was so pleased to have another tool for his collection that he did not stop to wonder how a hammer could have survived the burning waste water, nor why it felt so cold against his skin.

Chapter 10

IT WAS NEARLY THREE O'CLOCK IN THE MORNING by the time Ana returned to her room. She should have been exhausted, but she was so bewildered by everything she had witnessed, and so angry with Clarissa for keeping secrets, that sleep was the last thing on her mind.

She kicked open the door, snapped the glow lamps on to their brightest setting. Clarissa, who had been fast asleep, sat bolt upright.

"What are you doing?" she said, shielding her eyes from the glaring light.

"Oh, don't mind me. I'm just looking for my friend Clarissa," Ana said, slamming the door. "She used to be here, but now there's someone else in her bed."

"What are you talking about?" Clarissa said.

"I'm talking about the person who told Benjamin we were in that closet," Ana said. "The person who told him we were done now, and he could go on with his criminal activities."

Clarissa's freckles merged into a bright pink mass. "You—you saw him?"

"Of course I saw him!" Ana said. "If he had been anywhere but in the sewer, the entire planet would have seen him. I suppose he couldn't wait to do his nefarious business."

Clarissa hugged her knees. "He wasn't doing anything *nefarious*."

"He was stealing athen."

"He was *getting rid of it*. You Immortals don't want it, and it has to go somewhere. So we take it and use it in the ghetto . . . to—to fill holes in the streets and buildings."

"Then why be so secretive about it?"

Clarissa groaned in frustration. "What do you think your mother would do if she found out we can get in and out of the castle at will?"

Ana hadn't thought of that. But that was not the point. "You're stealing books, too—lots of them," she said.

Clarissa raised a finger to her lips. "We're not *stealing* them," she whispered. "They're ours. We brought them here hundreds of years ago, to preserve them. And now we're taking them back; that's all."

Ana shook her head. It was far too bewildering: mortals smuggling books in, smuggling books out, stealing athen, traipsing miles and miles through the sewers. From what Clarissa had said, this had been going on for hundreds of years, yet no one had ever noticed before.

Ana was not ready to forgive her yet, however. That the mortals had secrets was one thing; that Clarissa was keeping secrets from her was another. Ana changed into her nightgown. She snapped her fingers at the glow lamps, then flopped into bed, exhausted and angry.

"I don't have any idea who you are anymore, Clarissa," she said, punching her pillow to make it more comfortable.

"What are you talking about?" Clarissa replied from her own bed.

"You're so secretive these days. You get these strange looks on your face, as if you've seen a ghost. I can't trust you at all."

"Because I told Benjamin you were hiding in that utility closet?"

"No. Because Benjamin can talk and you never told me. Because mortals have been sneaking in and out of the castle for eons, and you never told me that, either. And you're taking books and athen and who knows what else. You're supposed to be my friend."

"I *am* your friend," Clarissa said. "But I'm a mortal. If I let slip that you went to the park without permission, your mother will take away your dessert for a week. But if you let slip that Benjamin can talk, or that people are coming and going through the sewers, or that we put mortal books in the library and are now taking them back, what do you think she'll do? We're friends, Ana, but we're not equals. You know that."

"You make it sound like we're enemies," Ana said. "We live in the same house, the same room. We eat the same food and share the same clothes. You've done everything but stick your tongue out at my mother, and she hasn't blasted you or turned you into a four-headed nematode. So why do you always keep crying 'Poor mortal me!' all the time?"

There was a loud rustle. Clarissa was suddenly on top of Ana, pinning her wrists to the bed.

"You don't understand a thing, do you?!" Clarissa hissed. Her eyes gleamed in the dark. Was it anger or tears or both? Ana could not tell. But she had not seen Clarissa like this since their fight on the battlements years ago.

She struggled to free her arms, but leverage and gravity were on Clarissa's side. And Ana knew from experience that if she used a spell to get Clarissa off her, it would only infuriate Clarissa more.

"I've done everything for you!" Clarissa said. "I put myself at risk every single day. If your mother hasn't blasted me out of existence, it's only because she's either too busy or too snobby to bother. I even fold your ratty underthings! And for what?"

"You don't fold them. You throw them in a drawer," Ana said.

"Look—just answer one question," Clarissa said. "When you've finished your schooling, what are you going to do?"

"My internship at AW—you know that," Ana grunted.

"And after that?"

"I don't know. Become a knight-errant, I suppose, if Mother will let me. . . ."

Clarissa groaned in frustration. "*That's* your plan? Hunt for amulets and magic mirrors and kill dragons who aren't bothering anyone?" She released Ana, collapsed back against the wall, hiding her face in her hands.

"What's wrong with that?" Ana asked, sitting up and rubbing her wrists.

"It's not even what knights-errant *do*!" Clarissa said, jerking her hands away from her face. "Not *true* knights-errant."

"I think I know more about the profession than you do," Ana retorted.

"Where do you think your people got the idea? From mortals. Thousands of years ago, there was a king named Arthur. He organized a group of knights and sent them out on quests. They went all over the countryside, battling evil kings and monsters and wizards and rescuing anyone who needed rescuing. They saved people. *That's* what knights-errant are supposed to do—*save* people. But you wouldn't know anything about that, would you? All that power in your stupid fingers and you—"

"Oh, please. Don't start another of your 'if I had your power' lectures," Ana said. Then she heard a sob escaping from Clarissa. Clarissa almost never wept, but when she did, it always frightened Ana. It sounded so desperate, so final.

"I'm sorry. I didn't mean it," Ana said, reaching for Clarissa's hand in the dark.

"What's going to happen to me, Ana?" Clarissa sobbed. "When you're gone—where am I going to go?"

So that's what this is about, Ana thought, putting her arm around

Clarissa. She almost laughed, but then realized she had never given the question any thought. She had always assumed Clarissa would go wherever she went. But it was not as easy as that. Mortals did not respond well to spotshifting or interstellar flight. A few times a year was as much as their bodies could tolerate. And Ana couldn't very well leave Clarissa behind, for a mortal with no one to protect her would have a very short life.

"You've never even thought about it, have you?" Clarissa said, wiping her tears away. "I'm just a pet to you. When Uno and I are dead, you and Barnaby will laugh and reminisce about the silly tricks we used to do."

"Stop it! That's ridiculous," Ana said.

And it was. But long after Clarissa had dried her tears, long after she had retreated to her own bed and fallen asleep, Ana lay awake, full of worry and shame. She had *never* thought of Clarissa as a pet. But she had never thought about Clarissa's future, either. Why? Because Clarissa was there. Clarissa would always be there. Yet Clarissa *was* mortal—she had been telling Ana that for years. And Ana had refused to listen. Now she had finally heard, but she did not have the slightest idea what to do.

Chapter 11

BARNABY HAD NOT PURPOSELY HIDDEN the hammer from Ana. She had simply dashed away while he was fetching Uno from the utility closet, and he had not caught up with her. He doubted she would be interested, in any case. Tools were his passion, not hers.

Now, locked in his room with a crude Privacy Spell on his door, he laid the hammer on his bed. He had never seen anything like it. The head and handle were of the same smooth, shiny metal, without a pit or seam or flaw of any kind. He gripped the formfitted shaft in his hand, raised it up and down, feeling the weight and the chill. If he had not known better, he would have said it was made of athen. But, of course, that was impossible. *It must be iridium or draconium,* he thought.

Uno, resting his head on the bed, groaned. "Not another tool. Why can't you collect useful things, like soup bones or small, edible animals?" He sniffed at the hammer. Every hair on his body suddenly stood on end.

"Do you know what that is?" he said.

"A hammer, obviously," Barnaby said.

"I mean, do you know what it's made of?" Uno said.

"Draconium, I think," Barnaby said. "But I'd have to ask who-ever dropped it."

"It's made of *athen*," Uno said. "Look at it."

Barnaby laughed. "That's impossible," he said. "You can't make anything out of athen."

"Touch it. Smell it," Uno growled.

Barnaby touched it. He sniffed at it. "I don't smell anything," he said.

"Exactly," Uno replied. "Draconium has a scent. Steel and copper have scents. Even hydrogen has a scent—at least for those of us with nonvestigial noses. The only thing in the Universe that has no scent is athen."

Barnaby stared at the hammer. If it were a lump of athen, he would have recognized it at once. But shaped liked this, made into something so practical . . .

"You're right," he said. "But how—how is that possible?"

"You said the mortals were stealing athen," Uno replied. "Per-haps they make things with it."

"They don't have the power," Barnaby said. "And if they have discovered some way, wouldn't our Immortal scientists have dis-covered it, too?"

"If they didn't have the collective intelligence of dead ice marmots."

Barnaby shook his head. "Someone else must have dropped

it—the Queen or Mr. Pound. Yes, Mr. Pound would make much more sense. He's got lots of power, and he knows nearly everything."

Uno's ears stood on end. "You'd better put it back," he said. "Mr. Pound will come looking for it, and when he discovers you took it, he'll split *you* open."

"I didn't take it. I *found* it."

"I'm sure the distinction will impress him greatly. Now please—put it *back*."

"No," Barnaby said. He reached under his mattress and removed his tool kit. "I'm going to hide it," he said. He laid the hammer beside the other tools, gazed at it once more, then rolled the canvas up and hid it beneath his mattress.

"Wonderful. Perhaps you should put a sign on the footboard, too: 'Nothing unusual under here,'" Uno said.

Barnaby frowned. Uno was right. The safest thing would be to return the hammer. But Barnaby could not bring himself to do that. He was not sure why Mr. Pound would go to the trouble of making a hammer out of athen, but if he could do it once, he could probably do it a thousand times. Whereas Barnaby was not likely ever to find another athen tool, much less make one, so he was not going to part with this one.

He rummaged through his dresser drawers, found some bits of dragon leather and wire. Within half an hour, he had fashioned a crude holster for the hammer. He removed the hammer from its hiding place, slipped it into the holster, and attached the holster to a spare belt. Then he strapped the belt around his waist, hiding it beneath his shirt.

"Oh, that looks cozy," Uno muttered as Barnaby slid into bed. "You might as well sleep on a bone."

It was, in fact, a bit uncomfortable, but Barnaby was too exhausted to care. He clicked his fingers to shut off the glow lamps. Within a minute, Uno was snoring loudly. But Barnaby could not sleep. His thoughts kept returning to the hammer. Had Mr. Pound really made it? Whatever for? And how?

Chapter 12

EVERYONE AWOKE OUT OF SORTS the next morning. Luckily, it was Saturday. The Queen had gone off to Sanctolonia, the spa planet, for a manicure and Golem mud massage, and Ana and Barnaby had no classes. They were expected to spend several hours in the SSCCR, of course, but neither Ana nor Barnaby had the energy for that.

"Let's go into the city," Clarissa suggested, when they had all gathered in Ana's room after breakfast. "We can talk there and decide what to do about you-know-who."

"The park? Can we have a picnic?" Uno said, his ears perking up.

"Why not?" Clarissa said.

Ana, tugging her hair back into what looked like a sheaf of wheat, studied her friend's sagging cheeks and puffy eyes. *She wants to get us out of the castle,* Ana thought, noticing the way Clarissa kept rolling and unrolling the edge of her apron. *She's afraid someone will ask about Benjamin.*

Clarissa had lied about Benjamin's activities, Ana had realized when she woke up. It made no sense for the butler to risk his life for a few books, nor for the dwarf to crawl through miles of sewers for a few lumps of athen. Even mortals could find better materials than that for patching holes. But she had not voiced these suspicions to Clarissa, for fear Clarissa would get upset again.

"Mother will lock us in the SSCCR if we go off without permission," Ana said. It was true. Once, she and Clarissa had gone to Alpha Centauri to see the annual migration of the giant blue-bellied rotifers. When they had returned to the castle, the Queen had been waiting for them. She had given Clarissa a week in the dungeons, Ana a week in the SSCCR.

"And I'm a bit tired," Barnaby said. "I thought I would just stay in my room and, um, study today." The truth was Barnaby could not take his mind off the athen hammer. It was burning against his skin, and he was desperate to test it out. He had already tried it once that morning, tapping it against a small lump of athen to see if it would make a mark. But the lump had made such a strange, ungodly shrieking noise, he had had to stop. If everyone were to go to the park, however, he could hammer away to his heart's content.

Uno, however, would not allow it. "I am not going to sit in this glorified kennel while everyone else frolics in the park," he growled. "And you're not going to sit in your room tinkering all day, either."

And that was that.

Clarissa changed out of her maid's uniform and prepared a picnic lunch. Ana cast Aura Duplication Spells to fool the castle's Monitoring Spells into thinking they were all still in their rooms. Then she spotshifted them into the city.

Spotshifting takes a fair amount of practice. Many novices have been known to spotshift themselves or their friends into a tree or rock or even one another. It was a testament to Ana's abilities, therefore, that she delivered them all into the park without mishap.

"It's beautiful!" Clarissa said as they materialized into fresh air and sunshine and the heady scent of flowers. She spun this way and that, her braid whipping about.

Ana laughed. "It's always beautiful," she said. It was true: The park could not be anything but beautiful. Every day, the sun sprinkled down upon it, never too hot and never too cold. The four or five square miles of lawn were always perfect, a bed of green, healthy grass that never grew too long and never turned dry or patchy. The tall beeches and willows and elms shading the paths never lost their leaves, and the shrubs and flowers—tulips and daffodils, mums, impatiens, glorious tangles of roses—were always in bloom, their petals full and radiant thanks to nightly rain showers.

Immortals—witches and warlocks and dwarves in business suits, hurrying from one glass tower to another—glanced at the little group in passing. A few mortals, dressed in the standard blue-and-white AW coveralls or red-and-black CNI ones, also glanced their way, puzzled by the sight of three children and a dog. But no one stopped to ask questions.

Uno trotted from tree to shrub to flower bed, sniffing at everything and performing all the necessary canine rituals. Clarissa led everyone away from the more populated western half of the park, around which all the business towers stood like a glassy picket fence, and down to the eastern end of the park. Here lay the city's tournament field and, not far beyond it, the ghetto, sitting like a stale crust of bread on the edge of the park.

Ana worried that Clarissa might lead them into the ghetto. She had done it once before, when Ana was about eleven. "I want to show you something," Clarissa had said, and the next thing Ana knew, she was standing in a disgusting little square full of broken cobblestones and smoking, iridescent puddles. The buildings had looked like dying giants, each leaning against the other and dropping bricks and glass like old, unwanted scales. And the air— full of ozone and sulfur and dozens of other smells Ana could not name—had been almost unbreathable.

Ana had expected a much quainter scene: huts and horse-drawn carts and perhaps some dirty-faced children running about, just like in the mortal books she had read with Clarissa. But this . . . Who could live here? There were people, though. Ana had not seen them, but she had felt their eyes upon her, staring at her from every broken window, every nook and cranny—fearful eyes; angry eyes. They did not want her there; that much had been clear.

And it was this feeling of hatred, so unfamiliar, so frightening, that had made Ana run out of the ghetto.

She certainly did not want to repeat that experience now. But just as she was about to say something, Clarissa led them off the path and into the canopy of an enormous weeping beech.

"We can have our picnic in here," Clarissa said, pushing aside the leafy curtain of branches. They followed her into the natural tent. Thick, winglike limbs radiated out from the trunk of the tree. They sat on these and opened their picnic sacks.

"I can't believe you've never been here before," Clarissa said to Barnaby as she pulled out a roast sandpig sandwich.

"Father promised to take me once, if I cast three spells in a row correctly," Barnaby replied, gazing up into the canopy of leaves. "Of course I didn't, so . . ."

Ana nodded. "My father brought me a few times, when he was home. I remember he said most of the Earth used to be like this—full of trees and flowers and grass . . ."

"Animals, too: dinosaurs and tigers and horses," Clarissa chimed in. "And do you know, I saw puppies once. They were in the ghetto, and they were so tiny and beautiful—all furry and warm. But they died. Everything dies in the ghetto. Even the stupid mice." She stared at her sandwich as if it had suddenly turned to paper.

Ana was not surprised that everything died in the ghetto. She had never understood why anyone lived there in the first place, nor why it was kept so decrepit and unhealthy. "Much too costly to extend the Environmental Management Shield over the ghetto," her mother had explained once. But Ana was sure it had more to do with indifference than with cost.

Well, after last night, Ana had a new vision. She would follow in her mother's footsteps. She would become chairwoman of AW, and the first thing she would do would be to extend the Environmental Management Spell over the ghetto. Then the mortals would have the same clean air and water as the rest of the island. And she would make it illegal to harm or enslave a mortal. *Emancipate*—that was the word: She would *emancipate* the mortals. Then she could go off on an occasional knight-erranting weekend without worrying about Clarissa.

"Speaking of dying," Barnaby said, tossing a sandwich to Uno, "I had an idea why Mr. Pound's been hollowing out all the prisoners in the dungeon. Perhaps he wants a new body."

They all stared at him as if he had suggested Mr. Pound wanted ballet lessons.

"Well, look how ugly and clumsy he is," Barnaby said. "He's supposed to be a demigod, yet he moves like a zombie. If I were him, the first thing I would do is get a new body."

"Couldn't he just make one?" Ana said.

Barnaby shrugged. "He must not be as omnipotent as he pretends. Otherwise, he wouldn't have an Immortal for a master, would he? Unless your mother has a way of controlling him— you know, like a genie with its lamp. I remember there was a genie in one of my father's ambrosia bottles once . . ."

Clarissa rolled her eyes. "Well, before you go off on another one of your *fascinating* stories," she said, "I'd like to suggest we tell the Queen about Mr. Pound—before it's too late."

"Right," Uno said, gulping down his fourth sandwich. "'Excuse me, Your Highness—that decrepit but all-powerful tutor you hired? He's snacking between meals. Could you please make him stop?'"

Clarissa shot him a withering glance. "You wouldn't be so glib if it were dogs being killed," she said.

"Clarissa's right," Ana said. "The longer we wait, the more prisoners he's going to kill. But we still need proof."

"I thought of that. What if we search his room?" Clarissa suggested. Mr. Pound had been given a room in the castle. Why he would need such a thing, no one could guess, for he did not sleep, and he was not likely to sit up nights knitting or reading a good book. Nevertheless, they sometimes heard him clomping about up there late at night. "Uno could go in while Mr. Pound is teaching."

This, of course, elicited a very impolite response from Uno as well as renewed charges of anticanine discrimination. "Why don't *you* search his room?" Uno growled.

"I will," Clarissa said, tossing the remains of her sandwich back into her bag. "But I thought someone who's always bragging about how much better his sight and hearing and sense of smell are would have an easier time. Or was that just a lot of dog nonsense?"

"I hear the cogs clicking in your evil little brain well enough.

Does that count?" Uno said. But Clarissa had hit her mark. After lengthy negotiations, in which Ana promised Uno at least one outing a week to the park, Clarissa promised to get an entire roast sandpig for Uno, and Barnaby promised not to kick Uno off the bed at night, he finally agreed to search Mr. Pound's room.

Chapter 13

UNO PROCRASTINATED FOR NEARLY A WEEK, but at last he kept his promise. He searched Mr. Pound's room, and when Ana and Barnaby and Clarissa rushed upstairs after class, they found him hiding beneath Barnaby's bed.

"Don't ever ask me to do that again," he said when they had finally convinced him to come out of his hiding place. "That room . . . There's something terribly wrong with it."

He recounted how he had gone in expecting some sort of macabre decor—a coffin, perhaps, or skulls for candlesticks, or even a gate of fire leading to the netherworld. Instead, he had found the same furnishings as in all the other guest rooms: a large iron bed, a dresser, a desk and chair, a carpet on the floor, and various decorations on the walls. Except every line was sharper and brighter and straighter than any Uno had seen before. Every angle met at exactly ninety degrees, not one-millionth more or less. Every plank in the wooden floor ran straight and true, and every spot of red or blue or yellow or green in the ornate carpet stood out as brilliant and distinct as its neighbor. The sight alone had made Uno dizzy.

But the smells and sounds had been even worse. An armada of odors, each scent exactly as powerful as all the others, had made it impossible to breathe. And though he had been the only source of sound in the room, every click of his nails had pricked his ears, like a needle. His sneezes had almost deafened him.

"But did you find anything?" Clarissa asked.

Uno reached under the bed with a paw. He flicked out two stony objects: the petrified halves of an animal—a mouse.

"He eats mice?" Barnaby said, staring at the hollow remains.

"He eats *intruders*. Look," Uno said, nudging the mouse forward. There was a note tied to one of the mouse's half legs. No one wanted to touch it. Finally Clarissa, with an exasperated growl, snatched it off and opened it. The note said: *Misery and Hope awaited Pandora. See what awaits you.*

"He knew all along!" Barnaby said, clutching at Uno's fur. "He could have split Uno in half!"

"But he didn't. And now we have proof!" Clarissa said, holding up the note.

Ana did not think a petrified mouse and an unsigned note constituted proof. But she agreed they were not likely to find anything better, given that Mr. Pound was on his guard.

The next morning, as she slipped into her seat at the breakfast table, Ana laid the broken mouse and note before her mother.

"This is what your wonderful tutor has been doing," she said, unfolding her napkin.

The Queen glanced with distaste at the mouse halves. "Dissecting mice? How awful, Anatopsis. I'll have him sacked at once." Then, to Ana's dismay, she spotshifted the mouse's remains away.

"He's doing the same to the prisoners in the dungeons, Mother," Ana said as the Queen returned to tapping her soft-boiled roc's egg with a spoon. "He splits them open and scoops them out, just like that mouse."

"He can bake them into pies for all I care," the Queen said. "They're only prisoners, Anatopsis."

"What about that note? It doesn't bother you that he's threatening me and my friends?"

"You were snooping in his room, Anatopsis. You can hardly expect him to leave you *encouraging* notes."

Ana growled in frustration. "I don't understand you, Mother," she said. "Here's this awful person attacking prisoners and threatening your daughter, and you're not the least concerned. Don't you wonder what he's doing here? Doesn't the fact that he's a thousand times more powerful than you but wants to spend his time tutoring Immortals seem odd to you?"

The Queen laid down her spoon. "What Mr. Pound chooses to do with his time and abilities is none of my business. He obviously does not provide these services gratis, however. There are conditions, ones which I will be happy to share with you—as my mother did with me—once you have completed your education."

"Conditions? Like eating his fill of prisoners, you mean?"

"I don't have time for your little dramas, Anatopsis. If you find that Mr. Pound is committing acts I have not expressly permitted, I will be happy to listen to you. But I can assure you, there is nothing about him I do not already know."

She finished her egg and patted her mouth with her napkin. "I must go," she said. "But there is something else we need to discuss. Mr. Pound informs me that you and Prince Barnaby have been spending time together. Is this true?"

The question surprised Ana. Did her mother know about their outing to the park? "Not really," she lied. "I mean, we have classes together, and we talk sometimes. He's actually a rather interesting person, you know, once you—"

"There is nothing interesting about him," the Queen snapped. "He's a dim-witted bore from a long line of bores, and he'll be lucky to make it to the Bacchanalian exams. He is also the son of King Georges, in case you've forgotten."

"But you said yourself he's harmless."

The Queen rose. "I said he was an imbecile. That does not mean he is harmless. You will treat Prince Barnaby as a classmate, and when you are not in classes, you will keep your distance from him. Is that clear?"

Ana nodded. She had no intention of obeying her mother, but she knew there was no point in arguing.

The Queen spotshifted away, leaving Ana alone at the table. *Stay away from Barnaby. Don't ask about Mr. Pound. Don't bother your busy mother,* Ana thought. *The only thing she didn't order me to do is stop playing with Clarissa.*

She picked up the toast on her plate and tore at it with her teeth. *Conditions,* her mother had said. What sort of conditions? Were they only what Ana had already seen in the dungeons, or was there something more? *There is nothing about him I do not already know.* Ana doubted that. In fact, the more she saw of Mr. Pound, the more convinced she was that no one knew what his true business was.

She had a few minutes before class. She went to find Clarissa and tell her what the Queen had said, but as she was passing through the entrance hall, an envelope with the UCSB logo leaped up from the mail cauldron and stowed itself in the pocket of her jumper. Ana rushed upstairs to her room, overjoyed.

Dearest Ana, the letter said, when the envelope had finally opened and handed its contents to her.

How wonderful to hear that my missives are finally reaching you! I hope our secret is still safe and that you receive this letter soon.

How are you? Are your studies are going well? Only a few more months until your exams—you must be very excited! (As am I!)

Yes, I did finally enroll in the engineering school. (UCSB, by the way, stands for Union of Concerned Sentient Beings—no doubt you have heard of them.) They seem to think I have some natural talent for this sort of thing. Unfortunately, I am now so busy with classes that I hardly have time to breathe, let alone write letters. But I am squeezing this one in while awaiting my new field supervisor.

One thing: The chief librarian here—a wonderful chap!—thought he remembered a reference to Mr. Pound in a book about the Os Divinitas. The O.D.—as we in the Guild used to call it—is one of those perpetual hoaxes: a bone that supposedly contains the power of the gods. No one's ever seen it, of course, but the knights always fought over the O.D. jobs because there's nothing like the quest for a mythological object to keep one employed.

Obsession with the O.D. could indicate some insanity on Mr. P.'s part, of course. But it doesn't make him dangerous. Nevertheless, if he threatens you at all, let me know and I'll bring the entire UCSB down on him!

Write back soon. I miss you terribly!

Much love,

Your Father

Tears welled in Ana's eyes. She had hoped, after the strange goings-on she and Clarissa and Barnaby had discovered, that her father might come home. But she had only just mentioned Mr. Pound's predations in her last letter, and there was a chance he had not received it yet.

She read the letter again, wiping the tears from her face. *He's probably right,* she thought. *Mother would never have brought Mr. Pound to the castle if she thought he was dangerous.*

Still, Ana did not feel safe around Mr. Pound. It was not just the strange cracking in his eyes and the light shimmering behind them, the way he could paralyze her with just a glance. It was the sense that what lay inside Mr. Pound bore no resemblance to the outside, that what she saw was no more than a shell—and it was growing thinner every day.

Chapter 14

SOLOMON CASTLE WAS CHANGING, but whether it was for better or worse, Ana could not tell. On the one hand, Mr. Pound's predations had drawn her closer to Barnaby and Uno. They joined her and Clarissa in nearly everything now: Armor Bowling, Moatmonster Baiting (in which they tried to get the moatmonsters to leap as high as possible by tossing bits of melonfish down from the battlements), and, of course, Barnaby's favorite, Desert Island, where they used the SSCCR to create a tropical island and then spent the entire day sailing and swimming and lying about in the hot sun.

On the other hand, the Queen had taken to monitoring Ana's education more closely than ever, commenting frequently on Ana's abysmal performance, or her overly casual attitude, or her poor study habits. And Benjamin's glances had graduated from disdain to utter contempt, such that Ana could not pass him in the hallways without feeling as if he were about to poison her. No doubt Clarissa had told him what Ana and Barnaby had witnessed. And Clarissa, too, was behaving very oddly. One day, as Ana and Barnaby were coming into the kitchen for lunch, they overheard her saying to Benjamin, "I've looked everywhere! It's not here!" But as soon as Benjamin and Clarissa saw Ana and Barnaby, Benjamin left and Clarissa suddenly became very preoccupied with stirring the Uranian snakeleaf stew.

On top of everything else, the prisoners were still perishing in the dungeons. And every one of them had the same expression on his or her divided face: despair on one side, peace on the other. But no matter how often Ana protested to her mother, the Queen ignored her.

Weeks went by, then months. The Bacchanalian examinations drew closer, and Ana and Barnaby were beginning to grow anxious. Mr. Pound handed them dozens of new scrolls every morning, and every afternoon he took them down to the SSCCR, where they practiced cursing for so many hours that Ana wished Mr. Pound would just curse *her* and get it over with.

Unfortunately, despite all their efforts and the ceaseless criticism offered by Mr. Pound, neither Ana nor Barnaby seemed able to achieve a level of even modest proficiency in the casting of curses. Barnaby was hampered by a lack of natural skill or power, not to mention difficulty remembering the curses, and the malevolence of them frightened him so much, he tended to flinch whenever he cast one.

Ana's difficulties, however, were both more and less subtle.

That is to say, she had no trouble remembering the curses, and she had skill and power to spare. But whenever she cast a curse, it would explode out of her fingertips and ricochet off the walls in such a wild, uncontrolled burst of magic, Mr. Pound sometimes had to spotshift them all out of the SSCCR to avoid being hit. Worse yet, odd things kept appearing in the wake of Ana's curses: slime molds and mushrooms, mounds of writhing worms, even a puddle filled with jellyfish. It drove Ana mad.

"I can't stand it!" she said one day, after she had blasted a minotaur with a Midas Curse and, in the process, created dozens of snapping, bubbling mussels. "I might as well be doing this blindfolded!"

"Your performance has grown more erratic," Mr. Pound agreed. But he offered no suggestions. In fact, the general tenor of his tutoring had changed over the last few weeks. He no longer harangued or threatened Barnaby. He showed little interest in him at all, it seemed, except when Barnaby committed some grievous error or spoke too much. And though he was clearly watching Ana's efforts with great interest, he did not correct her or criticize her as much as he had been doing. He only made her throw the same curses over and over and over again, until she thought her arms would fall off. Then, after each failure, he would spend several minutes inspecting whatever bizarre plants or molds or slimy creatures had appeared, as if his secret love were botany or zoology.

"Erratic?" Ana said, stepping over the mussels. "I can't get a single—"

A flock of spheroidal toothbats suddenly appeared above her. They dove swiftly, their melon-shaped bodies opening to reveal row upon row of needle-sharp teeth. Ana fired a Cyclone Curse at them, but perhaps because she had reached her limit of frustration, or perhaps because the speed with which they attacked had put her in a panic, the Cyclone Curse went completely out of control. It roared through the cavern with such force that it not only shredded the toothbats to bits, but brought enormous showers of rock and dust and, worst of all, *goldfish* raining down from the ceiling.

"What was *that*?" Barnaby said when the rain of goldfish had finally stopped.

"I—I don't know," Ana said, her ears ringing. Goldfish were everywhere, flipping and flapping and gasping for breath. "I didn't mean to do that."

Mr. Pound's eyes lit upon her. She saw that same awful light she had seen on Mount Olympus, and it made her shiver. She was afraid he was going to subject her to another of his paralyzing probes, but instead he shut off the SSCCR and dismissed them.

The pieces of toothbats and other targets had vanished, Ana noticed as she and Barnaby hurried out the door. But the goldfish remained.

Uno was sitting in the corridor. When they climbed up the stairs, they found Clarissa waiting for them at the top.

"I've found it!" she said, looking very pleased with herself.

"Found what? Your sunny side?" Uno replied.

"The Os Divinitas," Clarissa said. "Ever since your father mentioned it, Ana, I've been trying to find out what it is."

"Nonexistent, I should think," Uno said. "That's what most myths are."

They followed her into the library. Clarissa locked the doors and asked Ana to cast a Privacy Spell on the room. Then, having secured the room against eavesdroppers, they all gathered around the study table.

A dozen volumes from various encyclopedias and dictionaries lay sprawled across the bloodwood surface. *Harrison's Book of Signs and Symbols,* the definitive guide to ideograms, was open to a page titled "Os Divinitas," and there, below the title, was a picture of the mythological object:

Ana and Barnaby gasped. "That's the symbol on Mount Olympus!" they said together.

Clarissa rolled her eyes. "Of course—what did you think it was?" she said.

"I don't know. I just hadn't connected them," Ana said.

"Well I did. 'Os Divinitas,'" Clarissa read from the book. "'Also known as: Thelosteum, Quayanis Vinacalum, Aruk Teledik . . .'

There are at least a hundred names for it. And look at all the different descriptions: 'In biblical lore, breastbone of God, split to create angels and devils. In Hellenic lore, sternum of Kronos, torn out by Olympians and stolen by Prometheus. In Quintanic lore, Lord Quiana's *furcula,* split in two when impaled on Quintanic sun; one half became Quayada the Destroyer, other half, Vinada the Creator; in Teledoran lore—'"

"Oh please! We're not going to go through every religion in the Universe, are we?" Uno said, standing with his paws on the table.

Clarissa skipped to the "Detailed Mythologies" section. "Since Mr. Pound took you to Olympus, I think we can assume he prefers the Hellenic version," she said. "So, according to this, Kronos created the Olympians. Then the Olympians turned on him, and Zeus, knowing where Kronos got his power, tore the Os Divinitas right out of Kronos and set it into the top of Mount Olympus. See, it says here: 'And Zeus set the Os Divinitas into the rock of Mount Olympus, and he said unto the gods, "Behold, the Os Divinitas: our life and our death, our power and our destiny. While it is whole, so are we whole. If it is broken, so shall we be broken." ' "

"And everything was fine until Prometheus came along," Ana said.

"Right," Clarissa said. "He was a Titan, and he wanted revenge, or he liked Man better than he liked the gods, or something like that. So he stole the bone and broke it. And to really humiliate the gods, he gave the pieces to Man. The gods couldn't get the pieces back, then, and with their power gone and no one to worship them, they just sort of withered away."

"But if this thing exists, why would Mr. Pound be searching for it?" Barnaby said. "It can't be of any use to him. I mean, the gods are gone, and finding the Os Divinitas or Thelosteum or whatever it's called isn't going to bring them back, is it?"

Clarissa shrugged. "I don't know. The book says that different parts of it have distinctive properties: One confers Life, the other Death; one gives Knowledge, the other Power—that sort of thing. The parts joined back together are supposed to confer all the power of the gods, so whoever found them and put them back together would become a god, I suppose."

"I thought Old Wax Face was already a god," Uno grumbled.

"A demigod," Ana reminded him. "Sort of like a slag deity."

"I see," Uno said. "And now he's tired of the other gods making fun of him, not letting him join in their Olympic games, and he thinks this overgrown wishbone will change everything?" He nudged Barnaby with his great, furry head. "If you're nice to him, perhaps he'll let you split it with him."

"Very funny," Barnaby said.

Clarissa flipped the book to the next page. "It says here, under 'Historical Evidence,' that no one's ever seen the Os Divinitas. So perhaps it's more of a symbol than a thing."

"Well, that *symbol* is carved into Mount Olympus," Barnaby said. "In fact, it looked exactly as if someone had torn it out of the wall. No, I think it's real—to Mr. Pound, at least. And now he's going about slicing people open one by one and rummaging through their insides, just like that wizard who came to the castle once, the one Father had to behead because he was slicing open all the moatmonsters looking for an amulet . . ."

Barnaby would have continued on in this vein for quite some time, but suddenly there was a muffled explosion from outside the doors. The Privacy Spell collapsed like tinkling glass, and in walked the Queen, looking angrier than Ana had seen her in years.

"What is the meaning of this?" the Queen said, eyebrows arched into arrow points.

"We—we were just studying, Mother," Ana said, feeling as if she had been caught drinking ambrosia.

"I see. And you need Privacy Spells in order to study?"

"N-no," Ana said, blushing.

The Queen glanced at Barnaby and Clarissa. "Go! Both of you. Before I change you into bookmarks," she said.

Barnaby, Uno, and Clarissa did not need to be told twice. They hurried out of the room, leaving Ana under the withering spotlight of her mother's gaze.

"I thought I was very clear, Anatopsis," Queen Solomon said. "I do not want you fraternizing with Prince Barnaby. It's bad enough that I still allow you to play with that chambermaid. I will not watch you jeopardize your future by being naive about the enemy."

"Naive?" Ana said. "Mother, Barnaby has been here eight months, and so far the only dangerous thing he's done is spotshift himself into the ceiling."

"Don't argue with me!" the Queen snapped. "He doesn't have to be a wizard to be treacherous." She approached the table. "Take these books . . ." She picked up the volume of *Harrison's Book of Signs and Symbols,* glanced at the entry, and laughed. "Ah yes, the Os Divinitas."

"You know about it?" Ana said, surprised.

"Darling, you are not the first to have Mr. Pound as a tutor. Of course I know about the Os Divinitas. It's the only reason he comes here."

"Mr. Pound thinks it's *here?* And that doesn't worry you?"

The Queen laughed. "You know I never speak well of your father if I can help it," she said. "But he *is* the best knight-errant in the Guild, and he has taken on at least twelve quests for the Os Divinitas since I've known him. If he can't find it, I assure you, it does not exist. But if Mr. Pound thinks tutoring our families will lead him to this fantastical relic, I am certainly not going to dissuade him.

"Back to my original point, however," she said, dropping the book onto the table. "Prince Barnaby, despite his imbecility, has done a remarkable job of distracting you from your studies. And if you never pass your Bacchanalians, will that be any less a victory for him and his father than if they blasted you into dust?"

Ana hadn't thought of that. Yet it was a ridiculous notion.

Barnaby could no more play the saboteur than Ana could cook. "If he worries you so much, why did you bring him here in the first place?" she said.

"*I* did not bring him here. Mr. Pound did. It is a condition of his agreement, one that he will not waive. But if you disobey me again, I assure you I *will* send Barnaby back, Pound or no Pound. Now please put all these books away and go change for dinner. I'm famished."

The Queen left. Ana, angry and confused, sent the books crashing into the shelves. The only Immortal friend she had ever had and she wasn't even allowed to speak to him. Why? She remembered one of her mother's favorite sayings: *Friends are enemies waiting to reveal themselves.* But how could the least offensive Immortal she had ever met be dangerous, yet a half-dead god who devoured people be perfectly safe? It made no sense.

On her way to her room, another letter leaped out of the mail cauldron. She raced upstairs with it and locked herself in her room, eager for news from her father. But the letter was short this time—little more than a page. Father was beginning his internship and had been given a "planetary engineering" project on a planet called Arthur B. He was very excited about it and hoped to be able to send spirit projections of his work when he was done. The rest of the letter was filled with trivial consolations, such as *Cheer up! Only two months to go!* and *It will all be over soon!*— which, not surprisingly, did not cheer Ana up at all.

She opened her dresser drawer and stowed the letter with the others. She wished her father would come home. She wished the Bacchanalians were over and done with and Mr. Pound were gone. But then she remembered that Barnaby and Uno would have to leave, too. *What will happen to them?* she wondered. Perhaps they could stay at Solomon Castle. But no, Ana's mother would never allow it. *And what will happen to Clarissa?*

She sighed and shut the drawer. She could make goldfish rain down from the ceiling. But she could not make the simplest wish come true.

Chapter 15

ONE MONTH BEFORE THE Bacchanalian examinations—everything changed. Ana and Barnaby and Mr. Pound had just completed the day's exercises in the SSCCR. Mr. Pound was shutting down the illusion-generating mechanisms, erasing various creatures, when Ana noticed a strange thing. All the mice—liberated from their unwilling participation in the illusions—were scurrying this way and that, trying to hide behind scattered lumps of athen or disappear into crevices in the wall. But one tiny white mouse was standing still. It had its forepaws atop a piece of athen and, most surprising of all, it was staring directly at Ana.

Its pink nose sniffed at the air. As soon as it saw it had Ana's attention, it opened its mouth and whispered, "Princess!"

Ana jumped. Had it really spoken? No, it must have made some mousy noise that only sounded like "princess." But its tiny, garnet eyes were still fixed on her, as if it were waiting for a reply.

Did you talk? she said, mouthing the words so that Mr. Pound would not hear her.

The mouse held one paw to its mouth. "Shh!" it hissed.

Ana approached the mouse. She knelt, pretending to take a pebble out of her shoe, and whispered, "You talk!"

"Yes. Yes, I do. Thank you for noticing, Your Majesty," the mouse replied, gripping its tail and making a little bow. "I'm very sorry to bother you like this, but . . . well, I don't suppose you remember me?"

"Remember you?" Ana said. "Have we met before?"

"Yes. Yes, in point of fact, we have," the mouse said. "My name is Charles, you see, and . . ."

He drew closer, but the light in the cavern was very dim. Ana held out her hand. Charles sniffed nervously at it for a moment, then climbed into her palm.

Ana raised him to her face. He seemed a very nice mouse, she thought, even handsome. But apart from his ability to speak and his pink-and-white coloring, she could find nothing that distinguished him from all the other mice she had seen in the cavern.

"I'm sorry. I don't remember," Ana said.

"Oh," Charles said, looking crestfallen. "That's all right . . ." Suddenly he stiffened, as if he were about to jump. Ana cupped her hand around him. In the same instant, she felt the chill of Mr. Pound's presence behind her.

"What is in your hand, Princess?" Mr. Pound asked.

"Nothing," Ana said, grimacing as Charles's claws dug into her palm.

Mr. Pound glanced at her closed hand. His eyes seemed to bore through skin and bone. She was sure he knew what was in her hand. Why did he ask, then?

"You may go, Prince," he said to Barnaby.

Barnaby, who had been waiting by the door, gave Ana a worried glance. He left slowly, reluctantly. When the door had shut behind him, Mr. Pound said again, "What is that in your hand, Princess?"

"Just a mouse," Ana replied. She suddenly felt very alone. Mr. Pound could do anything to her he wanted, she realized. No one could stop him. She clutched Charles tighter in her hands.

"Show it to me," Mr. Pound said.

"No. You'll hurt him," Ana said.

Mr. Pound's pupils suddenly snapped open. Two brilliant white beams of light shot out and struck her fingers. They burned only for an instant, but it was enough. Her fingers flew open. Charles fell to the ground and scurried away as fast as he could, squeaking in terror.

"Where did you get it?" Mr. Pound said as Charles vanished into a crevice in the wall.

"In here," Ana said, clutching her stinging fingers. "You saw me . . ."

Mr. Pound's eyes flared again. The light struck Ana full in the chest this time, a brilliant glassy fist that seemed to knock her back against the wall. It clutched at her heart, squeezing, crushing. She gasped with the pain. She could not breathe.

Then suddenly the pressure eased. She could breathe again. But the light was not gone. It had shifted to her forehead, a thin, burning blade that would cleave her in two if she so much as blinked. *Just like the prisoners in the dungeons,* she thought.

"You are divided, Princess," Mr. Pound said, his voice booming in the cavern. "Mortal and Immortal, child and adult, warrior and witch, creator and destroyer. All of these things are unbound within you. Were I to open you right now, your nature would spill out like dust. Would you like to see?"

No, Ana pleaded silently. She did not dare to shake her head or move her lips.

"Then do not lie to me again, Princess," Mr. Pound said. "Where did that mouse come from?"

Ana would gladly have told him, but she did not know what he was asking. The cavern was full of mice. How should she know where they came from? But she was afraid he would split her in two if she gave that answer.

Suddenly the door to the SSCCR swung open.

"Sorry. I forgot my books," Barnaby said, then froze when he saw what was happening. Uno, waiting in the doorway, began to snarl for all he was worth.

The light from Mr. Pound's eyes vanished. Suddenly Ana could move again.

"Barnaby!" she said, rushing to his side. "It's—it's time for our study session! Come on! Quick!" She grabbed his arm and tugged him out the door, and as soon as they were free, she shouted, "Run!" No one needed to be told twice.

Chapter 16

ANA AND BARNABY COLLAPSED on the floor of Ana's room, their backs against the twin beds. Uno crawled under the desk.

"Are you—are you all right?" Barnaby gasped.

Ana nodded. "Thanks," she said, trying to catch her breath. "I don't know what would have happened if you hadn't come in." She got to her feet and went to the mirror. The spot on her forehead still burned, but there was no mark on it, as far as she could see.

"What was he doing? Was he upset about practice?" Barnaby asked.

Ana shook her head and sat down again. "There was a mouse in the cavern—just an ordinary white mouse. But Mr. Pound wanted to know where it came from . . ."

Uno snorted. "Where *don't* mice come from? That's what I'd like to know," he said.

The door suddenly swung open. "You're not going to believe this," Clarissa said, walking in with a pair of books under one arm. "I've been going through every shelf in the library, and I found this journal—" She stopped. "What happened to *you?*" she asked.

Ana recounted what had happened in the SSCCR.

"He attacked you in your own home? He threatened to split you in half for a *mouse?*" Clarissa said.

"Information *about* a mouse, I believe," Uno muttered.

Suddenly Barnaby laughed. "Actually, when you think about it, it's perfect."

"What's perfect?" Clarissa said, frowning.

"Well, Mr. Pound has attacked dozens of prisoners, and Ana's mother doesn't care in the least," Barnaby said. "But now he's attacked the *Princess.*"

Ana's face lit up. "That's right! And he can't deny it, because the Monitoring Spells will have recorded everything." She rubbed her hands together. "Oh, I can't wait for Mother to come home."

The door suddenly swung open. The Queen stepped into the room, followed by Mr. Pound.

"That's wonderful, darling," the Queen said. "Unfortunately, I am not pleased to be home—especially when I see you disobeying my orders again."

Ana jumped to her feet. "He attacked me, Mother," she said, pointing at Mr. Pound. "He was going to split me in half—"

The Queen held up a hand. "Please, Anatopsis. It's impossible for anyone to attack you without the Monitoring Spells notifying me. And it was Mr. Pound who summoned me."

Ana was speechless. Mr. Pound had summoned the Queen?

Why would he do that? And why hadn't the Monitoring Spells reported the attack?

"As I explained, Your Highness," Mr. Pound said, "the Princess and I had a misunderstanding. She believed I intended to harm her, whereas I only wanted to dispatch the rodent she was holding. It was diseased, I believe. The young Prince interfered, however, before I could make myself clear."

"That's a lie!" Ana said. "You attacked me! And if it wasn't for Barnaby—"

"That is enough!" the Queen snapped. "Frankly, Anatopsis, Mr. Pound can incinerate every mouse in the castle for all I care. My concern is that I gave you an express order to stay away from Prince Barnaby, and once again I find you disobeying me."

"But, Mother! Listen to me!" Ana said.

"No. You listen to me. Your behavior has been atrocious. You are lax in your studies. Your performance is adequate, at best. And you continue to waste your time on juvenile games—even now, with the examinations less than a month away. Since my orders obviously mean nothing to you, I am forced to take drastic measures."

She turned toward Barnaby. "Prince Barnaby. Your presence at Solomon Castle can no longer be tolerated. Please go to your room. I will speak to you later."

All color drained from Barnaby's face. *No longer tolerated?* What did that mean? Back to Georges Castle? His father would throw him into the Maelstrom!

"Please, Your Highness," he said, trembling. "I won't be a bother. I promise. I'll let the Princess study. I won't talk to her. I won't even share classes with her. Just please let me stay!"

"Oh, stop your sniveling. I am not sending you back to your father. But if you don't go to your room at once, I'll throw *him* into the Maelstrom," the Queen said, pointing to Uno.

"Let's see you try," Uno snarled. But Barnaby did not want to see anyone try. He grabbed Uno by the collar and hurried out the door before the Queen could change her mind.

"Now then," the Queen said, turning to Clarissa and pointing to the books in her arms. "What are those?"

"Books, Your Majesty," Clarissa said, bowing her head. "I was—"

"I know what you were doing with them," the Queen said. "The question is, who gave you permission?"

"I did," Ana said, putting herself between her mother and Clarissa.

"Did you?" the Queen said. "Then I think I've had enough of this nonsense as well. As of tonight, Anatopsis, your pet will sleep in the dungeons. And be thankful I don't obliterate her. She distracts you from your studies far more than Prince Barnaby does."

She nodded to Mr. Pound. Ana fired a stream of curses at him. But though the force was enough to send Mr. Pound crashing through the wall, the curses themselves had no effect on him. He recovered quickly, stepping over a mound of leeches Ana's curse had produced.

"Really, Anatopsis," her mother said, looking more amused than angry. "I will not have you attacking the employees without my permission. Now I think I've put up with enough adolescent behavior for one afternoon."

She snapped her fingers. Suddenly Clarissa was gone!

"What did you do?!" Ana cried.

"Don't worry. She's quite comfortable, darling—for the moment," the Queen replied. "However, should your bad habits continue, I might allow Mr. Pound to use her for his classroom demonstrations. Now, if you'll excuse me, I have work to do."

The Queen spotshifted away, leaving Ana alone with Mr. Pound.

"Get out!" Ana shouted at him, shaking with fury. She was on the verge of tears, but she would not let him see her cry.

"You have not answered my question, Princess," Mr. Pound said. "Where did the mouse come from?"

"What difference does it make?" Ana shouted. "It's just a stupid mouse! I've never seen him before, and I'll probably never see him again! Now get out!"

"I am sure you *have* seen it before, Princess," Mr. Pound said, gazing at her. "The question is: Where does a talking mouse come from, when there are no talking mice?" And with that, he turned on his stiff legs and thumped away.

Chapter 17

BARNABY STAYED UP HALF THE NIGHT waiting for the Queen to come and pass sentence on him. She did not appear. When he awoke the next morning, however, he was not in his bed, but sitting in an ornate velvet chair, Uno snoring loudly at his feet.

His first thought was that they had both dozed off in class. But it was Saturday, and the turret did not have velvet chairs or intricately woven carpets, or a window through which the morning sun, already high in the sky, could shine so blindingly.

He raised a hand to shield his eyes. The window dimmed automatically. As his vision adjusted, he made several disturbing discoveries. First, he was still in his pajamas, a most discomfiting realization given that he was clearly not in his room anymore. Second, Queen Solomon, sitting no more than a few feet away from him and looking quite at home behind her gigantic witchadder desk, was smiling at him in a manner he found very unwelcoming.

"Good morning, Barnaby," she said, clasping her hands together. "I hope you slept well?"

Barnaby shifted nervously in his seat. He knew the Queen well enough by now not to be lulled by her pleasant tone.

"Not really. I mean, yes, thank you," he mumbled.

"I apologize for the abrupt transfer. I'm sure you would have liked to say good-bye to everyone, but a quick departure is best under the circumstances; don't you think?"

"Circumstances?"

"Your stay at Solomon Castle has not been quite as productive as your father had hoped. And given the degree to which you hinder my daughter's progress, you could hardly expect me to keep you there."

Barnaby's heart sank. "You're sending me home, then?" he asked.

"Not yet. Your father shows very little interest in having you returned."

Barnaby nodded. He had not seen his father in nearly three months, not since the last time the King had summoned him home to demonstrate what he had learned. Even then, the King had made it clear he did not care anymore what happened to Barnaby.

"Tell me, Barnaby: Are you aware of the specifics of the Bacchanalian examinations?" the Queen asked.

The sudden change of subject confused Barnaby. "Um, there's a written test, I think, and a practicum," he said.

"Exactly," Queen Solomon said. "And the Competition, of course."

"Competition?" Barnaby said. He had never heard anything about a competition.

"Yes. It's not usually mentioned until just before the Bacchanalians, because we don't like to frighten the young people. But it's very important. Not only does it test the candidates' prowess, but it also provides certain opportunities for . . . shall we say 'career advancement'? You see, the victor wins everything: family fortune, castle, market share, control over AW and CNI— *everything*. Of course, such a thing has never happened before. The contestants have always been far too evenly matched, and every Competition, alas, has ended in a draw. But this one promises to be different."

Sweat broke out on Barnaby's forehead. *A sorcerers' duel—that's what it is,* he thought. *Against Ana.* Why had no one ever told him? Why hadn't his father said something? No wonder the King used to turn scarlet every time Barnaby botched a spell. He probably saw the Georges family dynasty vanishing before his eyes.

"Oh, don't worry," the Queen said. "Your father is not ready to surrender yet. In fact, he has requested that he fight in your stead. Naturally, I'm reluctant to accept such an arrangement, but Mr. Pound tells me I have little choice. The rules allow another family member to participate if the heir apparent is deemed incompetent."

This is even worse! Barnaby thought, stomach churning. His father had centuries of experience; Ana had none. The King would vaporize her.

"You—you can't allow it!" he stammered.

"I'm afraid I have no choice," the Queen said. "But you know

I don't like to take chances—especially where my daughter's welfare is concerned. Therefore, I've decided to adopt a little contingency plan."

Barnaby did not like the sound of that. "What—what sort of contingency plan?" he asked, trying to ignore Uno, who had suddenly begun chasing something in his sleep.

"You," the Queen replied, grinning. "Oh, don't worry, I won't be dangling you over boiling oil or chopping your fingers off. That would be far too crude, and your father would hardly notice. But I've recently discovered another way in which you might be useful. You might even benefit from it. Who knows?"

"What do I have to do?" Barnaby asked, afraid to hear the answer.

"Nothing at all. You simply remain here at AW until the Competition is over. I will inform your father, of course. I'm sure he'll agree that a period of 'internship' at AW will do you some good—especially if I make it a condition for his participation in the Bacchanalians."

Barnaby breathed a small sigh of relief. The Bacchanalians were less than a month away. He could probably manage that, assuming the Queen didn't put him in chains or keep him on the rack. But what about Ana? Would the Queen tell her about the Competition? What if the King, despite all the Queen's precautions, still blasted Ana into oblivion?

"Now then, your stay can be pleasant or unpleasant," the Queen said, rising. "If you promise to behave yourself, I will see that you are treated like an employee and given work to do. If you misbehave, however, or attempt to leave, I will have you placed in a cage in our testing laboratories. Is that clear?"

Barnaby nodded.

The Queen touched a crystal ball on her desk. The doors to her office swung open and a tall, heavyset woman with square shoulders and a well-oiled beard entered. By the baggy silk trousers and curved sword at her side, Barnaby guessed she was a high-ranking member of the Assassins Guild.

"Put him in the basement with the other executive trainees," the Queen commanded.

The woman drew her sword and pointed it at Barnaby.

"And do remember, Barnaby," the Queen said as Barnaby half carried, half dragged Uno toward the open doors, "I am the only reason you are not sitting at the bottom of the Maelstrom right now."

Chapter 18

ANA CRIED HERSELF TO SLEEP THAT NIGHT. There was nothing else she could do, for the Queen, fearing Ana might run away, had set a Time Lock Charm on her room. Curses, spells, spotshifting, even a lump of athen smashed against the door had no effect. Ana was trapped.

The Time Lock Charm wore off at sunup the next morning. When the door—damaged by Ana's smashings and bashings—fell off its hinges, Ana leaped out of bed and flew down the stairs, her nightgown flapping around her legs.

Where was Clarissa? In the dungeons. The Queen had said she was sending Clarissa to the dungeons. But only when Ana reached the first level of the dungeons did she remember she had no idea what cell Clarissa was in. So she dashed back upstairs to Barnaby's room and pounded on his door. There was no answer.

"Hello? Anyone home?" she called, opening the door. Barnaby's clothes were still on the chair. His shoes were on the floor, and the bed had obviously been slept in. But there was no sign of him, or of Uno. She checked under the mattress and found Barnaby's tool kit still in its hiding place. It had been months before he trusted her enough to show it to her. And he had been so proud when he finally unrolled it for her. She knew he would never have left it behind—not willingly. So either he was still in the castle, or the Queen had broken her promise and sent him back to his father.

Tears stung Ana's eyes. She had not felt so alone since the days before Clarissa arrived at Solomon Castle. But she could not waste time feeling sorry for herself. She wiped her eyes, opened the drawer to Barnaby's nightstand. The locating device was still there, much to her relief.

She snatched up the little metal box and ran down to the dungeons. She had never used it—Barnaby had always been in charge of the device—but it did not seem very complicated. Unfortunately, as she fiddled with the knobs, she realized she needed Clarissa's cell number to make it work. If she knew the number, the device would lead her directly to the cell. But without the number, the box was of no use at all.

Frustrated, Ana resorted to rushing down the corridors, calling Clarissa's name. She could have asked the other prisoners if they had seen Clarissa, but there were very few left to ask, thanks to Mr. Pound. And when she peered into a few of the cells, she saw waste trickling in from all sides, the floors awash in curse fragments and spell effluents, and it reminded her that not all of the cells in the dungeons were benign. Immortal prisoners often had a difficult time protecting themselves from such hazards. A mortal would have no chance at all.

Ana quickened her pace, almost in a panic. But luck was with her. After half an hour of searching, she heard Clarissa's voice answering from cell 237. The cell vanished almost at once, but Ana had the number now and was able to program it into Barnaby's locating device.

"What took you so long?" Clarissa asked when Ana finally arrived in front of her door.

Ana, peering through the tiny barred window, almost wept with relief. "Is—is everything all right in there?" she asked.

"Very cozy," Clarissa said, moving aside. The cell was clean and dry, Ana saw. There was even a carpet on the floor and several glow lamps, and, against the far wall, a cot with two books. She told Clarissa about the Time Lock Charm and Barnaby and Uno being missing and how she had had to run through the dungeons, calling Clarissa's name.

"Well, now that you've found me, you can get me out," Clarissa said.

"I can't. You know that," Ana said. "There's half a dozen curses on the door alone. And if I spotshift you, the Warden Spells will sound every alarm in the castle."

"Then dig a tunnel under the floor or blow up the castle. Do something," Clarissa said. "Mr. Pound was prowling about all night. I don't want to be here when he runs out of other victims."

"You don't think he'd . . . ?" Ana asked, afraid to finish the thought.

"I don't know. But look—I found something in those books yesterday." She ran to fetch them and passed them through the food hatch. The first was a thin, brittle volume with a few crumbs of a cover left. The other was a heavy tome bound in dragon leather, with *Cecil's Guide to Divine Objects* stamped in gold leaf across the cover.

"Look at that thin one first," Clarissa said.

Ana opened the book to a dog-eared page full of tight, hand-scrawled lines. It was a mortal journal, she realized—and nearly two thousand years old, if the date at the top was to be believed.

Four dead this morning, the entry said. *Split in half and hollowed out. Witnesses say shadowy creature flew out of Maelstrom, cut victims with its eyes.*

"You see? Just like in the story," Clarissa said. "And look at the date: exactly a year before your grandmother's Bacchanalians. Who comes every thousand years? Who comes exactly one year before the Bacchanalians? Mr. Pound, that's who."

Ana could not believe it. She flipped to the next entry, and the next. Each described a similar attack. Perhaps there was *something* in the Maelstrom. But there was no description of the "shadowy creature" in any of the entries, and it was hard to imagine Mr. Pound sitting at the bottom of a whirlpool for a thousand years at a time.

The last entry was the most troubling: *Half the ghetto gone.*

Reliquum almost destroyed. No place to bury victims, and can't bear to throw them in harbor. No attacks last night. Pray he's gone.

"That would have been two days after your grandmother's Bacchanalians," Clarissa said as Ana shut the book. "Who leaves as soon as the Bacchanalians are finished? Mr. Pound. It's him, I'm telling you."

"But it doesn't make any sense," Ana said. "Why would he attack all those mortals?"

"Not just mortals," Clarissa said. "Benjamin told me the maintenance workers in the park have been finding Immortals every morning—at least one or two, split in half." Seeing Ana was still not convinced, she said, "Look, it's all very simple: He wants the Os Divinitas. Only he has to *collect* it first. Look in that other book."

Ana opened *Cecil's Guide to Divine Objects* to the page Clarissa had marked. There was a drawing of the Os Divinitas, similar to the other drawing they had seen, except the little dot in the middle was missing and the bone was split into dozens of fragments, each fragment labeled with a different attribute:

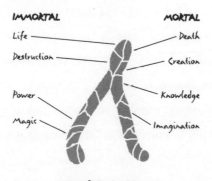

Os Divinitas

The information beneath the illustration was slight—a brief historical account, similar to what they had found in *Harrison's*, then a discussion of the various theories pertaining to its possible recovery. *There is widespread disagreement on whether the Os Divinitas exists,* the author wrote. *However, all sources agree that if it does exist, it was shattered by Prometheus and distributed to humankind. Therefore, any attempt to restore the Os Divinitas must begin with the recovery of its parts. To date, no part of the Os Divinitas has ever been found.*

"You see? He's searching for the pieces," Clarissa said. "Maybe he even has some."

"But it says no one's ever found any part of it," Ana said, closing the book. "And if Prometheus really *did* distribute the pieces to mankind, wouldn't Mr. Pound have to split *everyone* open to get them all back?"

"I don't know," Clarissa said. "When he's splitting me open tonight, I'll ask him: 'Excuse me, how many fragments is this so far?'"

"Stop it. He would never hurt you—not as long as Mother needs you," Ana said. But she was not convinced of this anymore. Hadn't Mr. Pound attacked her in her own castle? Hadn't he convinced the Queen it was all Ana's and Barnaby's fault? He could do whatever he wanted, and the Queen could not stop him.

"I'll go talk to Mother," Ana said. "I'm sure if I make a solemn vow to do nothing but study from now until the Bacchanalians, she'll release you."

Ana ran off to speak to her mother. When she reached the dining hall, however, only Mr. Pound was there, staring at the food-laden table as if it were a puzzle.

"Your mother has gone to her office, Princess," the demigod said before Ana could run off again. "She instructed me to keep you in classes until she returns."

"But it's Saturday!" Ana protested. And she was still in her nightgown. And she had not had breakfast yet. But Mr. Pound did not care. He spotshifted her to the SSCCR, and there she stayed—in her nightgown, without breakfast or lunch—until her mother returned.

Dinner that night was a torturous affair. Ana wanted to run down to the dungeons as soon as she was released, to make sure Clarissa was all right. But she was famished and needed to peti-tion for Clarissa's release, and, in any case, Mr. Pound could not have harmed anyone because he had been in the SSCCR all day with Ana.

So she dutifully changed into a dress, and devoured her roast questing beast, and listened patiently to her mother's gleeful discussions of the day's activities at AW. Then, after a second helping of fairydust mousse, she put on her most contrite "I'll be responsible from now on" face and begged her mother to let Clarissa go.

The Queen was not moved. "You've made these promises be-fore, Anatopsis," she said. "With your little pet in the dungeons, however, I think you'll be more likely to keep them. I'm sorry if that upsets you, but it's my responsibility to make sure you have a long and prosperous future, not a carefree adolescence."

Ana scowled. "All you want is to make me as pinch-faced and miserable as you are."

The goblet in front of the Queen shattered. A charred, smoldering ring appeared in the tablecloth around her plate.

"Everything I do is for your own good, Anatopsis," she said. "I may have made one or two minor mistakes along the way, but I have saved *you* from hundreds of terrible ones. Now, having your little pet locked up and that walking disaster of a warlock sent away may seem like the cruelest of fates, but let me assure you, there are far worse ones lying in wait for you. When you have triumphed over them, as I'm certain you will, I hope you will remember to get down on your bended knees and thank me for the strength and dignity and independence I've given you. Because, honestly, Anatopsis, those are the only things that will save you, the only things that have ever saved anyone."

The Queen went back to her dessert, eating her mousse in the smallest bites possible and making Ana sit until she was finished. Only after she had made a great show of wiping her mouth and folding her napkin did she finally excuse Ana.

Ana leaped out of her chair. She raced down to the dungeons, fuming over her mother's lecture. *Perhaps I'll blast Clarissa out of that cell after all,* she told herself. *Then we'll see how much Mother values strength and dignity and independence.* But when she reached the cell, Clarissa was gone.

Chapter 19

Barnaby and Uno's new room was a stark concrete cube in the basement of AW. It was not kept locked and it had far more amenities than one usually finds in prison cells, including a bed, a chair and desk, a plasma-reactor hot plate, and a small spirit-projection mirror. Nevertheless, they were prisoners.

"It's all your fault," Uno grumbled, sniffing about the room for something edible. "If you had woken me up, we could have made a run for it. Now we're trapped—and without breakfast."

"If we had made a run for it, the Queen would have chained us to the floor," Barnaby replied. Their escort, Mrs. Tamburlane, had made it very clear that escape was impossible. All the exit doors had locked as they had walked past them. A crystal ball had shouted "Illegal use!" when Barnaby had touched it. And when she had forced him to write a note and throw it into the post, it had materialized seconds later in her hands.

Barnaby sat on the bed. He surveyed the high, dwarf-sized windows, the dirty white walls. *Might as well be the dungeons, he* thought. Except here, at least, they did not have to worry about Mr. Pound visiting them.

"Do you think that hammer of yours could smash one of those windows?" Uno asked.

Barnaby pressed his hand to the lump beneath his pajamas. The hammer was still there, thank goodness. "I don't know, but what would be the point?" he said. "We can't go home, we can't go back to Solomon Castle, and no one else will take us in. We might as well stay here for the moment, or spotshift to another planet entirely."

"And end up with our heads buried in Martian sand," Uno groaned.

Barnaby ignored him. He was thinking about what the Queen had told him: Ana was going to fight his father. Did Ana know? Probably not. The Queen would wait until the last moment to avoid any chance of Ana refusing or running away.

Then I have to warn her, Barnaby thought. *But how?* He could not use the crystal balls, and he could not send a letter. He remembered a story Clarissa had once told him about mortals using birds to carry messages. He searched through his desk, found an AW memo pad and Ink-O-Matic quill, and sat down to write a quick note.

Dear Ana, he wrote.

How are you? Uno and I are fine. At present, we are living in the base-ment of your mother's company. She has kindly offered us a place to stay and employment until after the Bacchanalians. I have been disqualified from the examinations, unfortunately, because of the _duel_. (You must ask Mr. Pound about this. It's _very important_.) The rules allow another family member to take my place, however. I think you can guess who that will be.

Please be careful, and write back as soon as you can. I hope you and Clarissa are safe and well.

Your friend,

Barnaby

P.S. Uno asks that you send two sandpig dinners and whatever desserts you have available. He doubts the cafeteria here is up to his standards.

Barnaby rolled the letter into a tight cylinder and tied it with a strip of cloth torn from the bedsheet. He tried to summon a carrier pigeon, but he did not know what they looked like or where he could find one. The birds he did manage to conjure—chickens, a dodo, a pair of squabbling lovebirds—were of no use either, for the building's Security Spells prevented them from materializing in his room, and instead they appeared outside his window, pecking at the glass. Finally, he managed to call forth an aging, disgruntled phoenix, which, perhaps because of its relative rarity and harmlessness, was not blocked from entering. The phoenix seemed less than pleased with its task, however, and as it did not speak anything but an obscure dialect of ancient Egyptian, Barnaby was not sure whether it understood the address he had given it.

"I hope it isn't its nesting season," Barnaby said when the

phoenix had vanished. "Perhaps I should have written the letter on something more flame retardant."

He then went to the closet and donned one of the five sets of identical AW blazers, shirts, shoes, and neckties placed there for him. Mrs. Tamburlane had told him she would be back to escort him to his new post. The Queen tolerated idleness in no one, it seemed—not even hostages.

Barnaby's assignment was in the Research & Development Department, or R&D, as it was generally known. A dozen very busy Hibernian bees—all slightly shorter than Barnaby, round, with brilliant black-and-yellow stripes, wobbly antennae, and oddly cherubic faces—ran the laboratories. Their director, Dr. Zivvini, was a rather thin but jovial type with rumpled antennae and vestigial wings, and he seemed very pleased to have both Barnaby and Uno there. In fact, when he learned Barnaby had a talent for building things, he literally buzzed with joy.

"Wonderful, wonderful! Oh yes, we can certainly use that here!" he said. First, he gave Barnaby and Uno a tour of the laboratories. There were dozens of sections and subsections, all devoted to the discovery and development of one form of magic or another, and Barnaby was especially intrigued by the Space-Time Discontinuum Project.

"A few days ago, we thought we'd discovered a portal into another universe," Dr. Zivvini said as they stepped around the maze of pentagrams, door frames, and flaming circles. "But it turned out we were spotshifting things into the cafeteria's gelatin cups. Had a good long buzz over that one, yes, we did."

Finally, they arrived at the largest and most complex of all the sections: Competitive Research. ("Or 'I Spy,' as we call it," Dr. Zivvini said.) The R&D Bees here were charged with keeping abreast of CNI's latest developments, and they did this by means of special antennae called "sniffers." These intricate structures could detect traces of curses and even, by a process of reverse engineering, tell the R&D Bees how to reproduce them.

Unfortunately, each sniffer had to be built to exacting specifications, and as the R&D Bees were extremely clumsy with their hands, they needed others to build the devices for them. Mortals could not be trusted to do the work, and the only Immortals willing to perform such menial tasks were gnomes and brownies, who were small and tended to lose their tempers easily. Thus, Barnaby was like a gift from the gods to the R&D Bees.

"Now, let's see what you can do," Dr. Zivvini said, leading Barnaby to a shining zinc bench over which hung shelves and shelves of jars and bins and bottles. He gave Barnaby a sheet of instructions and watched as Barnaby painstakingly assembled his first sniffer—an ivory pentangle covered with pieces of ghost skin and dragon's tongue.

When Barnaby had finished the sniffer, Dr. Zivvini buzzed with approval. "That's a talent, my boy—quite a talent," he said. "Now let's see if it works."

He had Barnaby pick up the device and follow him into the

teleshifting tubes—large shafts designed to spotshift people up and down the various floors. They emerged on the rooftop of AW, high above the city. Barnaby was surprised to see the edges bristling with sniffers of every size and shape, and even more surprised to see a gigantic mound of athen in the center.

"Competitive Research produces a lot of athen," Dr. Zivvini explained as he led Barnaby to an empty socket at the edge of the roof. "That's just one day's worth there." He directed Barnaby to set the base of the sniffer in the empty socket and hold it by its shaft. Then he told him to slowly rotate it.

After less than one revolution, the sniffer suddenly grew warm in Barnaby's hands. Pieces of athen began to fly everywhere—a sign that it had attracted a curse—and Dr. Zivvini stopped him. He recorded the composition and state of the sniffer, and then, when they had returned to the laboratory, showed Barnaby how to compile these elements into the written version of the curse.

"Now for the testing," Dr. Zivvini said. He patted the pockets of his lab coat, searching for something. When he didn't find it, he went into his office—a small, glassed-in area adjoining the laboratory—and searched through the masses of paper on his desk. But whatever it was he was looking for, he did not find it there, either.

"I seem to have misplaced my key. Excuse me a moment," Dr. Zivvini said, and bustled off, leaving Barnaby and Uno alone beside the workbench.

There were, of course, many other workbenches, most of them manned by teams of gnomes, who had to stand on the benchtops to assemble the sniffers. Uno, who was ravenously hungry, kept licking his chops as he stared at the bite-sized creatures.

"We'll get something to eat soon. I promise," Barnaby said, holding tightly to Uno's collar.

Uno nodded toward Dr. Zivvini's office. "You don't suppose she's delivering lunch, do you?" he said. Through the glass partition, Barnaby could see a weary-looking mortal in blue-and-white coveralls pulling a cart into Dr. Zivvini's office.

"Not unless you like paper for lunch," Barnaby said, watching her empty Dr. Zivvini's waste bin into her cart. The woman suddenly stopped and peered into her cart. She removed a brightly colored card about the size of a napkin and slipped it into her pocket. But as she was glancing about to see if anyone had witnessed the theft her eyes met Barnaby's. She froze, her face turning absolutely gray. She backed away, never taking her eyes off of Barnaby, and bumped into the cart, and then she and the cart went sprawling onto the floor.

Barnaby and Uno rushed to help the woman.

"Are you all right?" Barnaby said, helping her up. She nodded, but she was shaking from head to toe and would not look at Barnaby.

"Don't worry. We're not going to report you," Barnaby said.

"No, no. Pilfer all you want. We don't care," Uno said.

The woman nodded again, but she seemed dazed and confused. Only when Barnaby had righted her cart and began to scoop up the mess did she snap out of her trance.

"I—I can do that. Thank you, sir," she said, taking the broom from her cart.

Barnaby stepped aside. "Are you sure you're all right, Miss . . . ?" He glanced at her name tag: ISAK. *A strange name,* he thought. He stole a quick look at her face. She had been pretty once, he could tell. Yet it must have been some time ago, for her hair was gray and brittle and her face had a weathered look to it. He introduced himself and Uno.

"Don't suppose you have anything to eat in there, do you?" Uno said, sniffing at the cart.

Isak shook her head. She reached into a pocket of her coveralls, however, and produced a crust of bread. But as she held it out for Uno, he suddenly backed away, growling low in his throat.

"Uno! What's got into you?" Barnaby said, grabbing Uno by the collar. He apologized to Isak. "I'm afraid he gets a bit testy when he misses breakfast."

Isak nodded and finished sweeping up the mess. Then she mumbled her thanks and hurried away.

"There's something not right about her," Uno said when she was gone. "She has power in her fingers. I smelled it."

"That was only bread. She was trying to be nice to you," Barnaby said.

Uno was about to say more, but Dr. Zivvini suddenly reappeared, a strange-looking troll following close behind him. The troll had red fur, a bulbous nose, and an undersized lab coat stretched across his thick shoulders, but he was much smaller than any troll Barnaby had ever seen. In fact, if not for the protruding teeth and the unmistakable gleam in his eye—that greedy, hungry look, as if everything he encountered could be a meal—Barnaby would have mistaken him for a very hairy dwarf.

"Barnaby, this is Sandborn. He's in charge of the Testing Floor," Dr. Zivvini said.

Sandborn grinned and pulled a brightly colored card from the breast pocket of his lab coat. "Key! Sandborn have key! Not you," he said.

Dr. Zivvini blushed. "Yes, yes. What he means is that no one can access the Testing Floor without the key. Very important, very important indeed. Unfortunately, I seem to have misplaced mine today. Don't know where it is. I'm sure it will turn up. Quite sure."

"Isn't that what the cleaning woman took?" Uno whispered to Barnaby as they followed the troll to the teleshifters. Barnaby nudged him. They had promised they would not report her.

They materialized in a warehouse full of cages. Each cage was no more than six feet in length and width and depth, and there were row upon row of them, stacked three or four high. Sandborn, skipping and grunting with excitement, led them down the aisle. Barnaby peered into the first ones, expecting to find mice or sandpigs or perhaps Deodoran rabbit-hens. But, to his horror, the cages all contained mortals.

"Mice are used for the preliminary evaluations," Dr. Zivvini explained. "But we need mortals for the final testing phases. Seems terrible, I know, but it's all in the interest of science, isn't it? And they're treated humanely. Yes, very humanely."

Barnaby was not sure what Dr. Zivvini meant by *humanely*. Some of the mortals appeared intact, but most had been transformed or disfigured in frightening ways—their skin turned to tar, extra limbs sprouting from their torsos, feet turned to anvils, or hands changed to soup spoons. Those still aware of their surroundings recoiled whenever Sandborn drew near. Others stared impassively at him, their eyes full of a dark lethargy.

Barnaby stopped looking after the first few cages. It was not just the terrible effects of the curses that nauseated him; it was the terror and hopelessness in the mortals' faces. But even with his eyes averted, Barnaby could smell the musty odor of their fear, hear the omnipresent sighs of their despair.

"I think I'm going to be sick," he whispered to Uno. And he was.

Chapter 20

ANA COULD NOT EAT. She could not sleep. She had looked every-where for Clarissa. She had confronted her mother, who claimed she had not moved Clarissa. She had questioned the dungeon mas-ter and servants, sent Summoning Spells into the far corners of the castle. She had cast every Locating Spell in the *Sorceropaedia Universalis,* and they had all led her to the same place: the very last cell in the dungeons. Except the very last cell was not the very last because the dungeons were constantly shifting. And, in any case, Clarissa was not in any of them.

Frustrated, Ana realized she had to question Mr. Pound. She had not forgotten the incident in the SSCCR, however, and there-fore decided to confront him in the hallway after class, where the possibility of witnesses might deter him from attacking her. She expected him to deny everything, but, much to her astonishment, he admitted having moved Clarissa.

"Your mother expressed concern that you might spend all of

your free time in the dungeons," he said. "Therefore, I took the liberty of removing your friend to a more discreet location."

Ana was furious. "That was for Mother to decide, not you!"

"Your mother has given me complete authority over your education," Mr. Pound said. "I will release your friend when you finish your Bacchanalians, not before."

"Then I won't take them!" Ana shouted. "I won't study! I won't do a single thing until you bring her back. Do you hear me?"

Mr. Pound's eyes flashed that awful white again. Ana jumped back, terrified that he meant to attack her.

"You will do exactly as you are told, Princess," Mr. Pound said. "You will follow my commands to the letter, or you will never see your friend again. Do you understand me?" Before she could reply, he thumped away, leaving her frustrated and shaken.

She burst into tears. *Why is he doing this?* she thought, burying her face in her hands. Did he really care whether or not she did well in the Bacchanalians? Was he only intent on tormenting her? She felt as if she would explode, as if her heart and her head had grown too small, too tight.

Suddenly something touched her shoulder. She jumped. There stood Benjamin, a tray of silverware balanced on one hand, a note in the other. His face was neither full of its usual disdain nor friendly. It was just blank.

He thrust the note toward Ana. Clarissa had always said she trusted Benjamin with her life, Ana remembered, but Ana had never been able to find anything trustworthy about him. He was a sneak and a thief. He was a liar. He hated Immortals, and he seemed to hate her most of all. Hadn't he said Clarissa and Ana were as likely to become friends as a cat and a mouse?

He thrust the note at her again, his scowl returning. Ana forced herself to take it. She expected some sort of accusation: *This is all your fault. You should have known. You should have helped her.* Instead, the note said, *We'll find her. I promise.*

Tears sprang to Ana's eyes. "Thank you," she said, gripping the note tightly. But Benjamin was already gone.

A week passed. Ana heard nothing more from Benjamin. And then, suddenly, Benjamin was gone, too. He did not appear for breakfast, or lunch, or dinner one day. He was not in his quarters. The Queen sent two Security Trolls to find him, but they returned empty-handed.

Did this mean he had found Clarissa? Ana prayed he had. Perhaps they had escaped to the ghetto together. But her heart told her it was much more likely that Mr. Pound had gotten rid of Benjamin, too. Certainly, the demigod did not seem surprised by or concerned about the butler's disappearance.

Then Ana did not know what to do anymore. If Benjamin had managed to free Clarissa, there was no reason to stay at Solomon Castle. But if Clarissa was not free . . . Ana walked about in a state of utter confusion, one moment making plans to run away, the next convincing herself she had to stay, for Clarissa's sake. She wrote a letter to her father, detailing all that had happened.

But as she had not heard a word from him since he began his fieldwork, she did not expect help from that quarter.

She grew more despondent. She lost weight and took to sleeping in Barnaby and Uno's old room, for she could not bear to be in her own room with that empty bed next to hers. She still attended her classes, but only because she was afraid of what Mr. Pound might do if she stopped.

Mr. Pound did not seem to care what state Ana was in. He worked her even harder than before, putting Ana through scenario after scenario in the SSCCR—in preparation for the practicum portion of the Bacchanalians, he said. Ana moved through the battles as if she were half-drugged, and yet, by the end of the third week, she had defeated dozens of elves, fairies, trolls, ogres, witches, warlocks, and even massive Rajhan jellytroopers (who bloat themselves on thousands of pounds of food in order to absorb even the most powerful curses). And in the process, she had acquired innumerable rings, swords, slippers, scepters, and one clairvoyant pig.

The one encouraging development was that Ana's curses had at last begun to obey her. They still struck their targets with far more force than was necessary, and she was still plagued by unwanted materializations—brine shrimp and minnows, puffballs, an enormous termite colony, even a swarm of bees. But at least they now achieved their desired effects.

"Absence makes the heart grow stronger, Princess," Mr. Pound said one morning. It was the next to last Friday before the Bacchanalians, to be exact. The examination was now a week and a day away.

"What do you mean?" Ana said, resting her hands on her knees and trying to catch her breath. Her arms were sore, and she thought she must have strained something, for her sternum felt tender and bruised.

"The loss of your friends has improved your performance," Mr. Pound replied.

"Then it's all worthwhile, isn't it?" Ana snapped.

"Fear and longing fuel the heart, Princess. They make the soul burn. And it is the burning soul that forges change."

"I don't want a *burning soul!*" Ana retorted. "I want my friends back. What do you care what happens to me, anyway? All you want is that *stupid bone*—though I don't see why. You can do everything you want already."

A blast of cold air suddenly swept through the cavern. Ice formed in a perfect circle around Mr. Pound's feet.

"You have been to Olympus, Princess," Mr. Pound said. "Did you see my kind there?"

Ana shook her head, frightened.

"And my form: Is it one a god would choose?" Mr. Pound said.

Ana shook her head again.

"Then you understand why I need the Os Divinitas. It will restore the gods. It will transform me into a full and living deity. It may even aid you and your friends."

"What do you mean?" Ana said, her teeth beginning to chatter.

"Mortals and Immortals were one people, Princess, before Prometheus divided them. When the Os Divinitas is re-joined, all such divisions will vanish again, and the tyranny of Immortals and the suffering of mortals will vanish with them."

Ana stared at Mr. Pound. He did not care about her or her friends, she was sure. And yet she wanted to believe him. To escape the nonsense of mortals and Immortals, slags and servants, to be free of her mother and the Bacchanalians and all the other monstrosities that had crept between her and her friends—she would like that more than anything.

"Why are you telling me this?" she said, shivering. "I don't have your precious bone, and I don't know where it is."

"No, you do not," Mr. Pound agreed. "But it will reveal itself. When it does, you will have a choice to make. And you will not have long to make it."

He clomped out of the cavern, leaving Ana frozen and confused. Was that a threat or a prediction? She did not know. Nor did she understand why he seemed so sure the Os Divinitas would appear. *Not just appear—appear here, Ana thought. He must have some sort of map or guide or—*

The prophecy! she thought, suddenly remembering the lines on Prometheus's rock. Why hadn't she remembered that before?

"Because it seemed like a lot of nonsense, that's why," she muttered to herself. But it obviously wasn't nonsense to Mr. Pound.

She rushed to the library, forgoing lunch. The warm, musty

air revived her a bit, and she climbed to the second balcony and searched through the various books on mythological objects. None of them contained a copy of the prophecy, however.

Then she remembered her father's journals. Sir Christopher had kept detailed records of all his quests. Ana was sure she would find a copy there. She retrieved the collection of his small, leather-bound journals and sent them floating down to the table. But as she went to open the first one, she heard a strange chittering noise. There, standing atop the dragon-leather cover, was a small white mouse with pink eyes and a very pink nose.

"Charles!" Ana cried.

Chapter 21

EACH MORNING, Barnaby dragged himself out of bed. He dressed in a daze. He followed Uno to the cafeteria and listened to him devour his food. He went to his workbench and began piecing together one sniffer after another, using Hibernian spruce, sandpig tongue, wraith's breath—whatever was listed in the instructions. He dragged the sniffers up to the rooftop and prayed they would not work. But they almost always did, and if they did not, the R&D Bees had him fix them. Then he had to go to the Testing Floor.

His trips to the Testing Floor were never long, thank goodness, because Sandborn was a jealous guardian of his domain. He always snatched the curse formulae out of Barnaby's hands and sent him off, saying, "Sandborn do it. Only Sandborn." But the visits were long enough for Barnaby to smell the smells, and hear the sounds, and see all the mortal fingers clutching desperately through the wire cages.

Barnaby wished Uno could accompany him. But on their first

visit without Dr. Zivvini, Sandborn had grinned at Uno and said, "Nice doggy. Love doggy." Barnaby had assumed the troll had a soft spot for dogs, but Dr. Zivvini had later told him it was not a soft spot—it was a *taste*. After that, Barnaby kept Uno far away from Sandborn.

The one silver lining in Barnaby's sojourn at AW was that the R&D Bees were very friendly to him. In fact, they tended to praise him lavishly, and when one of his efforts led to an important discovery, Dr. Zivvini even invited Barnaby to join in their traditional Eureka Dance—a buzzing mêlée of wings and wiggling abdomens. To Barnaby, who had never been treated so well, let alone praised for anything, this sort of camaraderie was almost intoxicating, and now and then he found himself forgetting that the laboratory's successes were the Testing Floor's horrors. But then he would bring another curse formula down to Sandborn, and it would all come flooding back to him.

"We have to get out of here," he said to Uno one night as they were making their way through the crowded cafeteria. They had been at AW nearly three weeks by then, and Barnaby's head ached so fiercely every night, he would have forgone dinner altogether. But skipping a meal was unthinkable to Uno.

"How do you propose we do that?" Uno asked, settling himself under a table to eat his stuffed minotaur flank. "We've tried everything short of diving off the roof."

It was true. In the first week alone, they had sent four letters, made three unauthorized crystal-ball calls (all of them refused), tried nearly every exit, and climbed out numerous windows. They had even tried to spotshift to Solomon Castle, but this had ended in disaster, as the Security Spells had redirected them into Mrs. Tamburlane's office (under her desk, to be exact). Any future attempts, she had warned them, would land them squarely in Sandborn's cages.

But Barnaby could not stay here. The R&D Bees were very nice to him, and assembling the sniffers was interesting, at times even challenging. But he could not forget what the work was for. More urgently, he could not forget that, come Saturday, the Competition would be exactly one week away. Had Ana gotten his message? Was she preparing to fight his father even now? And what would the Queen do, once the Competition was over? Would she keep her promise and release him? He doubted it. More than likely she would leave him to rot in the laboratories of AW, a slag, a slave.

He chewed nervously on a piece of toast while he waited for Uno to finish his dinner. Then they teleshifted downstairs for their evening constitutional. The constitutional was really nothing more than a short stroll through the marble-clad entranceway of the building. Uno would sniff and mark every one of the four towering Solomon queen statues, and then he and Barnaby would stand for a while by the giant glass doors and watch the black silky shadows fall over the flowers and trees.

It looks so peaceful out there, Barnaby thought, gazing through the glass. He remembered the picnic with Ana and Clarissa. He longed to sit under the weeping beech again, breathe in the scent of lilac and cherry blossoms. But he drew too close to the glass. The locks on the doors suddenly engaged with an ominous clank. The AW logo began to flash.

"Go on. Just smash them," Uno said, growling in frustration. "Use the hammer. What have we got to lose?"

Nothing, Barnaby thought. It was not the first time Uno had made the suggestion. But Barnaby always hesitated. He did not know what effect an athen hammer would have on magical doors. Perhaps it would smash them; perhaps not. But if it did not, then Mrs. Tamburlane would appear, as she always did, and she would confiscate the hammer. And though he knew it was little use to anyone, he could not bear to part with it. He didn't know why.

"Look—you said yourself we can't stay here any longer," Uno said. "Do you want to go back to that Testing Floor again?" Barnaby shook his head. "Then smash it!"

Barnaby reached under his shirt. He felt his belt, a scrap of leather, some rivets, but no hammer. "It's gone!" he said.

"Oh, brilliant!" Uno said. "The first time we need that stupid thing, and you've gone and lost it."

They retraced their steps. They went back to the cafeteria, the washroom, the R&D laboratories, their own room, but they could not find the hammer.

"It might be on the Testing Floor," Barnaby said when they

had exhausted their search. "That's the only place we haven't looked."

"We'll have to go in in the morning," Uno said.

But the next day was Thursday, always the busiest day of the week in the laboratories. And Sandborn was in a foul mood, growling and barking and gnashing his teeth about someone or something that had been breaking into the Testing Floor at night and killing test subjects.

"Sandborn cut *him*! Sandborn split *him* in half!" the troll shouted, nearly decapitating Barnaby with a large knife he had been waving about all morning. Barnaby thought it best to tele-shift at once back to the laboratory.

"Split in half?" Uno said when Barnaby returned to his workbench. "You don't suppose Old Wax Face is coming here now to get his midnight snacks, do you?"

Barnaby did not know and did not want to think about it. All he wanted was to get his hammer back. "We'll try later, when Sandborn goes to lunch," he whispered to Uno.

Sandborn did not go to lunch, however. And the R&D Bees kept Barnaby so busy that he almost forgot about the hammer.

By midafternoon, his head ached again. He glanced up from his bench and saw the cleaning woman, Isak, entering Dr. Zivvini's office. She came every day, always with the same grim, purposeful expression on her face, her eyes hammocked with weariness.

She nodded to Barnaby as she wheeled her cart into Dr. Zivvini's office, and he waved. He sometimes caught her staring at him, through the glass, and once, when he had asked her if she was all right, she had smiled. But it was the smallest, saddest smile Barnaby had ever seen.

"What about her?" Uno whispered, getting to his feet. "Do you think she has it?"

"The hammer?" Barnaby asked.

"No, my water dish. Of course I mean the hammer," Uno said. "She took that card, remember? I'm sure she'd pocket your hammer."

"She's only a mortal, Uno—"

"No, she's not. I can smell power in her every time she goes by. I can feel it. She must be a slag or something—probably a spy for the Queen, or Mrs. Tamburlane, or your father. See? She's snooping through the waste bins right now."

Isak was only emptying the waste bins into her cart, as she always did. *If she is a spy,* Barnaby thought, *she's a very bad one. Whatever's in that waste bin can't be as valuable as what's on Dr. Zivvini's desk.* And she had not given the desk so much as a glance.

He returned to the sniffer he was building. He had five more to do, and his last trip to the Testing Floor had left him shaking and nauseated. He had no energy for Uno's intrigues.

"I think we should follow her," Uno said as Isak departed.

"Leave her alone," Barnaby said. "She's not a spy."

"That's what you said about the bats at Georges Castle. Then suddenly your father was blasting your door off the hinges, and poor Alexander was in the dungeons."

Barnaby frowned. He did not like to think about that. "All right—the bats really were spies. But I've got five more of these blasted things to build, and I don't have the energy to worry about every suspicious person who glances our way."

Uno sniffed. "I'm only looking out for your welfare—a job that seems to be well beyond *your* capacity."

The frame of the sniffer suddenly collapsed, sending pieces of Hibernian spruce scattering across the floor.

"Look what you've done!" Barnaby said.

"Me? You're the one who can't talk and hold things at the same time," Uno said.

"And you're the one who never *stops* talking. 'Do this. Do that. Watch out for her. Don't go near him.' You're the only pet I know who lectures his master!"

"I wouldn't have to lecture *master*, if dear *master* paid more attention to what's happening around him. Who got Alexander locked up? Me? Who lost the hammer? Me? No. It was *you*. No wonder Ana and Clarissa thought you were a nut-brained—"

"That's it!" Barnaby shouted. He picked up a broken piece of Hibernian spruce and waved it at Uno. "Get out!"

"Fine. I'm going," Uno said, sauntering away. "I'm sure I can find more interesting people to talk to in the Waste Disposal Department."

Barnaby threw the piece of wood just as Uno stepped into the teleshifting tubes. But then, seeing Uno vanish, Barnaby was instantly sorry.

"Wait! Come back!" he shouted. But it was too late. Uno was gone.

Uno wandered for hours through the halls of AW—not to punish Barnaby but to prove to him that this cleaning woman, Isak, was not what she seemed. Unfortunately, Uno had no idea where Isak had gone. He had to teleshift from floor to floor and search for her scent, and this proved doubly irritating. One, he detested teleshifting. It did not require hands or skill—one simply thought the number of the floor one wanted, and *zoom!*—but it was similar to being sucked through a laundry chute, with one's molecules tumbling through the molecules of whoever else happened to be in the teleshifting tube—a very unpleasant sensation. Two, Isak's scent seemed to be everywhere: the cafeteria; the Sales Department; Production, Marketing, Accounting; even the executive offices. Given that there were over four hundred floors, it seemed unlikely that one mortal could have responsibilities on every one of them.

At last, Uno found her emptying waste bins in the Promotions Department. He followed her from a distance, using his nose more than his eyes to track her. But though she wandered nearly everywhere, he did not catch her doing anything suspicious. She did not linger outside office doors. She did not peek through key-

holes or rifle through papers on desks. She *did* glance at the odd
scrap of paper now and then before tossing it into her cart, but
this seemed more of a precautionary measure than anything else:
A mortal who threw away important memos could be sent to the
Testing Floor.

By supper time, Uno was tired and frustrated and hungry. *This
is all Barnaby's fault,* he thought, watching Isak disappear yet again
into one of the teleshifting tubes. *If the ostrich head would only learn
to look after himself, I wouldn't have to waste my time following a cleaning woman about the building.*

But Barnaby could not look after himself. That was the point,
wasn't it? Uno was the one who had to snoop and sniff and listen.
Uno was the one who had had to stand up to the King whenever
the King threatened to roast Barnaby in his own skull. And Uno
was the one who had been tied up and muzzled and nearly blasted
out of existence, all because Barnaby could not defend himself.

*If it wasn't for me, the idiot would be at the bottom of the Maelstrom
by now,* Uno thought. His stomach growled. He decided to sus-
pend his search for the moment and treat himself to a generous
supper. But when he stepped out of the teleshifting tube near the
cafeteria, there was Isak.

"Hello, Uno," she said, smiling. "Is everything all right?"

She looked different, Uno noticed. Her eyes almost glowed—
green amulets that only an hour ago had seemed dull and lifeless.
And there was a strength in her voice that had not been there

yesterday. *This woman is definitely not what she appears to be,* Uno thought, tensing.

Isak extended a hand. Uno backed away, growling, but the scent of her fingers set off a sudden explosion of memory inside his head: a man limping; steam and blood and disinfectant; Isak's voice ringing like a bell over everything. He had met her before! But where? When? The realization only confused him more.

"It's all right," Isak said, stretching her hand closer to him. Now he could feel the power radiating from her fingertips—strong, so much stronger than any mortal could be. She was a slag. He was sure of it. Was she trying to catch him? Was she going to curse him?

He snapped at her and fled back into the teleshifting tube, directing it to take him to the R&D laboratory. He hoped Barnaby would still be there. But when he stepped out of the tube, the laboratory was dark and empty, the only light coming from a few phosphorescent jars on the shelves.

"He probably went to bed," Uno muttered, turning to reenter the teleshifting tubes. Then, suddenly, he was jerked into the air by his collar. A furry hand covered his muzzle, and a familiar voice growled in his ear, "Nice doggy. Sandborn love doggy."

Chapter 22

"CHARLES! WHERE HAVE YOU BEEN?" Ana said, staring at the little mouse standing on her father's journal.

"Sorry, Your Majesty," Charles said. "I—I'm afraid I had a difficult time getting out of the cavern. Terrible place!"

"Well I'm very glad to see you again. Only we'll have to be careful," she said, glancing this way and that. "Mr. Pound has a bee in his derby about you. I don't know why." She started to put a Privacy Spell on the doors, then realized it would only attract Mr. Pound's attention.

"He seems to think I should know where you came from," she said, sitting down. "Only I don't, or I don't think I do. But you said we'd met before?"

"Yes, yes!" Charles said, clearly pleased that Ana remembered their conversation. "It was months ago, in the dungeons."

Ana bent low to get a better look. He did look familiar, but most mice looked alike, didn't they? "I'm sorry. I really don't remember," she said.

Charles clutched his tail in his paws, looking crestfallen. "No, I don't suppose you would. I only thought, since you created me . . ."

Ana blinked. "Since I did *what*?" she said.

"Created me. In that passageway—when you and the boy were spying on the nasty gray-haired man . . ."

"Benjamin? That was . . . Wait! The little mouse I conjured up when Barnaby fell? That was you?" Ana said, astonished.

Charles jumped up and down. "Yes! Yes! That was me! But you didn't conjure me. You *created* me. I saw you when you turned visible again, but I couldn't catch up. And then, of course, I got trapped in the cavern with the other mice . . ."

Ana was not listening. *I created a mouse?* she said to herself. *A talking one?* It wasn't possible. Immortals couldn't create anything. Hadn't Mr. Pound told them that on Mount Olympus? Even the masses of insects and worms and plants that seemed to accompany her every curse were only summoned, not *created*. Or so she had assumed. But if she truly had created them . . . No wonder Mr. Pound wanted to know where Charles had come from.

"This—this is all very, very confusing," she said. "But why did you want to see me?"

"Well, at first I was only hoping you would get us out of the cavern," Charles said.

"Us?"

"Myself and the other mice. I'm a bit politically involved, you see. The others—well, they've been transformed so many times they've lost all sense of mousehood. A complete loss of cultural and personal identity. So they asked me to help them escape. But then Mr. Pound attacked you, and what with all the goings-on in the SSCCR lately . . ."

Ana blushed. "I'm sorry about that," she said.

"It's not your fault, Your Majesty," Charles said. "In any case, I did manage to find a way out of the cavern. But then I got hopelessly lost in the dungeons, and in the middle of it all, who should I run into but a friend of yours."

Ana's heart nearly stopped. "A friend? What friend?" she said.

"A girl, Your Majesty," Charles said, startled. "Clarissa was her name, I believe. She asked me to find you."

Ana could not believe it! She snatched Charles up in her hand. "Where is she? Is she all right? Take me to her! Now!"

"Please, Your Majesty! You're squeezing me," Charles gasped. Ana loosened her grip, but she did not let go of him. "Of course. I—I'll be happy to take you to her. But you must understand, it's been weeks. I'm not sure—"

"Just show me where she is!" Ana shouted, nearly frantic now.

Charles directed her down into the dungeons. Down and down they went, into parts Ana had searched dozens of times before. *How could Clarissa be here and my spells not find her?* she thought.

Finally, they arrived at the lowest level—a dead end. Except where before there had been a stone wall, now there was an opening the size of a man. Ana stepped through the hole. There was a hidden corridor here with four more cells, all of them

ancient-looking and unnumbered. An emerald light emanated out
of the viewports, and the air had a foul, acidic stench to it.

"That one," Charles said, directing her to the very last cell.

Barnaby waited all night for Uno to return. When Friday morning came, there was still no sign of his friend. He went to the
cafeteria, sure that Uno's boundless appetite would bring him
there. But Uno did not appear.

Perhaps he got locked in the laboratory last night, Barnaby thought.
He rushed up to the R&D Department, sure that he would find
his friend asleep under the workbench. But Uno was not there—
only Dr. Zivvini, waiting with a dozen orders in his hands.

Where can he be? Barnaby wondered as he set to work. It was
not like Uno to stay away this long. And he would not have
left AW without Barnaby. *He must be trapped somewhere,* Barnaby
thought. And then, with a sickening feeling, he thought of Sandborn.

He had to get to the Testing Floor! He had no key, however,
and Dr. Zivvini never lent him his unless there was something to
test. Barnaby searched through the papers on his bench, found a
copy of an old curse. He changed the name at the top, then went
to get the key from Dr. Zivvini. But the R&D Bees were headed
out for a luncheon meeting.

"We'll have plenty of time to test in the afternoon," Dr. Zivvini
said. "And Sandborn's not there right now. He's being treated for
some sort of injury he received last night."

"Injury?" Barnaby said, alarmed.

"Yes, yes. It must be a bad one, because he's been ranting and raving all morning about an athen hammer he supposedly found." Dr. Zivvini laughed. "An athen hammer! Can you imagine? Might as well say he discovered a reversible curse."

Barnaby was sure now that Uno must be on the Testing Floor. He waited for the R&D Bees to buzz out the door, then raced to Dr. Zivvini's office. He touched the crystal ball on the desk and asked for the Testing Floor. There was no answer. He tried three more times, and still there was no answer.

This was Barnaby's chance. If he could only find Dr. Zivvini's new key, he could search the Testing Floor before Sandborn returned. He began rifling through the papers on the desk, carefully at first, then scattering them everywhere as he became more desperate. He pulled out the drawers, spilled their contents across the desk. He emptied the waste bin onto the carpet.

Then a voice in the doorway said, "Are you looking for something?"

Barnaby looked up to find Isak, the cleaning woman, staring at him.

"I—I lost something," he said.

"Can I help you look?" she said.

Barnaby did not want her help. "I need to find it myself," he said. "Please. Just go away."

Isak nodded. She stared at him for a moment, looked out into the laboratory. "Where's Uno?" she suddenly asked.

Tears flooded into Barnaby's eyes. "He's missing!" he sobbed, though he knew he shouldn't say anything to her. She probably *was* a spy. "I think—I think Sandborn's taken him! Only I can't find Dr. Zivvini's key, and Sandborn will be back at any moment, and then . . ."

Isak reached into the breast pocket of her coveralls. "Here," she said, pulling out Dr. Zivvini's old key.

Barnaby stared at it for a moment, wondering why she had it. Then he snatched it out of her hands. He ran into the teleshifter. Isak followed.

Within seconds, they were on the Testing Floor, racing down the aisles. Barnaby usually avoided looking at the prisoners, but this time he had no choice. He ran along, calling Uno's name and praying that the black lizardy thing in the top cages, or the blind thing with the cow's head and frog's body, or the strange, talking stones would not answer him.

Then, suddenly, he heard Isak calling to him from the far side of the warehouse: "He's here!" Barnaby raced toward her voice.

Ana hesitated. The door to the cell was hanging open, a green, foggy light drifting out. She set Charles down and stepped closer, anxious, fearful.

"Clarissa!" she called. There was no answer. She stepped inside. But she had no sooner crossed the threshold than she was struck by a wave of pain and terror such as she had never felt before. It sent her reeling into the corridor, blind, sickened, and as she waited for it to pass, she realized it was an aura that had struck her: Clarissa's aura!

She rose, shaking. She approached the doorway again, dreading what she would find. But it was far worse than she feared. The cell's floor lay foot-deep in poisoned water. A steady fog of sorcery drifted down from the ceiling. The stones themselves—pitted by the caustic air—had mouths and teeth and sucked hungrily at everything within reach.

This was not a cell meant to hold a prisoner, Ana realized; it was meant to torture and kill. And there, draped across a mound of athen, were Clarissa's clothes—scorched and torn and empty.

Ana cupped her hands over her mouth. An eerie, keening cry rose out of her, and she backed away from the cell, shaking her head. Then, suddenly, she bumped against something hard and cold.

"To witness one person's suffering is to witness the world's, Princess," a voice behind her said. "And it is truly bottomless."

Barnaby found Isak kneeling before a cage in the back of the warehouse.

"He's hurt," she said, fiddling with the lock. The cage door popped open, and Barnaby threw himself on Uno.

"Uno! Uno! It's me!" he said, pressing his face into Uno's thick, furry coat. Uno did not move. Barnaby felt something wet against his cheek. He pulled away, cried out at the sight of blood on his hands and shirt, on Uno's coat. There was a gash on Uno's head—a wound so deep, Barnaby could see the white of Uno's skull.

"He's alive," Isak said. "But we have to get him out of here." She spoke some words. To Barnaby's amazement, a roll of bandages suddenly appeared in her hands. *Uno was right!* he realized. *She has power!* But he did not care, so long as she saved Uno.

Isak bound the gash on Uno's head as tightly as she could, then told Barnaby to lift Uno onto his shoulders. But before they could make their escape, they heard the teleshifters start to hum.

"Quick! This way," Isak whispered. She dashed toward the farthest corner of the warehouse. Barnaby followed as best he could, Uno bouncing heavily on his shoulders.

"Sandborn smell!" a ragged voice suddenly cried from the far side of the Testing Floor. "Sandborn catch you!" The cages began to rattle as the troll dashed toward them.

Isak stopped before a set of rungs fixed into the wall in the back. "These go to the roof," she said. She scrambled up and Barnaby climbed after her, struggling to keep Uno from slipping off his shoulders.

"Mine! Mine!" Sandborn rasped below. Barnaby glanced down. One of the troll's hands was bandaged. There was a bloodier bandage around his throat. Uno must have bitten him, Barnaby realized. That was the only reason he was still alive: The troll had been too hurt to eat.

Sandborn watched Barnaby for a moment, then ran off.

When they reached the top, Isak popped open a hatch. "Emergency exit," she explained. She climbed out and took Uno from Barnaby's shoulders.

"Emergency exit for whom? The birds?" Barnaby asked, stepping onto the roof. They were at least four hundred stories above the ground. How would they get down?

"Go to the teleshifters. We'll take them to the basement," Isak said.

"Then where?" Barnaby asked.

"Home," Isak replied.

Ana leaped away from Mr. Pound.

"Why?!" she said, tears streaming down her face. "I did everything you asked! Everything!"

"It was necessary, Princess," Mr. Pound said. "So that you might understand. So that your choice will be clear, when the time comes."

Necessary—the word delivered so calmly, so precisely, as if the word itself could justify any injustice. Ana trembled. Her heart felt so hot she thought it could melt athen. And when she opened her mouth, what sprang from her lips was not a reply, but a curse—a curse she had never heard before, never learned, a curse that flew like the voice of death from her mouth.

Too late, Barnaby thought. The teleshifters were humming. Isak pulled him down with Uno behind the pile of athen lumps. The mound had not been cleared out all week and was at least four feet high. Still, it would not hide them for long.

The teleshifter stopped. Barnaby heard nothing but the pounding of his own heart and Uno's soft, ragged breathing. Then, suddenly, there was Sandborn at the top of the mound, staring down triumphantly.

"Sandborn smell you!" he rasped through his injured throat. He had a large net draped over the arm of his injured hand. But in his other hand he clutched something far more upsetting to Barnaby: the athen hammer!

Isak cast a fireball at Sandborn. The troll batted it aside with the hammer and cast the net down over them.

Then, as Barnaby struggled and twisted against the thick cords, a very strange thing happened. He heard a muffled boom in the distance. The sniffers lining the edge of the roof began to twirl and hum. And then, suddenly, the mound beneath Sandborn exploded!

Ana's curse struck Mr. Pound full in the chest. It sent him crashing through the wall. But the force rebounded off of him like a cataract off a rock and ricocheted wildly through the castle, destroying everything in its path. The foundation began to shake. The walls trembled and groaned. Suddenly the castle tore open from one end to the other. And as the Monitoring Spells shrieked their alarms, as stone and dust began to fall all around and sunlight sliced down into the farthest depths of the dungeons, Ana saw her chance. She leaped through rock and mortar, tore through the airy skin of spells. She rocketed up and up and up, into the sky, into the stars, into the beautiful black arms of space.

The blast slammed Barnaby against the roof's surface. It sucked the air out of his lungs, scoured his hands and face and clothes with a hot, searing wind. He was sure he would be blown off the roof at any moment.

Then, at last, the wind died. Barnaby staggered to his feet— ears ringing, clothes torn to shreds. Isak rose, too. Uno was still breathing, thank goodness, though his fur had been singed. But Sandborn was gone. And so was the mound. All that remained was a sheet of melted athen, crazed and cracked and warped. And as Barnaby stared at it, wondering what force could have done this, he saw a word forming in the athen, saw deep block letters spark and burn and etch themselves into the surface until they spelled:

ANATOPSIS

Part II

Chapter 23

ANA FLEW. Ana burned. Ana plunged through space like a diver, like a stone. Earth tumbled away behind her, Mars and Jupiter dodged aside. Andromeda sang past in a mist, musical and heavenly. Wolf 359, Sirius, Trenelaus, Amadeus, the Sardonin Galaxies, Claudia G, Imitramine—the stars and suns and planets in schools too dense to count swirled away from her like fish before a crashing prow.

She did not think about where she was going. She only wanted to get as far from Solomon Castle as she could, away from that cell, away from Mr. Pound. But his voice followed her, echoing in her head: *necessary, necessary, necessary.* For whom? For what? To punish her? To drive her away?

She pushed herself farther and faster, her face frozen with tears, her nose and throat full of cosmic dust. She thought of her father. He was out here somewhere—on a planet called Arthur B. Except she did not know where Arthur B was, or if he was still there. So she cast a Reunion Spell to spotshift her to wherever he might be.

She materialized on a muddy flat in some unknown place, her whereabouts obscured by rain and bolts of lightning. Drops the size of frogs pelted down on her, soaking her hair and clothes. She did not see her father anywhere, and not knowing what else to do or where to go, she shouted a Spell of Dehydration.

The rain stopped. The clouds vanished. The water evaporated quickly, and whatever tiny creatures had been flipping about in the puddles were now fossilized. Then, as Ana was about to conjure up a bed, a voice behind her bellowed, "What in the name of Alfze Embrahed the Beleaguered do you think you're doing?"

Ana whipped around. A middle-aged gentleman with white hair and green coveralls stood a few feet away from her, clutching a large clipboard. He seemed on the verge of bashing her over the head with it, but then suddenly dropped it.

"Ana? Is that you?" he said.

"Father?" Ana said. She could not believe it. What was he doing here? Was this Arthur B? She rushed into his arms, bursting into tears as he hugged her.

"Oh, Father!" she said. "I thought you were . . . ! I tried to find you . . . !" She dug her face into his chest, sobbing, and the more she cried the more she felt she would never stop.

"Have I been gone that long?" Sir Christopher said, bewildered.

Finally the tears subsided. Sir Christopher produced a handkerchief from his pocket and wiped Ana's face, and then she tried, as best she could, to explain all that had happened since his departure. But it was no use—every time she mentioned Clarissa's or Barnaby's or Uno's name, she would burst into tears again.

"I'm so sorry, Ana," her father said, catching the gist of what had happened. "I had no idea your mother or Mr. Pound would do anything like that. But you're safe now. And you'll feel better once you get some food in you. You look like you haven't eaten in months."

This was an understatement. Even had Sir Christopher not been away from Solomon Castle so long, he would hardly have recognized Ana. Her hair—never tidy to begin with—looked like dead grass, and her eyes had such dark circles around them, she could have been mistaken for a vampire. Worst of all, she had lost so much weight, she looked like a dryad pried out of a tree.

"I've got some rations in my pack," Sir Christopher said, pointing to the green UCSB rucksack hanging from his back, "but I'm afraid I can't offer you anything substantial until I finish my task. I'm a journeyman now, see?" He plucked at the insignia on the pocket of his coveralls. "Planetary Engineer, Third Class."

"Planetary engineer?" Ana said, blowing her nose.

"Or 'bio-artisan,' if you prefer. The younger students call themselves that, but it sounds pretentious to me."

"You mentioned that in your letters. What—what does a planetary engineer do?"

Sir Christopher blushed. "If you hadn't stopped the rain, I might have been able to show you. But essentially, we restore planets. Dead ones, that is."

"*Restore* planets?"

"Yes. Give them atmospheres, water, try to introduce life-forms—that sort of thing."

Ana had never heard of planets being restored. "And that's what you've been doing all these months?" she said. "When you said you were becoming an engineer, I thought . . . well, I don't know what I thought. So Arthur B is dead?"

Sir Christopher coughed. "Ahem—well, no. That is to say, Arthur B isn't dead anymore, but it might very well be again." Seeing Ana's confusion, he sighed and said, "I'm afraid I got into a bit of trouble on Arthur B. I was supposed to do the prep work—start the rain, prime the oceans, grow a few simple eukaryotes. But I got a little carried away."

"Carried away?" Ana said.

"Well, you know my fondness for dinosaurs. Amazing creatures. And, of course, one can't have dinosaurs without first having blue-green algae, and then various sea creatures, and a host of plants and trees. So I did all that. And I thought I'd done a bang-up job. But then the chief inspector came, and he said I'd botched the whole thing—skipped at least a dozen essential evolutionary steps—and they were going to have to start all over again. So now here I am, serving my sentence, as it were."

"But where is *here*?" Ana asked.

Sir Christopher laughed. "Earth, of course. Where did you think?"

"Earth?" Ana said. Everywhere she looked there was nothing but dried mud and hazy sky. What part of Earth could this be?

"Well, not the island, obviously. This is one of the continents. The UCSB cleared a practice area for me."

Ana shook her head. "I don't understand," she said. "Practice area for what?"

"Restoring planets, of course," Sir Christopher said. He glanced at his watch. "Look, why don't I show you? There are a few hours left before sunset." He picked up his clipboard where he had dropped it. "You can watch from the top of that cliff. Just don't go any farther than that. The Environmental Management Shield doesn't extend much beyond it, and if you step outside the perimeter, there's no telling what might happen. The UCSB's lost several engineers that way."

Ana glanced up at the cliff, a high, rocky promontory that looked very cold and lonely. Her eyes welled up.

"It won't take long," Sir Christopher said, seeing her distress. "It might even make you feel better." A few tears trickled down Ana's cheeks. "I could do a request," he said. "Is there some species you're particularly fond of? Drumfish? Palamanxes? Neutrinovores? I'm rather fond of dinosaurs myself, but—"

"Dogs," Ana said, wiping her eyes. "I like dogs."

Sir Christopher frowned. "Dogs." He studied his clipboard. "You wouldn't rather have bouncing hairbats?"

"If it's too much trouble . . ." Ana said.

"No, no," Sir Christopher said. "No trouble at all. It's just that I've never grown a dog before. But I'll see what I can do."

Grown a dog? Ana thought. *How does one grow a dog?* But before she could ask, her father had flown away.

There was not much to see, at first: only clouds and lightning and torrents of sulfurous rain. Then, after twenty minutes or so, the clouds parted a bit. Standing at the edge of the cliff, gazing two or three hundred feet down, Ana could see a lake forming below. The water rose and rose—thick and rust-colored at first, but little by little turning purple, then blue-green, then a deep, dark jade. Then, in the very center of the lake, a wild green fire suddenly bloomed—algae, Ana realized—and it churned and swelled and seemed to boil right out of the lake, spreading its tropical flame everywhere.

After an hour, the rain stopped, and the sun emerged. Sir Christopher, standing on the shore of the lake, called to Ana to join him. She flew down and landed on a soft, springy bed of moss. Horsetails and ferns were already beginning to unfurl from the earth. The air smelled of mud and grass and wet, steaming leaves.

"What do you think?" Sir Christopher said, mopping his face with a handkerchief. "I'm trying to go slower this time. If you go too fast, you risk getting 'mischronicities'—frogs evolving before there are insects to eat, that sort of thing."

Ana turned this way and that, speechless. Saplings were inching their way up around her. Flowers were exploding out of their stems, and vines snaked this way and that across the ground. The air literally cracked and popped with life.

"It's beautiful, Father," Ana said. "How did you learn to do this?"

"Oh, it's a long story," Sir Christopher replied. "Why don't we eat first?"

Ana followed her father a little way until they came to a small, green tent pitched near the shores of the lake. He took off his pack and brought it to a large, flat rock, where they made a picnic of sorts. Dried sandpig strips, purple Venusian potatoes, a half-dozen fresh apples: It was not a feast by any means, but it was enough for Ana.

As they ate, Sir Christopher told her about his conversion from knight-errant to planetary engineer.

"I had no intention of joining," Sir Christopher said. "But one night, my friend at the UCSB was reciting an incantation. It was supposed to create mushrooms, but he kept repeating it over and over again without any success. Finally I said, 'Look, even I can produce a mushroom.' I repeated the incantation, and *presto!*— the floor was covered in mushrooms.

"Well, you would have thought I had discovered magic itself. He grabbed my arm, dragged me all the way to the chief inspector's office, and made me repeat the incantation then and there. The next thing I knew, the school was offering me a scholarship."

"For conjuring mushrooms?" Ana said, taking a bite from her apple.

"For *creating* mushrooms," Sir Christopher replied. "That's what I'd done, you see. Only I didn't know because, like everyone else, I had been taught that Immortals can't create things."

Ana choked on her bite of apple. "But—but that's what happened to me," she said. "Remember? I told you in my letters." She described all the strange creatures that had appeared whenever she cast a spell or curse. She told him about Charles.

"Oh, I can't imagine it's the same thing," Sir Christopher said. "I mean, even the best engineers would be hard-pressed to create a flower, much less a mouse."

"But you created all these plants and trees."

"In point of fact, I didn't *create* them—I *grew* them. You see, it's too difficult to create everything from scratch, so instead we seed a planet with a few simple life-forms—algae, amoebas, that sort of thing—then accelerate the evolutionary process to generate the other species. One has to manipulate the environment carefully, of course, but it's still much easier than trying to create all those species from nothing.

"Now, to create a mouse, you would have to know everything about it—its internal and external makeup, its mating rituals and social structures, its feeding preferences. And then, of course, you can't just have one, you have to have a male and female, which introduces other complications. So the potential for errors becomes enormous. No, I think your mouse must have been conjured from somewhere else. He's just a bit confused about his origins."

Ana frowned. Perhaps she had only conjured Charles out of the SSCCR. But if so, why did *he* think she had created him?

When they had finished eating, Sir Christopher pressed Ana to tell him again what had happened at Solomon Castle. Ana did not want to; she was far too tired. But her father insisted. So she related her trials as quickly as she could in a flat, dispassionate voice, as if it had all happened eons ago. But when she came to the part about Clarissa, she burst into tears again.

Sir Christopher put an arm around her. "I'm so sorry, Ana," he said. "If I had had the slightest idea—"

"I told you, Father!" Ana snapped. "In my letters! I told you!" She was shaking, she was so angry.

"You mentioned some suspicions concerning Mr. Pound," Sir Christopher said, taken aback. "But I haven't received a letter in weeks. Of course, I've been out in the field—"

"You're always out in the field! You've been out in the field since the day I was born, either fighting dragons or searching for treasure or saving dead planets. And when I really need you, where do I find you? Growing weeds on a barren patch of dirt! I hate it!"

Her father looked as if he had been slapped. "I'm—I'm sorry, Ana," he said, blinking. "I always *wanted* to be with you. But your mother . . . you know how she can be."

Ana made a face. He was always blaming her mother. The Queen held all the power, it was true. If she ordered Sir Christopher to leave the castle, he had little choice but to leave. But it seemed to Ana that he had never once challenged her. He had simply flown off at the first flick of her fingers. *Of course, I haven't done much better, have I?* Ana thought gloomily.

They were silent for a while. Ana hugged her arms around herself, tired and shivering. The slap of the water in the lake was making her dizzy. She needed to lie down, but she was afraid that if she moved, she would tumble off the rock.

"I still don't understand this business about the Os Divinitas," Sir Christopher said, not noticing how pale Ana had become. "No one in the Guild ever took it seriously. Why does Pound?"

Ana shrugged. "There's some sort of prophecy," she said, her voice seeming to float away from her. "I can't remember it."

Sir Christopher unbuttoned one of his breast pockets. He took out a small, folded piece of paper and handed it to Ana. "There's not a knight-errant in the Guild who doesn't carry a copy of this," he said, "in case a job comes along."

Ana unfolded the piece of paper. The words bobbed up and down on the page, like little ships. *Half and half now borne away,* she read, and then everything turned white and she was falling. . . .

Chapter 24

BARNABY FOLLOWED ISAK through the crumbling sewers. His back ached. His eyes and nose and mouth burned from the foul air. He had Uno draped across his shoulders, and it was all he could do to keep up, yet he wished Isak would go faster. For Uno's breathing was growing more labored by the minute.

Where were they going? To the ghetto, Barnaby guessed. But it was at least two or three miles, even in a straight line, and here they were stumbling through a maze of tunnels that would have confounded the Minotaur. They hopped over green liquids and flotillas of spell fragments, detoured around curses stretched across their path, and everywhere a thick, yellow mist rained down, seeping through the rags tied around Barnaby's face, stinging his eyes and throat.

At last, Isak stopped. She clambered up a short set of rungs in the wall, opened a hatch, and hauled Barnaby and Uno into what looked like the inside of a cheese grater. Holes in the walls and ceiling sprayed warm water down on them. Holes in the floor drained the water away.

"Get as much of the muck off as you can," Isak said, taking off her rags and using them to wipe her hands and clothes and boots. Barnaby did the same for himself and Uno. Then the shower stopped. A hatch above them swung open, and hands reached down to pull them out.

At first, Barnaby could not see where he was. Steam filled the air, and a dozen or so mortals—each dressed in either blue-and-white AW coveralls or red-and-black CNI coveralls—were all crowding around him. He shoved them aside, looking for Uno. A group of mortals was carrying him toward an enormous oval pool in the middle of the floor. At least, Barnaby assumed it was a pool, though it was like none he had ever seen: carved of some strange black rock, with sloped sides and a shallow bowl. Steam wafted off the surface, making it look like soup, and his first thought was that they intended to cook Uno.

"Let him go!" Barnaby cried, grabbing hold of Uno.

"It's all right, Barnaby," Isak said, gently pulling at him. "It's just a bath—to decontaminate him. They won't hurt him. I promise." She pointed to a flight of wide metal steps not far away. "You can sit there and watch."

She signaled to one of the mortals, a dark, bearded man in a CNI uniform. The man guided Barnaby to the curving staircase and gave him a towel to wipe his hands and face.

Barnaby watched the mortals lower Uno into the pool. It was

all as Isak had said; they were only giving him a bath. And he could see now that Uno's fur was covered in glowing bits of waste. There was no telling what that stuff might do. *Best to get it off right away,* Barnaby thought.

The steam cleared a bit. Barnaby could see now that he was in some sort of enormous bathhouse—though it must have been a bathhouse for giants, for the pool alone was as large as the ballroom at Georges Castle, and there was a broad expanse of tile on every side, decorated in strange mosaics. The ceiling, too—a wide dome of metal and cloudy green glass—was unnaturally high, almost hidden beyond the clouds of steam.

Did the mortals build this? Barnaby wondered. He could not imagine it. And then he noticed the monstrosity beside him: an enormous metal tank as tall as the building itself. The bottom half was cylindrical, but the top sloped to a peak, like an alchemist's retort, out of which sprang a Medusa's hair of pipes. Except the pipes appeared to have been snapped off in places, and a rent in the top of the tank was releasing steam at an alarming rate. There were mortals clambering about on a platform halfway up, and others trying to get a ladder up to the top, and they were all waving hammers about and shouting at one another in panicked, hurried voices. But this only made the sight doubly astonishing to Barnaby. For as near as he could tell, the tank, pipes, valves, platform, ladders, and even the hammers in the mortals' hands were all made of athen!

How is that possible? he thought. But he did not have time to ponder the significance of his discovery. Isak and the others were now hoisting Uno out of the pool and onto a stretcher.

"Is he all right?" Barnaby asked, rushing to Uno's side.

"Yes, but you can't touch him yet," Isak said, pushing Barnaby away. She pointed to the pool. "Go decontaminate first. Then meet us in here."

A door at the far end of the room swung open. A team of mortals in coveralls and surgical masks took the stretcher and hurried away.

"What's in there?" Barnaby said, alarmed.

"The hospital. We have to stitch him up," Isak said. "But don't worry. My father's very good with animals."

Her father? Barnaby did not like the sound of that. "I'm coming with you," he said.

"No. You'll infect everyone in there," Isak said. "Go wash first."

Four burly mortals blocked Barnaby's way. He had no choice but to go rinse off in the pool and put on the coveralls and boots they gave him.

Once through the door, he found that what Isak called the "hospital" was little more than a corridor lined with cots, with two or three side chambers that served as operating rooms. He found Uno at the far end of the corridor, lying on an old mattress. Isak was holding his head while a second mortal—older, with heavily lidded eyes and skin like crumpled paper—finished putting in a line stitches from Uno's brow to the back of his ear.

"He's going to be all right, I think," the mortal said. "A

smaller dog wouldn't have had a chance, but Saint Bernards have very thick skulls." He finished the last stitch and wrapped Uno's head in thick layers of gauze. In the dim light, Uno looked like an old man in a turban.

As the mortal gathered his instruments, Barnaby knelt and pressed his cheek against Uno's shoulder. He could hear the thud of Uno's heart, his ragged, strained breathing.

"Is he going to wake up?" Barnaby asked, anxious.

"Not for a day or two, at least," the doctor said, slipping off his mask. He washed his hands in a basin on the floor, then introduced himself. "Dr. Azhkima—chief dog stitcher and father to the worst cleaning woman at AW," he said, winking at Isak.

Isak's father. He doesn't much look like her, Barnaby thought. *Or act like her.* Of course, he had no idea how Isak usually acted. She had seemed quiet and timid at AW, but since coming to the ghetto, she had done nothing but rush about and give orders. She *was* a spy; that much was clear. But whether she meant to harm him or not, Barnaby still had no idea.

Isak helped her father to his feet and handed him his crutches. Both of his legs were immobile below the knee, it seemed. When he walked, his footsteps made heavy, clunking sounds, like Mr. Pound's.

"A gift from King Georges," he explained. He rolled up his trousers on one side and showed a leg made of pure granite. Then he and Isak retreated to a corner while Barnaby lay down beside Uno.

A day or two, Dr. Azhkima had said. It sounded like an eternity to Barnaby. And what if Uno did not wake up? No, he could not allow himself to think about that.

He heard Dr. Azhkima whispering to Isak. ". . . every piece of athen within a mile," he said. "The Princess is gone, the castle's in ruins."

Ana gone? Solomon Castle in ruins? Barnaby thought. *How? Why?*

"Is she . . . ?" Isak whispered.

Dr. Azhkima nodded. "Still in the archives," he said. "Won't come out. Won't talk to anyone."

"I should never have sent her there," Isak said.

"No, you shouldn't have," Dr. Azhkima replied. And with that, he thumped away on his crutches.

Barnaby knitted his fingers into Uno's fur, his mind spinning. He remembered the sheet of melted athen on the roof, the letters that had appeared in it. And now Dr. Azhkima had said that Solomon Castle was in ruins. Could Ana have done that? It didn't seem possible. But then, if the mortals could make a tank out of athen, and pipes, and valves, and even steps, perhaps it wasn't so difficult after all.

The hammer must have come from them, Barnaby suddenly realized. But it was all too confusing. He needed to sleep. He would sleep for two days, like Uno. And perhaps when he awoke, Uno would be awake as well.

He closed his eyes. But just as he was drifting off, Isak returned. She handed him some gloves and boots and rags that looked as if they had been dragged through mud.

"Put those on. Wrap the rags around your head and across your face," she said. "I know you're tired, but there are a few things we have to do first."

"What about Uno?" Barnaby said, standing up. He did not want to leave Uno's side, not now.

"He'll be safe here, I promise. And I'll bring you right back when we're done."

When Barnaby was ready, Isak led him back out through the Bath (as she called the larger building) and up the staircase by the tank. A door at the top opened into a wide square of broken cobblestones and iridescent puddles. The air stung Barnaby's nose and throat. As he stopped to pull his rags tighter around his face, he noticed a rushing, grinding noise behind him.

He looked back and saw that the Bath rested on the very edge of the harbor. Its top half was level with the street, the rest sunk below the seawall. But beyond that, burning and roaring in the very center of the bay, lay the Maelstrom. Barnaby could see the fiery spray shooting from its mouth, a ruby halo burning in the mists above it. He shivered and hurried after Isak.

As she led him deeper and deeper into the ghetto, he was dismayed to find that Clarissa's stories about the ghetto had not been exaggerated. The buildings were little more than brick carcasses, ready to disintegrate, the streets so pocked and potholed they might as well have been struck by meteorites. And there were so many puddles of ooze that Barnaby hardly knew where to step.

"How can you live here?" he said as Isak led him through the maze of broken streets.

"Where else do we have to live?" Isak replied. It hadn't always been this way, she explained. Thousands of years ago, the ghetto had been just another part of the city. Land had been in abundance, and the oceans, if not perfectly clean, had been safe.

"There were Immortals, but they were interested in other worlds, back then," Isak said. "Earth was just their backwater birthplace, a planet to escape from. And then, for some reason, they returned—in droves. They brought their magic and their industry. They built their offices and castles and factories and poured their wastes into the sky and ocean. The air became unbreathable, the water undrinkable. The seas rose, and whatever land didn't vanish beneath the water became uninhabitable.

"That's when they put the Environmental Management Shield over the city. But they didn't bother to extend it to the ghetto. Which is why the rest of the island has clean air and water and we have smog and sludge."

They had progressed deeper into the ghetto now. They passed several mortals along the way, all of them dressed in coveralls and wearing the same brown rags around their heads. But there were other figures as well—shadowy forms that hovered in the windows and doorways. These wore cloaks and cowls and rags, and every part of them except their eyes was hidden.

Barnaby wanted to ask Isak who they were, why they were

dressed that way. But they had entered another square now, a much wider one. At the far end, in a gap between sagging tenements, squatted a large building—a former museum or library, Barnaby guessed. Its walls were black with time, the columns pockmarked and falling. The sight of it filled Barnaby with weariness. *This entire place,* he thought, glancing around the square— *it's like standing in the wound of a dying animal.*

Isak led Barnaby down a flight of stairs to the basement of the building. He followed nervously, wondering if it was a trap, if she was leading him into some sort of dungeon.

"No one's going to hurt you, I promise," Isak said, pushing open an old rusted door. "In fact, the Reliquum's more likely to attack me than you."

"The really what?" Barnaby said.

"The Reliquum. It's a sort of assembly," Isak explained. "They make all the decisions for the ghetto." She led Barnaby through a long, dim basement full of ancient bookshelves, then ushered him into a harshly lit room with athen walls and a wide, warped athen table in the center.

The room was full of mortals, a dozen of them seated around the table, a half dozen or more standing along the periphery. On the far side were two of the "rag people" (as Barnaby thought of them), also seated at the table.

Barnaby had never seen so many mortals congregated at once. Nor had he ever felt so unwelcome. They glared at him as he removed his rags, and he wondered if Isak had made a mistake in bringing him here. And then, through the sea of angry faces, he saw one that was smiling, a friend he had never expected to see again: Alexander!

Chapter 25

THE RELIQUUM WAS SILENT as Isak introduced Barnaby. Alexander, from his place at the back of the room, winked at Barnaby, as if to say, *It'll all be over soon, you'll see.* But Barnaby was not reassured. In the faces of the Curates, as the individual members of the Reliquum were called, he saw no hint of welcome.

One of the rag people stood. It was at least eight feet tall, but whether man or woman, mortal or Immortal, Barnaby could not tell, for every part was buried beneath cloak and cowl and rags.

"We're on the brink of destruction, Isak," the rag person croaked, each word sounding like a block of wood being scraped. "Now you add the King to our troubles?"

Barnaby shivered. If this person was their leader, it did not bode well for him. Would they imprison him? Would they torture him?

"I had no choice, Curate for the Deceased," Isak replied.

Curate for the Deceased?! Barnaby did not like the sound of that. Isak recounted their narrow escape from Sandborn and AW.

The Curates listened in stony silence, as if whatever story she told would never excuse her having brought Barnaby to the ghetto. Then, as she described how Sandborn had vanished in the mysterious explosion on the rooftop, the room suddenly erupted. The Curates were all on their feet, cheering and shouting and embracing one another. And it was only when Isak, grinning broadly, began to bang on the table and call for order that Barnaby finally realized *she* was the leader.

Of course, he thought. *That's why everyone here does what she tells them.* But then why did she spend her days cleaning the offices at AW? And why had she brought him to the ghetto?

The celebration finally stopped. Isak finished her report, and as soon as she was done, the taller of the two rag people stood again.

"What do you propose we do with him now?" the Curate said. "Keep him here?"

Isak frowned. "The damage is done, Curate," she said. "I didn't plan for Barnaby to come here. But now that it's happened, I think we can turn it to our advantage."

"Use him as a hostage, you mean?"

Isak blushed. "No. I mean let him join us. Then, if we're lucky, the Princess may join us, too."

The Curate made a barking noise. "The Princess destroyed her own castle. She melted half the athen in the city. She even broke the Crucible. And now you want to bring her here? It's not enough that my people are being cut to pieces? It's not enough that King Georges will come looking for the boy?"

Isak frowned. "It's not *your* people and *my* people, Curate. It's *our* people. And we need *help*. Do you understand that?" she said. "Not a century from now, not a thousand years from now, but today."

"Why should the Princess help us?" the Curate said.

"Because her friends are here," Isak said.

The Curate snorted. "For the first time in your life, it's your *heart* clouding your *mind*, Isak, and not the other way around."

Isak's face burned as the Curate sat down. Barnaby assumed the discussion had run its course, but in fact, each Curate had to be allowed his or her say. As the talking went on and on, Barnaby's head throbbed. His eyes felt like lead. He hardly noticed when the vote finally took place, but then, suddenly, Alexander was by his side, helping him out of his chair.

"Oof! That was deadly," the dwarf said, leading Barnaby out of the basement and up into the square. The sun had set. The ghetto was pitch-black now, except for the glowing spots of residue. "I don't know what everyone was arguing about. It's not as if we can return you to AW. In any case, you're an official guest now, and I've got something exciting to show you."

Barnaby, still groggy and confused, wished Alexander would wait until morning to show him whatever it was. He needed to get back to Uno. But Alexander said it would not take long. So

Barnaby stumbled along behind him, trying not to trip over the loose bricks or break a leg in a pothole.

As they walked, Alexander explained the rules of living in the ghetto. "You work if you can work. You share whatever there is to share, which isn't much usually. And if you spend any time in the streets or the sewers, you go to the Bath and decontaminate yourself.

"The most important rule, though, is no sorcery—not to save yourself, not to save a friend, not even to save the entire ghetto. We've had enough grief from that nonsense. If you cast so much as a Hand Washing Spell here, half the people will tear you limb from limb. The other half will pitch you into the Maelstrom."

"I don't know any Hand Washing Spells," Barnaby muttered. Still, the prohibition made him a little nervous. What if he cast something accidentally?

They walked for several blocks. The street opened into a wide boulevard that ran alongside the crumbling seawall. They followed this and eventually came to an old firehouse, its brick sides black with soot, the engine bays boarded up.

Alexander led Barnaby down a flight of stairs outside the building to the lower level, where the firehouse butted up against the Solomon River. Here, there were three more bays, two of them boarded up, the third open to the water.

"They had fireboats here once," Alexander said. "But the building's got a different purpose now." He opened the side door, switched on an overhead bulb. Torrents of light poured into Barnaby's eyes.

"What—what is that?" he asked, shielding his eyes with his hands.

"Athen," Alexander said. "A hundred tons or more, I would guess. This is where we store it."

Barnaby's eyes finally adjusted, and he saw that there was athen everywhere: athen plates on the floor, on the walls and ceiling, athen lumps in mounds higher than Barnaby's head. Two of the boat slips had been plated over, and these were piled high with athen as well. But the third slip was open, and bobbing inside it was the most amazing thing Barnaby had ever seen: a fireboat made of athen!

"Does—does that work?" he asked, pointing to the boat. It was at least thirty feet long, with a wheelhouse in the center and water cannons bolted to the fore and aft decks. It must have weighed as much as the building itself.

"That depends on your definition of *work*," Alexander said. "It floats, but it's got no motor, and it's too heavy to row. So it just sits there. One of my less successful ideas."

He led Barnaby past a pole that rose up through a wide hole in the ceiling. Barnaby could hear bangs and clatters and what sounded like Harpies being tortured on the floor above.

"What is that?" he asked nervously.

"You'll see," Alexander said. He led Barnaby into a small

freight elevator. They rode it up to the next floor, and when it stopped, he shouted, "Welcome to our workshop!"

Barnaby could scarcely hear him. The room was enormous, filled with mortals banging and sawing and drilling. And under every hand and every foot, above their heads and on the walls around them, gleamed the most fabulous machines Barnaby had ever seen: lathes of athen, drills of athen, band saws and scroll saws, planers, bits and gouges and chisels, all made of athen. Even the workbenches were made of athen.

"I found an athen hammer at Solomon Castle!" Barnaby shouted into Alexander's ear.

Alexander nodded. "It was mine!" he shouted back. "I dropped it that night you saw me. Clarissa tried to get it back, but she couldn't find it. And then you took it to AW."

The roar and clang of the machines slowly died. The workers, having noticed their visitor, turned and stared at Barnaby.

"So all of these people know how to smith athen?" Barnaby said to Alexander.

"Every person in the ghetto," Alexander replied. "It's the first thing we teach. But these people are the best at it."

"Should you be showing me this?" Barnaby said, feeling uneasy now.

Alexander laughed. "Isak told me to. Besides, I'm master smith here."

It seemed strange to Barnaby that Isak would trust him so

quickly. But he was too enthralled by the machines to dwell on her decision.

"This is—this is marvelous!" he said. "But how do you do it? That noise . . . I tried to hammer a lump of athen once. It nearly deafened me."

"It takes getting used to," Alexander said. "Here, I'll show you."

He walked over to a lathe, picked up a short bar of athen, and then, standing on a box, fixed the bar into the chucks. When the lathe began to spin, he took a gouge and slowly inched the tip toward the whirling bar. The athen screamed. It shrieked. It spat fire and smoke and filled the room with the most painful noises Barnaby had ever heard. It was not the sound of metal on metal. It was far deeper and more terrifying, as if Alexander were fighting a demon.

Just when Barnaby thought the noise would drive him mad, the shrieking began to wane. It softened a little at a time, until finally it settled into a pleasant ringing sound. Then Alexander moved the gouge back and forth, paring off long curls of athen as easily as if he were turning a bar of soap. When he was done, he severed the posts at either end and handed the finished piece to Barnaby.

"A bell," he said. "Just hollow it out and it'll ring nicely."

"Incredible," Barnaby said, inspecting the bell. "But what makes that noise?"

"The metal has a spirit. It's alive, really," Alexander explained. "With the wrong touch, it will scream forever and probably drive you insane. With the right touch, it eventually gives way. Then you can make whatever you want out of it."

"But how did you discover that? I mean, the noise is enough to stop anyone," Barnaby said.

"Well, necessity may be the mother of invention, but desperation's the mother of success. Nothing but athen could protect us from magic, so we just kept trying until we succeeded," Alexander said.

"What do you mean 'protect' you?" Barnaby said, confused.

"Athen's immune to magic, isn't it?" Alexander said. "You can blast every curse in existence at it, and nothing happens. So what better material is there for us to build with?"

Of course, Barnaby thought. Every Immortal knew magic was useless against athen. No one had ever seen that as a benefit, however, perhaps because no one had ever found a way to forge it into something useful. But if the mortals *could* forge it . . . The possibilities were endless!

"And the tools—they're made of athen, too?" he asked.

"Yes, but they hardly touch the work," Alexander said. "It's the athen itself that really does the shaping. You need the tools, though, because athen's very temperamental. If you're even a hair off in your instructions, it will give you back complete rubbish."

The other mortals finally turned back to their work. The air soon filled again with the noise of athen being smithed.

"Isak said I could put you to work tomorrow," Alexander shouted. "Do you want to give it a try?"

Barnaby nodded. He was going to learn to smith athen—he could not believe his luck!

Barnaby slept beside Uno that night. When he awoke, Dr. Azhkima was kneeling on the floor, changing Uno's dressing.

"How is he?" Barnaby asked, sitting up.

The doctor shook his head. "Still bleeding, I'm afraid," he said. "And his pulse is weak. Did he wake at all during the night?"

Barnaby shook his head, tears welling in his eyes. The doctor finished his work, gave Barnaby a friendly pat on the shoulder, then hobbled away on his crutches.

Barnaby pressed his cheek against Uno's shoulder. *You have to get better,* he said silently. *You have to wake up.* They had been together as long as Barnaby could remember. He could not imagine living without Uno. It would be like living in a grave.

An attendant brought Barnaby a bowl of cereal—stolen from AW. All of the food in the ghetto was stolen, it seemed, for nothing would grow there. Afterward, Alexander came and took Barnaby to the firehouse.

"Here's your workbench," he said, leading Barnaby to a long athen table. A stack of bars, each four or five feet in length, lay on the floor next to the bench. Alexander took one, gripped it with a pair of tongs—to protect his fingers; not because it was hot—and began banging it with an athen hammer. For a minute or so, there was nothing but screeching and sparking. Then, when the noise finally died away, the bar began to spread into a thin, flat sheet.

It looked easy enough. When Barnaby tried it, however, the bar made twice as much noise and turned less and less flat with every blow.

"It doesn't respond to brute strength," Alexander explained. "If you try to beat it into submission, it will change into exactly what you don't want." He showed Barnaby how to tap the metal firmly but with respect. "If you sing or talk, it goes even faster. Stories, jokes, limericks, nonsense songs, whatever you want. I know it sounds ridiculous, but it's a living metal. If it likes what it hears, it will turn as malleable as clay. If not, you could beat it all day and get nothing."

Barnaby tried again. Now that he had an idea what to expect and a better grasp of the rudiments, he proved fairly adept at smithing athen. He did not know very many stories, but thanks to his father's endless parties, he knew dozens of bawdy ballads and ribald drinking songs. The athen seemed to like the drinking songs best, and soon it was spreading itself beneath Barnaby's hammer like a dog begging to have its belly scratched.

Alexander left him to it, stopping by now and then to check on Barnaby's progress. By lunchtime, Barnaby had forged more than thirty sheets of athen. As a reward, Alexander took him on a quick tour of the fireboat.

"I built it from some ancient plans we discovered," Alexander explained. "I thought it might be useful for transporting athen. But it's so heavy, no motor can budge it."

He took Barnaby belowdecks to see the pumps and hold and the empty engine compartment. Then he took him topside to inspect the water cannons.

"I thought we could use the cannons against attackers," he said. "But the water's too dangerous to spray about."

Afterward, Barnaby returned to the hospital to check on Uno. But when he arrived, one of the rag people was crouched over Uno, a thick scaly claw peeking out from its sleeve.

"Get away from him!" Barnaby shouted. He threw himself at the creature with all his might. But the creature was like stone beneath its rags. Barnaby bounced off of it, almost breaking his shoulder.

"Stay away from him!" Barnaby shouted. "I'm warning you!"

The rag thing stood up, making a hoarse snuffling sound. Was it trying to say something? Barnaby could not tell. He caught a glimpse of greenish brown eyes and coppery fur. And then the creature pushed past him and ran away.

Chapter 26

ANA LAY IN A FEVER for two days. When she finally awoke, she was in a large, green tent with UCSB stenciled in white letters on the walls. Her father was sitting beside her, hunched over and looking as if he had not slept for a week.

"There you are. I was beginning to think I'd have to find a prince to kiss you," he said.

Ana sat up. She was drenched in sweat. Her limbs felt as weak as grass. "What happened?" she asked.

"Exhaustion," Sir Christopher said. "You young people always confuse Immortality with invulnerability. But the worst is past, I think. Are you hungry?"

Ana was surprised to find that she was. She devoured the remains of some leek soup her father had made and chewed some dried sandpig strips. Then, leaning on her father's arm, she went down to the lake to wash her face and hands.

The landscape had changed, she noticed. The saplings she had seen on the first day had grown into a forest. The moss had given way to grass and shrubs and wildflowers. There were new sounds, too—chirrupings and clicks and a disturbingly loud buzzing noise.

"Any dogs yet?" she asked, glancing around.

"Not yet," her father said. "Only insects and a few aquatic species. But dinosaurs should be along any day, and if the Environmental Management Shield holds, we might get to the birds and mammals by next week."

"What do you mean, if it holds?" Ana said.

"Well, it's a temporary shield, you see. A permanent one would be too costly to maintain. So, at best, I'll be able to muck about down here for a few weeks. Then the shield will deteriorate, and the mess AW and CNI have made will flow back in."

"But that's awful! All that work for nothing?"

Sir Christopher shrugged. "I can't make all the magical waste disappear, and it won't burn itself out for a million years or so. So this is the best I can do. Besides, this is meant to be a punishment, not a real assignment."

Sir Christopher escorted Ana back to the tent. He had to go check on some ant colonies, he said. He insisted Ana rest while he was gone, but Ana was not sleepy. As soon as her father was out of earshot, she crawled out of the tent and sat on a log beside the remains of last night's campfire. She was still a little weak. The sun and fresh air revived her, and she thought of going for a stroll through the woods. But then a golden-eyed dragonfly the size of an eagle roared over her head, and she realized a stroll might be a bit dangerous.

She cast a Campfire Spell. As she watched the crackling, popping flames and sprites leaping into the air, she thought of what she had seen in the dungeons: the poisonous mists, the burning water and spellsnakes. She thought of Clarissa's clothes draped like a torn skin over the stones, and Mr. Pound saying, "It was necessary . . ."

Necessary. The word rang in Ana's head again. *So that you might understand,* Mr. Pound had said. *So that your choice will be clear, when the time comes.*

What choice? Ana wondered. She suddenly remembered her father's copy of the prophecy. She crawled into the tent and searched until she found the slip of paper tucked inside a book. She sat down by the fire again and, with trembling hands, opened the piece of paper.

Half and half now torn away
Could yet be whole again one day,
When a dead heart seeks and a dead eye finds
Two of mortal and Immortal kind.
In ice from a sword, flames from a shield,
Two enemies united, one bearer revealed.
Then let fear meld creation, desire,
Hate stoke the hottest of fires
Enough to crack sword, shield, and stone,
Enough to melt athen, turn spirit to bone.

In the forge of Hephaestus let Man's heart meet
The white-hot fire of despair and defeat,
And if it melts, the gods shall reign,
And Mankind never dream again.

There was nothing about a choice. Nor was there any hint as to when or how the pieces of the Os Divinitas would be found.

She shivered. She wished her father would return. She needed someone to talk to. And then she thought of Charles, the little mouse. She saw him clutching his tail again, telling her—so gleefully, so gratefully, as if it were the most welcome miracle he could imagine—that she had created him. But she hadn't, had she? She had only conjured him from somewhere else. At least, that was what her father said.

On a whim, she muttered the words she had spoken that night when she and Barnaby had almost been caught by Benjamin. No mouse appeared. She was not surprised, but she decided to try one more time. She closed her eyes, tried to remember every nuance of that moment—her panic, the look of menace on Benjamin's face, the way the spell had seemed to leap out of her. She spoke the words again and felt the sharp snap of sorcery in her chest and arms and fingertips. But when she opened her eyes, there was still no mouse.

Now her father was back. "Some trouble on the western edge," he said, tossing his clipboard into the tent. "Trees drying up. I'm sure it's nothing that can't be fixed. What have you been up—" He stopped. "What on earth is *that?*"

Ana sat up. "What?" she said, turning around. And there it was: a mouse, sitting on the log beside her, washing its paws—a very small white mouse with pink eyes and a very pink nose. Ana scooped it up before it could run away.

"I did it! I really did it!" Ana said, cupping the mouse in her hands.

Sir Christopher stared. "That's a mouse, Ana," he said. "What is it doing here?"

"I made it, Father!" Ana said gleefully. "I truly did! You said I only conjured Charles from somewhere else, but I didn't. I *created* him. And I created this one, too." She stroked the trembling mouse with her finger.

Sir Christopher frowned. "That's not possible, Ana," he said. "In the entire history of the UCSB, no one's ever created anything more complicated than a walnut tree—and the tree never grew a single walnut. That mouse must have come from somewhere else."

"Well, I doubt I summoned it all the way from Solomon Castle."

Sir Christopher, still skeptical, stretched a finger toward the mouse. The mouse bit him.

"That'll teach you!" it squeaked. And as Ana stared at it in astonishment, it squirmed out of her hands and ran off into the bushes.

"It's true," Sir Christopher said, watching the mouse go. "I can't believe it. I mean, I'm half-mortal, but you're only one-quarter. It should be more diluted, not less."

"What should be?" Ana asked, confused.

"This . . . this talent," Sir Christopher said. He sucked at his bleeding finger. "It's the reason I was able to make those mush-rooms so easily. It's the reason I'm out in the field, after less than a year of training. But to create a *mouse*!"

He sat down on the log beside her. Ana noticed the mouse was still there, staring at her from beneath the underbrush.

"Immortals can't create anything," Sir Christopher explained. "You know that. But now and then a tainted Immortal—a slag, if you will—will inherit the right proportions of mortal craft and Immortal power. These people sometimes demonstrate unique abilities—such as creating life-forms. But a mouse! No one's ever done that. And since your mother's one hundred percent Immor-tal, I expected the ability to be diluted in you, not strengthened."

"Does Mother know about this?" Ana asked. "I mean, your ability to create things?"

Sir Christopher blinked. "I don't see how she could. I only just discovered it myself a few months ago. But now that you mention it, she was not terribly interested in me when we first met—not until I conjured a bouquet of Tasmerian humminglilies for her. Then she became quite amorous and made me conjure all sorts of things for her—flowers, toadstools, blue-green algae. I didn't know I was creating these things, but perhaps she did. Your mother's always been very perceptive, whatever else one might say about her."

And determined, Ana thought. Perhaps this explained why her mother, who had never shown the slightest affection toward Sir

Christopher, had chosen him. Perhaps she had wanted a touch of mortal creativity to enhance the Solomon family powers. *If so, she must be terribly disappointed now,* Ana thought.

She shook her head. It was all so very confusing. And she was too excited by her newfound talent to dwell on her mother's intrigues. Whatever the Queen's plans, they did not matter anymore. Ana was never going back to Solomon Castle.

The next day, Ana felt well enough to accompany her father. He would not allow her to create anything more complex than moss, for fear the area would be overrun with talking animals when the chief inspector came, but Ana did not mind. She was happy to be with him, happy to be wandering about, testing the soil, inspecting the bark and leaves on trees, tweaking the light here, the oxygen there.

By the fourth day, reptiles had begun to appear.

"Dinosaurs tomorrow," her father said that evening.

Ana could not wait. She finished her supper, then retired for the night, happy and exhausted.

But a little before dawn, she awoke with a terrible feeling of dread. Someone was calling her name, she realized. She poked her head out through the tent flaps. The air had turned cold and misty. When she stepped outside, the grass made crackling noises beneath her feet, pricked at her soles. And in the same moment that she realized it was frozen, she saw Mr. Pound standing a few yards away, his ghoulish bulk circled by frost.

"Father! Wake up!" Ana cried, her voice cracking with fear.

"He will not wake, Princess. And I have not come to harm you," Mr. Pound said. Dawn fanned out in a curtain behind him, purple shadows lapping at his coat and derby. He looked larger and more menacing than ever.

"What do you want?" Ana said.

"For you to return to the city, Princess, and complete the Bacchanalians."

"You must be joking!"

"It is not in my nature to joke, Princess. I have aided your families for thousands of years. I made them masters of mortal and Immortal alike, and I asked little in return. The Bacchanalians are my one condition. They are not negotiable."

"What if I refuse?" Ana snapped. She knew she should be careful. She did not want to provoke him into attacking her. Yet she could not believe he could speak to her about the Bacchanalians after all he had done.

Mr. Pound swept his arms to either side, drawing an invisible circle around the clearing and the lake and forests behind Ana. "Do you think your father's work is beautiful, Princess?" he asked.

The sudden change of subject confused Ana. "What do you mean?" she said.

"Which is more beautiful—the trees or the grass?"

"What difference does it make? All of it. It's all beautiful."

"Yet the trees kill the grass with their shade, do they not? And the grass smothers the seeds when they fall. And when the animal species appear, they will attack the plants, and the plants will poison the animals, and the animals will attack one another. And this is beauty?"

"It's the way nature works . . ."

"No, it is what you are accustomed to. Nature was not always this crudely balanced force, Princess. There was grace; there was beauty and perfection, once. What the gods created was united, and it will be united again."

"Why are you telling me this?" Ana said, shivering in the cold.

"Because I need you to understand, Princess. Your world is a fractured world. But when the Os Divinitas is restored, all will be made whole again. And it is you who will give me the Os Divinitas—gladly, willingly."

"The prophecy doesn't say anything about that."

"'Two of mortal and Immortal kind./In ice from a sword, flames from a shield,/Two enemies united, one bearer revealed,'" Mr. Pound recited. "The words refer to the Solomon and Georges family crests. The union of which it speaks will take place in two days, on the tournament field."

"What are you talking about?" Ana said, completely bewildered now. And then Mr. Pound told her about the Competition. Ana did not believe him. How could her mother keep such a secret for so many years? How could there not be even one image of the Competition in the family albums? And why would her family—generation after generation—have cooperated with such a bizarre arrangement?

"The Competition alone determines your family's fate, Princess—whether you believe me or not," Mr. Pound said. "It is the Bacchanalians. Or did you think dynasties were bought with practica and written examinations?"

Ana shook her head. "It doesn't matter," she said. "Even if it's true, I won't fight. And Barnaby won't fight me. He can't—you know that."

"The Prince is incompetent. But his father is not," Mr. Pound said.

"What?! King Georges?" Ana said, even more bewildered now. "I can't fight him!"

"You will, Princess. Or you will be declared forfeit. A contestant who forfeits sacrifices much more than the well-being of her family. But you will be there, I am sure. A good knight-errant never abandons her friends, does she?"

"What do you mean? What friends?" Ana said.

But the frozen circle of grass was empty now. No, not quite empty. Something fluttered in the center: a piece of paper. She stepped gingerly through the grass and picked it up. It smelled of smoke and bird dung, but there was writing on it, and when she spread it open, her heart nearly stopped.

Dear Ana, the note said. *How are you? Uno and I are fine. At present, we are living in the basement of your mother's company . . .*

"Father!" Ana shouted. "Father! Wake up! We have to go!"

Chapter 27

FIVE DAYS HAD PASSED. Uno was still unconscious, and Barnaby, beside himself with worry, refused to leave his side anymore.

"Two days, you said!" Barnaby snapped at Dr. Aẓhkima on the sixth morning. "And here it's been almost a week now. Don't you have any real doctors in this place?"

Dr. Aẓhkima, wrapping a new bandage around Uno's head, did not reply.

Isak put a hand on Barnaby's shoulder. "My father is doing everything he can, Barnaby," she said.

"Well it's not very much, is it?" Barnaby said. He sat on the floor beside Uno. "I'm not going to that firehouse today. Send someone else."

He expected Isak to give him another lecture about how everyone in the ghetto had to work, that he could not stay if he did not do something useful. But he had made himself as useful as he could. He had gone to the firehouse every day and hammered dozens upon dozens of athen bars into paper-thin sheets, and what good had it done? Uno needed him far more than the mortals needed more sheets of athen.

"All right," Isak said, rubbing her temples. "You can help out in the Bath today. That way you'll be close by."

Barnaby preferred to stay where he was, but he could see Isak was not going to allow that. At least if he worked in the Bath, he could check on Uno now and then. And he wouldn't have to wash up so many times. He nodded. Isak said someone would come for him. Then she rushed off to do whatever it was she did every day.

"Don't mind her," Dr. Azhkima said, tucking in the end of Uno's bandage. "She's a bit preoccupied right now. The Competition's only two days away."

"What's that got to do with her?" Barnaby asked, surprised that the doctor even knew about the Competition.

"Too much, unfortunately," Dr. Azhkima replied. "If the Princess wins . . . well, there's a chance she could change things for us. But if your father wins . . ."

Barnaby shuddered. "What do you mean, 'change things'?" he asked.

"We can't survive the way we are, Barnaby," Dr. Azhkima replied. "I think you can see that. But if the Princess wins, she'll control the entire Immortal world. AW and CNI will be at her command. She could force them to include us in the Environmental Management Spell. She could free us. She could move the factories to another planet. She could do anything."

"But she has to win first," Barnaby pointed out.

"That's why Isak's so busy. She has an idea how to help the Princess, if the Princess is willing to help us," Dr. Azhkima said.

The mortals seem barely able to help themselves, Barnaby thought. *How could they help Ana?*

When the doctor was done, Barnaby laid his head on Uno's shoulder. He hoped no one would come for him. But just as he was drifting off to sleep, a toe nudged him awake. He looked up to see Benjamin, of all people, standing over him. The butler's hair was badly singed in places, and he had a nasty cut on one side of his face that made him look even more sinister.

Barnaby sat up, startled. "What happened to you?" he asked.

"I was playing with matches. What do you think?" Benjamin replied. "Now get up."

Barnaby, not used to hearing Benjamin speak, rose quickly and followed Benjamin into the Bath. The facility was always in use by a few people, but today there were mortals everywhere—in the pool, around the pool, sitting on the floor, even clambering up and down the athen stairs.

"Where did all these people come from?" Barnaby asked.

"The offices and castles," Benjamin said.

He led Barnaby past the giant athen tank—the Crucible, the mortals called it. Alexander and some of the other craftspeople were climbing on top, trying to repair the pipes damaged by Ana's strange curse. It was more difficult than it appeared, for each section weighed several tons, and the ropes to hoist them could not be slung from the glass dome. But everything in the ghetto depended on the Crucible. It gave them fresh water and electricity. It gave them heat and light. And it was their only defense against the porridge of poisons floating all around them. Barnaby still did not know how it worked, but he knew that if Alexander could not fix it soon, the mortals were as good as dead.

Benjamin escorted Barnaby to the far end of the pool, where more mortals, dripping wet and exhausted, were climbing out of the hatch. Barnaby's job was to collect the contaminated clothing from the new arrivals and deposit it into a large athen bin. This proved to be more difficult than it sounded, for the clothes were spattered with dangerous wastes. Barnaby had to use athen tongs to pick them up, and as he ran back and forth between the newcomers and the bin, he grew painfully aware of how many of the mortals were injured—not just burns and bleeding heads, but hands turned to fins, faces turned to stone, whole limbs missing or transformed. It reminded him of the Testing Floor, and he had to look away, for fear he would be sick.

Whenever there was a lull in the stream of refugees, Barnaby would wash and run into the hospital to check on Uno, but there was never any change in Uno's condition. On his way back from one of these trips, he ran into Alexander, resting on the steps.

"Is it done?" he asked the dwarf.

Alexander, wiping his face with a towel, shook his head.

"Something happened to the pipes in that blast. They don't fit together anymore." The Crucible suddenly let out a deafening bang, as it tended to do every few minutes. "And we can't weld the pipes back to the peak until it stops doing that."

"When will that be?" Barnaby said.

Alexander shrugged. "A day if we're lucky. Three if we're not."

"I don't understand."

"It's just a boiler," Alexander explained, "but a boiler filled with ocean water. We pump it in from the harbor, then add organic matter—paper, grass, leaves, human waste, whatever we can find. The spells and curses in the water react with the organic stuff, and *poof!* Steam.

"The steam's supposed to get shunted to the generators and storage tanks and into the pool, but we've got the outlet capped right now, to fix the pipes. If we take the cap off before we drain the Crucible, the Bath will get sprayed from top to bottom with wastewater. But draining the Crucible takes a day, and filling it takes another day. And our batteries and water supplies are already running low. So we've been feeding the Crucible more organic matter instead, hoping the magic will burn itself out quickly."

The dwarf picked up his hammer. "It's a crude sort of machine to depend on," he said, starting back up the stairs. "But it works."

Barnaby did not think it was crude at all. An engine that could transform poison into power, waste into water—he could not imagine anything more brilliant than that. He wished he could take a closer look, but the stream of refugees had grown again.

Barnaby worked all morning and all afternoon. He ate his lunch—dried sandpig strips and biscuits—at his post, as did everyone else. Whenever there was a break in the line, he would steal a glance at the Crucible. A bucket brigade of mortals was bringing load after load of organic matter to the platform. Two mortals would spin open the hatch, let four or five buckets be unloaded, then spin the hatch closed again. As soon as they pulled a lever on the side, the Crucible would jump and give off another deafening bang.

Finally, near suppertime, all of the refugees had been taken care of. The pool was empty. Barnaby, impatient to see Uno, decontaminated himself. But just as he was changing into clean coveralls, the bell rang again.

"Oh no, not more!" Barnaby groaned.

Benjamin and the others rushed to open the metal hatch. Barnaby could not face another swarm of refugees. He watched from afar as the cover swung open and two people emerged. The first was Isak, looking wet and pale and at the end of her patience. The second, hair dripping like limp sheets, her clothes soaked and stained and torn in places, and looking even more frustrated than Isak, was Ana.

Chapter 28

ANA WAS EXHAUSTED. She and her father had searched nearly every floor of AW. They had questioned every employee they could find. No one had had any idea where Barnaby and Uno might be.

Finally, Sir Christopher had decided to ask the Queen. Ana thought this was a terrible idea, but he would not be dissuaded. Nor would he allow her to accompany him.

"There are some discussions children should not witness," he said.

Thus, while he went off for his a tête-à-tête with the Queen, Ana had continued her search. Eventually, she had tracked Barnaby and Uno's auras to the R&D laboratories. But from there, the trail had vanished again. If Isak had not appeared then, with Uno's collar in her hand . . .

Ana had followed the strange cleaning woman down into the sewers, unwinding a Breadcrumb Spell (which left tiny glowing spots only her father would be able to see) behind her. Who Isak was, where they were going, why it was necessary to hop through miles of magic-infested tunnels to get there, Isak would not say. Nor would she allow Ana to cast a Membrane Field over them. But one thing Ana was sure of: Isak had power. Ana could feel it in her aura.

Now, climbing out of the hatch into a giant steambath filled with gawking mortals, Ana wondered if she had made a mistake. Perhaps Isak didn't know where Barnaby and Uno were. Perhaps it was all just a trap.

"Where are they? You promised they would be here," she snapped, water dripping down her face.

Isak nodded behind her. The circle of mortals parted. A familiar figure clutching a soggy towel in his hands slowly approached, looking as if he had seen a ghost.

"Barnaby!" Ana cried, rushing to him. "Where have you been? What happened? Where's Uno? What are you doing here?"

Barnaby could not possibly answer—she was hugging him far too tightly. But at last she let go and stepped back. And now she saw how wan and tired he looked, as if he had been locked in a tower for forty years.

"What . . . what happened?" Ana said, brushing strands of dripping hair from her eyes. "What are you doing here? Your note said you were at AW." She pulled the crumpled, soiled, and now very soggy letter out of her pocket and showed it to Barnaby.

Barnaby's eyes widened. "I wrote that weeks ago," he said.

"I know. But I only got it this morning," Ana said. She glanced about the Bath. "What is this place? And where's Uno? I've missed his big slobbery face terribly. Is he eating?" The look on Barnaby's face stopped her. "What? Something's happened?"

Barnaby told her about Sandborn and the hammer, how Isak had rescued them and brought them to the ghetto. "It's been six days now," he said, fighting back his tears. "The doctor said he would wake up, but he hasn't, and now he's—"

"That's all they've done? Stitch him up like a ratty sock?" Ana said. "Where is he?"

Barnaby pointed to the door at the far end of the Bath. "You have to wash first . . ."

But Ana was already halfway to the hospital's door. She was certainly not going to let Uno die simply because the mortals did not know the first thing about Healing Spells, she thought. Barnaby and Isak and the other mortals chased after her. Two guards tried to stop her, but Ana knocked them aside with a Repelling Charm, then rushed into the hospital.

I'm too late! she thought when she finally found Uno. But no, he was still breathing. She cast half a dozen Healing Spells over him. One second passed, then two, then three. Then, finally, after what seemed an eternity, his legs began to twitch. He groaned. His lids fluttered, and his eyes slowly opened.

"Oh. Not you again," he muttered, peering groggily at Ana.

Ana laughed, tears flowing down her face. The others had caught up to her by now, and Barnaby, seeing Uno awake, nearly smothered him.

"I was so worried!" Barnaby cried.

"Then perhaps you should let me breathe," Uno grunted.

Barnaby loosened his hold, only to bury his nose in Uno's neck. Ana was about to do the same, but Isak suddenly grabbed her by the arm and yanked her to her feet.

"What are you doing?!" Ana shouted, jerking her arm away from Isak.

"You're contaminated!" Isak said. "You've been walking in the sewers, and you're covered with all sorts of magical muck. You've just infected everyone in this hospital—including him!" She pointed to Uno.

Ana, who had been about to blast Isak to the other end of the corridor, glanced down at her clothes. Her dress was spattered with ooze. Smoke was curling up from the bottoms of her shoes.

"I'm sorry," she said, blushing. "I didn't know."

"Well, now you do," Isak said. "No one comes in here without decontaminating first. And no one uses magic in the ghetto. Those are our rules. Do you understand that?"

"That's ridiculous," Ana said. "Uno would have died if I hadn't—"

"God forbid the dog should die," someone rasped. Ana saw a strange, rag-covered figure approaching. It was at least eight feet tall, impossibly thin, with a single golden eye shining out from the depths of its cowl.

"Who are *you*?" Ana said.

The figure bowed its head. "Curate for the Deceased, *Princess*," it said, stressing the last syllable.

"The Deceased? What is that supposed to mean?" Ana asked.

But Isak flashed the Curate a withering look. "Not now," she said, and dragged Ana and Barnaby back to the Bath.

Afterward, when everyone (including Uno) had been decontaminated again, and Ana and Barnaby had put on clean AW coveralls, Ana sat with Barnaby in the hospital, running her fingers through the clots and tangles of Uno's fur. Uno had fallen asleep again, but he was snoring, and the sound comforted Ana, as it seemed to comfort Barnaby.

They each tried to recount all that had happened since leaving Solomon Castle, but it seemed like years since they had last been together. Barnaby told Ana about his stay at AW, the R&D Bees and the Testing Floor, how Isak had rescued him and Uno. Ana told him about Mr. Pound, and Charles, and, finally, Clarissa.

"But—but Benjamin is here," Barnaby said when Ana told him how the butler had disappeared shortly after Clarissa. "You don't think . . . ?"

Ana shook her head. "I saw her cell, Barnaby," she said. "No one could survive that. Not even your father."

Then, to change the subject, she began to tell him about finding her father, and the prophecy. But Isak suddenly arrived, carrying a bundle of rags and a pair of boots.

"Oh no—she's taking you to meet the Reliquum," Barnaby whispered.

He had already told Ana about his encounter with the

Reliquum. She was not eager to meet the Curates herself. But she did as she was told.

Outside, Ana followed Isak down one dark street after another. She stepped carefully around the glowing pools of waste, dodged strands of wraith's breath in the air.

"Wouldn't Membrane Fields be a good idea?" she asked as a spellsnake shot out of a pothole. But Isak did not reply.

They passed deeper and deeper into the ghetto. Ana began to notice what looked like clusters of stars peering out at her from cellar windows and landings and rooftops. *Eyes,* she realized. She remembered the time Clarissa had brought her into the ghetto, how she had felt as if there were hundreds of eyes watching her.

"Who are they? Mortals?" she asked, gesturing toward the glimmering eyes.

"The Deceased," Isak replied without stopping.

"That's what you called that other person," Ana said. "Are they really *deceased*?"

"As good as," Isak said. They had arrived at a dead end now. Isak reached down and pulled open a heavy trapdoor. In the dim, brown light that spilled out, Ana could see a ramp leading down into the cellar.

"Follow me," Isak said. And before Ana could protest, she'd vanished into the gloom.

Chapter 29

ANA STUMBLED DOWN THE RAMP behind Isak. She could barely see, but Isak seemed unaffected by the darkness. They entered a crumbling, abandoned cellar, passed through a hole in the wall into another cellar, then another and another, the dirt floors of each littered with planks and plaster and the remnants of ancient, corroded pipes.

The labyrinth ended at a wall of athen that stretched from floor to ceiling and from one side of the cellar to the other. There was no window or grate in the wall, only the vaguest outline of a door, and, to one side, a large button.

"The Archives," Isak said.

"Your Reliquum meets in here?" Ana said, recalling what Barnaby had told her about a room in a basement. Isak shook her head. She pressed the button on the wall. There was a loud click. Then the door slowly began to swing open.

For a moment, Ana could see nothing but glaring light. Then, as her eyes adjusted, she saw books—on the shelves, on the floor, in metal boxes, stacked ten or twenty high in the corners, and scattered across an athen table in the center of the room. Above the table hung a crude lamp, and under its harsh cone of light sat a single, rag-covered figure in an athen chair, hunched over a book.

The Curate for the Deceased! Ana thought.

Isak stepped into the room. "I brought someone," she said. Ana followed, bracing herself for some acid comment from the Curate. Instead, the figure dropped its book, let out an unearthly howl, and retreated to the far corner of the room, clutching its rags and robes tightly to itself. Only then did Ana realize this was not the Curate for the Deceased; its shape beneath its rags was too short and thick. *It must be one of the other Deceased,* Ana thought.

"I'm sorry," Isak said, stepping slowly toward the ragged figure. "I know you don't want us here. But we don't have any more time."

The creature unleashed another spine-chilling howl and covered its face with a pair of scaly claws. Isak laid a hand on the creature's head, but it shoved her away, sending her sprawling across the room.

"All right. I deserved that," Isak said, struggling to her feet. "But it doesn't change anything. The Competition's in two days. If Ana doesn't help us, we're as good as dead."

"I don't care!" the creature said, startling Ana with its cracked, scraping voice.

"Yes, you do," Isak said. "That's why you're still here. But we can't wait any longer. So just show her. Please. Get it over with. If she runs away, at least she'll remember. That's what you want, isn't it? For her to remember?"

Ana had no idea what Isak was talking about, but judging from the way the creature kept shaking its head and trembling and moaning, she did not think she wanted to know.

Isak continued to plead and cajole. Finally, after several agonizing minutes, the rag person stood up. It fumbled with its claws, slowly loosened its cloak, untied its rags, unwrapped layer after layer from its arms and legs. And what emerged was unlike anything Ana had seen before: arms wiry and scaled; claws where hands should have been; legs thick and powerful as an ogre's, with feet that bulged from the weight they carried. The creature lifted the edge of its torn, distended shirt, and underneath, Ana saw knobs and stony spikes, burns running up and down the ribs.

It was only then that Ana realized this truly *was* a person, that somewhere beneath the layers of spells and curses was a human being. And though she had studied the effects of hundreds of curses, knew the baleful purpose behind each and every one, she was horrified by what she saw here. For there was no logic behind this magic. It was just harm for harm's sake, like slop poured over a painting.

"Who—who did this to you?" Ana said, her voice weak.

"You," the rag person replied.

Ana blinked. "Me? But I've never . . ." And then, as the cowl began to slip away, Ana understood. Yes, there was the face, burned and cut, but still fair, still freckled; the hair, singed down to a ragged brush, but still thick, still coppery; and those eyes— still wide and bright and glowing their polished, nutty hue, but full of so much bitterness now, so much pain.

"Clarissa?" Ana whispered.

Clarissa winced. "No. Yes. Does it matter?" she said.

Ana burst into tears. "Of course it matters!" she said. "How did you . . . ? I saw your clothes. I thought you were *dead*."

"Benjamin got me out," Clarissa said. "He found the old plans for the dungeons. He broke a hole in the wall; he chopped through the door—all those things you were too busy to do."

"I looked for you, Clarissa! I looked everywhere!" Ana said.

"Then why is it Benjamin found me, and you didn't?" Clarissa spat. "All those marvelous powers, and you can't even . . ." She began covering herself again. "I don't care what Isak says. We're all doomed anyway." She pulled her cowl back over her head. "But I want to see you lose, first. I want to see your face when King Georges takes all *your* powers away."

"Clarissa!" Isak barked.

Clarissa ran out of the room, nearly knocking Ana down as she passed her.

"She doesn't mean it," Isak said.

But Ana knew Clarissa *did* mean it. *I should have torn that castle apart,* Ana thought, sinking to the floor, weeping. *I should have blasted through every wall until I found her.* She felt a terrible ache growing in her chest—a physical pain, as if something had lodged inside her heart.

"It's not your fault," Isak said, watching her, arms folded.

"No? Then whose is it?" Ana said, wiping her face with the back of her hands.

"Mine. I'm the one who sent her to the castle."

Ana was not sure she had heard right. "What do you mean? Father gave her to me for my birthday."

"Your father told Benjamin you needed a playmate. He meant an Immortal one, but when I heard, I thought, *Why not a mortal one? Why can't the Princess's best friend be one of us?* So I sent Clarissa and had Benjamin present her to your father."

Ana could not believe her ears. Isak had sent Clarissa to Solomon Castle on purpose?

"You have to understand, Ana; we were dying," Isak said. "There were five thousand of us back then. Now there are less than two thousand. You were our only hope. You *are* our only hope."

Ana felt sick. All those years she had trusted Clarissa. All the things they had done together.

"I was just an assignment to her, then," Ana said. "Befriend the stupid Immortal Princess. Gain her trust. Make her help you."

"No. Clarissa was your *friend*. That's all she was and all she ever wanted to be. And she's still your friend, even if it's hard for her to remember right now."

Ana did not believe Isak. She did not think she could believe anything the woman said anymore. *She's no better than Mother,* Ana thought, *always plotting, always manipulating.* Sparks trickled from Ana's fingertips. If she did not get out soon, she might blast Isak into dust, she thought.

"Clarissa wants me to lose," Ana said. "She wants King Georges to take all my powers away. That hardly sounds like a friend, does it? And what did she mean by that?"

Isak nodded toward the books on the table. "She's been going through everything we have on the Competition, and the Os Divinitas, and Mr. Pound. She told me she'd found a copy of the rules for the Competition, the original agreement with Mr. Pound. Do you know what it says?"

Ana shook her head.

"Whoever loses the Competition loses her powers. *All* of them."

It took a moment for this to sink in. It took a moment for Ana to understand who she would be without her powers, what would be left. And then she ran out the door.

Chapter 30

ANA MATERIALIZED IN THE PARK. She threw the rags off her face and sucked in deep drafts of air. Lilac and apple and honeysuckle—the scents filled her, calmed her pounding heart. But she could not get Isak's words out of her head.

Whoever loses the Competition loses her powers. All of them. How was that possible? What purpose would it serve? Surely Mr. Pound had no use for an impotent Solomon or Georges. Or had Isak only been trying to frighten her? *Yes, that makes more sense,* Ana thought. Isak was a manipulator. She wanted Ana's help, and what better way to get it than to make Ana believe she was in danger, too? Hadn't she sent an eight-year-old girl to Solomon Castle to spy for her? Hadn't she all but doomed Clarissa?

Ana winced, remembering Clarissa's poor deformed body. She heard the broken, bitter chords of Clarissa's voice: *Why is it Benjamin found me, and you didn't?*

Suddenly the temperature dropped. The mist all around Ana

froze into a crystal skin on her hair and clothes. And there was Mr. Pound.

"Welcome, Princess," he said. The moon sat like an icy horn over his head. Where before there had been nothing but grass, now a circle of mortals—stiff and brittle as ceramic dolls—surrounded him, spaced like the marks on a sundial. "I see you have decided to compete."

"What do you mean?" Ana asked, dismayed by his appearance.

"Do you not know where your wanderings have led you?"

Ana glanced around. She was standing in the middle of the tournament field. The Solomon and Georges pennants had been raised over the grandstand. Tents and tables and chairs lay in orderly stacks beside the fence, waiting to be erected. Why had she spotshifted herself here? she wondered.

"I—I didn't come here to compete," Ana said. "I only came to help my friends."

"Have you helped them?" Mr. Pound said.

Ana blushed, thinking of Clarissa. "Why are you doing this?" she said.

"Why do you think? Look at me, Princess. What do you see?"

"Someone I wish were dead. Someone who's half-dead already."

"And yet I am a god, am I not?" Mr. Pound said. "And if I am a god, how can I be dead? If I am dead, how can I be a god? There is the paradox, Princess—the godhead trapped in the corrupted leavings of mortality."

His eyes flashed. One of the mortals cracked in half. Every-thing within turned to burning light, and the light flew to Mr. Pound and seeped into him the way water seeps into the ground. His body swelled and stretched. His eyes swirled with color. And then he was the same gray, passionless ghoul he had been a moment ago.

What did he do? Ana wondered. *Did he feed on the mortals? Would he die if there were no mortals left?*

"Survival is the goal of animals, not gods," Mr. Pound said, reading her thoughts. His eyes flashed again. Two more mortals cracked in half, and as before, the light flew into him.

"You wonder why I come here, why I involve myself in the petty dance of insects," he said. "The Competition is my inven-tion, Princess. It was I who began the tradition and I who made the rules. Do you know why?"

"To find the Os Divinitas," Ana said. "You think it's here, but—"

"I do not *think*," Mr. Pound said. "I *know*. The fragments are here, and when I have gathered the last and forged the Os Di-vinitas anew, my destiny will begin."

Clarissa was right! Ana thought. *The Os Divinitas is in fragments.* Was that why Mr. Pound was splitting open mortals? Was he searching for the last piece? Then why didn't he split them all open? And why did he attack Immortals sometimes?

"I will not repeat the mistakes of my father," Mr. Pound con-tinued.

"Your father?" Ana said, surprised. It was the first time she had heard him mention any parent.

"The greatest of all deities," Mr. Pound said. "The one without whom all the others would have been as nothing. Out of *his* hand came lightning and fire. Out of his hand came Eros's love and Ares's temper, Athena's bravery and Apollo's brilliance. While the others were fighting, he was *creating*. And I will resume his dream."

Which god is he talking about? Ana wondered. *Zeus?*

"Complete the Bacchanalians, Princess. Restore the Os Divinitas. Then you will see what Creation can be, what it should have been but for the treachery of Prometheus."

"What if I refuse?" Ana said.

Mr. Pound's eyes flashed. He split open two more mortals. Their halves clattered upon the ground, hollow and stiff, and everything inside turned to light.

"You *will* compete, Princess," he said. "You will strive your utmost to win. Because if you do not, you will lose your powers. And I do not think you would enjoy such a life—you, who have tasted the greatest gift of all, the creation of a living being."

So it's true, Ana thought, her chest tightening again. He would take away all her powers. She would never cast a single spell or curse again, never fly or spotshift again. She could not be a witch or knight-errant. And she would never create another thing again. She would just be Ana, ordinary Ana.

"You understand now," Mr. Pound said. "But let me show you

how simple it is." He split open another mortal. The two halves fell away, and the light leaped toward him, as before. But this time he held up his hand. The light stopped. It hovered in front of him, a glowing, eager orb.

Ana could see now that the light was not uniform. There was a center to the radiance, a greater brightness, and as she peered hard into it, she saw what looked like a tiny, ghostly Y.

"What is that?" she asked.

Mr. Pound closed his fist around the light. "Everything," he said.

And then Ana was alone again.

Ana hid beneath the bower of a weeping beech. She cried herself to sleep, and her dreams were full of broken bodies and the awful scything light of Mr. Pound's eyes.

Hours later, she awoke to the noise of hammers pounding and Decoration Spells popping. She peered through the branches to see mortals from AW and CNI putting the finishing touches on the tournament field and grandstand. Two Security Trolls watched over them, while a half-dozen Promotions Elves in glittery blue suits rushed here and there, casting Bunting Spells. Then the Queen suddenly appeared, wearing a brand-new sapphire fiber suit and looking very chipper.

Ana stepped out of her hiding place. The elves jumped, but the Queen smiled in delight.

"Anatopsis—darling! What a wonderful surprise," she said,

then wrinkled her nose. "You know, even your father used to freshen up after his little expeditions."

Ana glanced down at herself. Her AW coveralls were muddy and torn. Her boots had muck from the ghetto on them. But she did not care.

"Why didn't you tell me about the Competition, Mother?" she said. "Why didn't you tell me I could lose my powers?"

"I'm afraid I couldn't, darling," the Queen said. "Mr. Pound's quite strict about that sort of thing: what the contestants can know, when. But it wouldn't have made any difference, would it?"

"And when were you going to tell me about King Georges?"

"Last weekend, actually. But you left the castle in such a huff, I didn't have a chance. Our *former* castle, I should say. It's going to take months to rebuild, darling."

"The King is going to destroy me, Mother. You know he will. I can't believe you would do this to me."

"Oh, Archibald won't do anything of the sort," the Queen said, smiling. She reached into one of her suit pockets and pulled out, of all things, a piece of athen. It was the size of an apple and covered in hairline cracks, as if it had been dropped very hot into ice-cold water.

"Do you see this?" she said. "Do you know who did it? You, my darling. It's the most brilliant piece of sorcery in the history of witchdom, and tomorrow I expect you to do the same thing to Archibald. So let's not talk about *him* destroying *you*."

"What about Mr. Pound?" Ana said. "He thinks the Os Divinitas is here, Mother. He thinks I'm going to lead him to it."

The Queen smirked. "Honestly, darling, you're becoming positively hysterical about this silly myth. Mr. Pound will leave as soon as the Competition is over, as he always does. And if he does not, well . . . *When* you win this Competition—notice I don't say *if*—you will become the most powerful being in the history of Immortaldom. If Mr. Pound is still bothering you, you can simply send him packing. It's not a course of action I would recommend, but—"

"Stop it, Mother," Ana said.

"I am perfectly serious, Anatopsis. When you win the Competition, Archibald surrenders his powers *to you*. You will acquire his genius and his prowess and his raw magical force, and in combination with your own, you will become the most powerful Immortal the Universe has ever seen. Now, doesn't that sound like a wonderful birthday gift from a mother to her daughter?"

"Birthday *gift*?" Ana said.

"Yes, it's your birthday tomorrow. Remember? Now run along, dear. Mummy has work to do." And with that, she went off to inspect the bunting.

Chapter 31

THE IDEA CAME TO BARNABY as he was waiting for Ana to return. The mortals had finished all their bustling, and Dr. Azhkima had come to check on Uno one more time, and Barnaby had nothing to do now but sit in the hospital and listen to Uno snore. He was thinking about Clarissa and about what Ana had discovered in the dungeons. It seemed so long ago that they had all been together, and yet it could not have been more than a month. And now Clarissa was dead. Or so Ana believed.

He wished they had all run away when they'd had the chance. They could have spotshifted to another planet, or perhaps to that UCSB place Ana had mentioned. Then Uno would not be hurt, and Clarissa would not be dead, and they would not be hiding in this rotting mass of buildings.

Could he convince Ana to go now? Probably not. And he had no more chance of spotshifting himself and Uno to another planet than he did of sailing across the Maelstrom in a paper boat. *If only the Crucible could be made to suck up all the water and waste, he* thought. Then he and Uno could walk to another continent, make their home in a cave or jungle or atop a mountain somewhere. Or if they had a smaller Crucible of their own, they could take it with them and—

The idea hit him then. It seemed so obvious, he could not believe no one had thought of it before. If a large Crucible produced enough power for the entire ghetto, then surely a smaller one would generate a lot of power, too. He began to work out the design in his head—levers and chambers and pipes floating before him like the pieces of a jigsaw puzzle.

Finally, too excited to sleep, he jammed his feet into his boots and found some rags to protect his face. After making sure Uno was resting comfortably, he went off to the firehouse to tell Alexander his idea.

It was already well after dinnertime. He expected to find the master smith and one or two other craftspeople still at work. But, in fact, the workshop was running at full tilt, every bench and lathe and drill occupied by a mortal.

Barnaby wandered about, searching for Alexander, but he could not find him anywhere. *Perhaps he's still working on the Crucible,* Barnaby thought. But he did not want to go all the way back to the Bath. He was too eager to try out his idea.

He went to his workbench and pounded out a few sheets of athen to allay the suspicions of the mortals watching him. Then, when he felt no one was paying attention, he took one of the athen sheets and rolled it into a cylinder. He shaped another into a cone and welded the two athen pieces together. (Welding, luckily, did not require a flame or torch. One merely had to beat and smooth the pieces together, like lumps of clay.) Next, he cut some holes in the sides of the cylinder. He fit an athen box behind one of the holes, then made two sliding doors for it, one on the outside, one on the inside. The entire process took at least two hours, for he had to pause now and then to forge some blank sheets of athen so that the mortals would not become suspicious.

As he was beating an athen bar into a lever, Alexander suddenly appeared behind him.

"What in the world are you doing?" Alexander said.

Barnaby jumped, dropping the tongs. "N-nothing," he stammered. "I—I couldn't sleep and . . ."

Alexander lifted Barnaby's work off the bench, turned it this way and that. "A miniature Crucible," he said. "To take to the King and Queen?"

"No!" Barnaby said, alarmed. "It's—it's for the boat. You said you couldn't find an engine powerful enough to drive it, so I thought . . . I didn't mean any harm."

Alexander set the Crucible down. "Look," he said, "we need every piece of athen we have right now. And I don't think anyone's in the mood for a pleasure cruise."

Barnaby's heart sank. "I'm sorry," he said. "I just wanted to—"

"However," Alexander continued, "you give me one hundred

sheets—one hundred perfect ones, mind you; nothing rushed. And then, if we're not both dead tired, I'll help you hook it up. It might be useful yet."

Barnaby beamed with pleasure. A hundred sheets, five hundred sheets, a thousand—he would have agreed to any number, just to have this chance. And he knew that Alexander must be intrigued by the idea, for the master smith would never have allowed him to continue otherwise.

Barnaby set to work, hammering and humming so fast and furiously that the mortals nearest him were sure he would smash a hand off.

The night was half over by the time Alexander returned. Barnaby had completed his one hundred sheets and finished assembling his miniature Crucible.

"That's good work," Alexander said. "Now go get some sleep."

"No! You promised we could put it in the boat," Barnaby said.

Alexander ran a hand across his forehead. "Do you have any idea what's going on here?" he said. He studied Barnaby's face for a moment, then sighed. "No, of course you don't. All right. I'll show you what to do, but I can't stay."

Barnaby carried the miniature Crucible to the fireboat. Alexander opened the engine compartment and showed Barnaby where the propeller shaft was. It was not a perfect fit, by any means. The Crucible stuck out of the compartment, and Barnaby had to fit a new flange to the driveshaft before it would connect to the propeller shaft. But an hour or so before dawn, he finally finished.

He would have liked to start the engine, to see if it really worked, but Alexander had forbidden him. "Just hook it up, and go to bed," the dwarf had told him. "We don't need any explosions in here—especially not tonight."

So Barnaby returned to the Bath, exhausted and bleary-eyed. He washed the athen dust off, then went into the hospital. Uno was sleeping peacefully. The bandage on his head was clean— thanks to Ana. But where was she? She could not still be talking to the Reliquum.

Perhaps she left, Barnaby thought, lying down next to Uno. He hoped not, for he did not relish being alone with the mortals again. On the other hand, the Competition was only a day away now. If Ana stayed, she would have to fight his father. Barnaby did not think that was a good idea.

He was not sure how long he had been asleep, but he suddenly awoke to barking and snarling. Uno had pinned one of the rag people to the floor, and the only reason the rag person was still alive was because it had a thick, scaly claw against Uno's throat.

Barnaby jumped up to help his friend, but the rag person shoved Uno hard into him, and he and Uno went tumbling across the floor.

"It's me, you idiots!" their attacker croaked. "Clarissa!"

She pulled her cowl back. Barnaby and Uno stared at the hacksawed hair, the burns on her cheeks, the long, puckered cut across her forehead.

"It can't be! Ana said you were dead," Barnaby stammered. "How—"

"I'm not here to explain," Clarissa said. "I need to find Ana. Where is she?"

"I don't know," Barnaby said. Something in Clarissa's eyes made him nervous. They kept slipping out of focus, then sharpening again.

"Not here to *explain*. I see. Well, it's wonderful to see you, too," Uno growled. "My head's healing nicely. Thank you for asking."

"Stop it, Uno," Barnaby warned.

"Well, if she's going to sneak in here and scare the living daylights out of us, the least she can do is tell us where she's been, what happened to her, why she looks as if a family of rats is gnawing away inside her."

Uno was right, Barnaby realized. It was pain that kept flashing in and out of Clarissa's eyes. She was hurt.

"Look, I have to find Ana. It's about the Competition," Clarissa said. "When she comes back, tell her to come find me."

"I don't think she's planning to go to the Competition."

Thick yellow tears welled up in Clarissa's eyes. "I'm sure she is," she said. Then she turned and walked out through a back door.

"That was awful," Uno said. "Did you see her eyes?"

"Of course I did," Barnaby said.

"I mean what was behind them," Uno said. "When you said Ana wasn't going to compete—I swear I felt a spark going through her. I could smell it burning."

Suddenly the door to the Bath swung open. In walked Isak and Dr. Azhkima and a tall, elderly man in a too-small AW uniform. His wrists and ankles protruded from their cuffs and his hair was dripping wet, and he glanced this way and that as if every inch of the hospital were fascinating to him.

When they reached Barnaby and Uno, the man extended a long, lanky hand. "Prince Barnaby, I presume?" he said. "Delighted, delighted! I'm Sir Christopher—Ana's father."

Chapter 32

ANA RETURNED TO THE BATH, exhausted and angry. She washed off and made her way back into the hospital, and there, to her astonishment, was her father talking to Barnaby!

"Father!" Ana cried, rushing to him.

"There you are," Sir Christopher said, putting down a map he had been showing to Barnaby. He threw his arms around Ana. "I was just getting acquainted with your friends here. Barnaby's interested in my little project . . ."

"Where have you been?" Ana said. "I thought Mother had thrown you in the dungeons."

Sir Christopher laughed. "Don't be silly. She hasn't even rebuilt them yet. No, I got lost down in the sewers. I followed your Breadcrumb Spell for a mile or so, and then it disappeared. I got quite turned around. In fact, if it hadn't been for a roving band of mice—"

"Mice?"

"Oh yes. Hundreds of them. I told them I was lost, and they led me right to the entrance to this place. Very decent of them. Their leader was quite well-spoken, too, for a rodent."

"Well-spoken? You don't mean a little white mouse with pink eyes and a pink nose?" Ana said.

Sir Christopher nodded.

"Father—that was Charles! The one I told you about!"

"Oh, bother," Sir Christopher said. "Now there are all sorts of things I wish I'd asked him."

Ana peppered her father with questions, but all Sir Christopher knew was that the mice had fled Solomon Castle when it collapsed and were emigrating to the park.

"They seem to think it's a mouse paradise there—grass, shrubs, all the seeds they can eat," Sir Christopher said.

A mortal arrived with lunch—pitifully small bowls of stew. Ana, Sir Christopher, and Barnaby sat on the cots, while Uno ate his lunch on the floor. As they devoured their meals, Ana told them about her encounters with Mr. Pound and her mother. Barnaby was especially dismayed to hear that Ana would lose her powers if she forfeited or lost the Competition.

"Does—does that mean I'm going to lose mine?" he said. "I mean, it's not really a forfeit, is it, if Father decides for me?"

"I think they declared you *incompetent*," Uno growled, lifting his muzzle out of his bowl. "That means you don't have any power to lose."

Barnaby blushed. Uno was right, he realized. If his powers were taken from him, he would hardly notice—nor would anyone else.

"What I don't understand," Ana said, putting her bowl down, "is why this is so important to Mr. Pound. It's just a duel. And Mother behaves as if I've already won the Competition."

"Well, you did break all that athen," Barnaby said. "I'd say that was impressive."

"I didn't *know* I was doing it!" Ana said. "I don't even know where that stupid curse came from. In fact, if I didn't know better, I'd swear Mr. Pound put it in my head."

Isak arrived, suddenly, followed by Alexander and Benjamin and a few of the Curates from the Reliquum. Isak looked harried and impatient, and when she spoke, it was in a tone that left no room for argument.

"Go with these gentlemen," she said to Barnaby and Sir Christopher. "They'll explain our plans for tomorrow. Take Uno with you, please. I need to speak to Ana alone."

Ana watched the others shuffle out the door. She wished they would stay. She was not afraid of Isak, but she did not particularly want to talk to her, either.

"You spoke to your mother and Mr. Pound last night," Isak said, once the others were gone. "They told you the same thing, didn't they?"

Ana did not reply.

"You can't defeat King Georges by yourself," Isak continued. "Your mother couldn't. The best she could do was a draw, and that was a thousand years ago. King Georges is ten times more powerful now."

"Yes, but can he crack solid athen?" Ana said.

"No, and neither can you. Not reliably, at least. But if you want to prove me wrong . . ." Isak pointed to one of the athen lamps hanging from the ceiling.

Ana blushed. She could not even remember the words to speak, much less how to do it.

"Yes, that's what I thought," Isak said. "Now listen, Ana. There are two thousand people here who would just as soon see *you* blasted as King Georges. I've just spent five days convincing them we're going to help you instead. So tomorrow you're going to fight King Georges. You're going to defeat him. And if you can't do it by yourself, we'll step in and help you."

"What do you mean 'step in'? How? Why?" Ana said, staring at Isak.

"I can't tell you how," Isak said. "And you already know why. We won't last another thousand years, Ana. We won't last another hour, if King Georges wins." With that, she turned and walked back toward the exit.

"What about Mr. Pound?" Ana shouted after her. But Isak did not reply.

After a moment, Barnaby and Uno returned. Sir Christopher

had gone to the firehouse with Alexander, Barnaby told Ana. Ana recounted her conversation with Isak, then asked what Alexander and Benjamin had said to them.

"They didn't really say anything," Barnaby said. "They just measured us."

"Measured you? For what?" Ana said. "Rags?"

"I don't know. They measured Uno, too. But that reminds me. Clarissa was here. She said she needs to talk to you—something about the Competition."

Not knowing what else to do, they went in search of Clarissa. Ana cast a Locating Spell. It led them to an old brick boardwalk running between the Bath and the firehouse. They found Clarissa standing by the seawall, her cloak and rags fluttering in the breeze as she stared out into the harbor. In the distance, the Maelstrom swirled and roared, pulling the waters of the Solomon and Georges Rivers down into its throat. The fiery halo above it was brighter than ever now, burning a hole in the clouds above.

"*Don't ever* do that again," Clarissa croaked as they approached.

"What?" Ana said.

Clarissa pulled her cowl back. "The Locating Spell," she said, glaring at Ana. "I felt it."

Ana blushed. *It was only a Locating Spell,* she thought. But she had only to look at Clarissa to know there was no such thing as a harmless spell anymore—not to Clarissa.

"I'm sorry. I wasn't thinking," Ana said.

Clarissa rested her arms on the wall's rusted railing and looked out over the water. Shades and spirits were leaping in fiery arcs. Spellsnakes streaked the water with their phosphorescent plumes. For a long time, she did not say anything. Then, suddenly, she lifted her chin toward the water.

"I used to come here when I was little," she said. "I used to climb on this wall and pretend I was Immortal. I would throw pieces of athen into the water and pretend they were curses I was throwing at the monster in the Maelstrom. I wasn't afraid. I wasn't afraid of falling in. I wasn't afraid of the Maelstrom, or the monster. I was sure nothing could happen to me."

Clarissa squeezed the railing with her claws.

"It was the same when Isak asked me to go to Solomon Castle," she said. "I'd get to live in a castle, have all the food I could eat. I'd make friends with a real witch. And it didn't matter how much Isak warned me of the dangers. I never once thought anything terrible would happen. Just like standing on this wall."

She squeezed the railing tighter with her claws. It crumbled into rust and dust. "But now all I feel is afraid. I look at that thing, and it sickens me; it makes me want to run and hide. I look at you and Barnaby, and all I see are Immortals, people who make everyone else suffer, but never suffer themselves—*never*."

She turned to Ana. "But nothing's changed, has it?" she said. "Not the ghetto, not the Maelstrom, not the mortals or Immortals. It's just me that's changed. I can't see anything the way I used to, Ana. I look at the ghetto, and I hate it. I look at Isak, and I hate her. I look at you and Barnaby, and I hate you, too. Except it's always flickering. One moment you're the enemy; the next you're my friends; the next you're witches and warlocks swimming in power. And I'm sick of power, Ana. I'm so sick of it I'd destroy you and everyone else who has it if I had half the chance."

She leaned heavily against the railing, her body sagging with weariness. Ana and Barnaby glanced at each other, frightened. Ana put a hand on Clarissa's shoulder, but almost pulled it away again. Clarissa's body was hot!

The curses aren't done yet, Ana realized. They were still moving through Clarissa, burning away. Ana put her arms around her friend, and she could feel how much it hurt Clarissa just to stand upright, how her bones—heavy and misshapen—were straining to hold themselves together.

Clarissa buried her head in Ana's shoulder. "What am I going to do?" she sobbed, her tears burning into Ana's coveralls.

Barnaby, standing on the opposite side of Clarissa, put a hand on her shoulder. It was not an easy thing for him to do, for he did not like to be touched and was not used to touching others. But he understood what it meant to feel the way Clarissa did. People with power *knew* they would survive, but the powerless could only *hope*.

Suddenly Uno, standing with his paws on the wall, barked, "What is *that*?"

"What?" Barnaby said. Then they all saw it, the bright beams of light cutting like swords through the clouds.

"Let's get out of here," Clarissa said, pulling the cowl back over her head.

She led them to the nearest entrance to the cellars, down into the dust and darkness. Murmurs and whispers followed them. Shapes appeared, then vanished again. And always there were the eyes—gleaming and hungry and hopeless.

"Who are they?" Uno growled.

"The Deceased," Clarissa said.

"That's very morbid," Uno said.

"It's from centuries ago, when the cursed were considered dead," Clarissa said. "Now we can work and live with the others, if we want. And we have our own Curate, thanks to Isak. But everyone's still happier when we stay down here."

Suddenly the walls of the cellar began to shake. The ceiling and pipes above them flew away. And then two brilliant white needles of light scythed down toward Ana.

"Run!" Clarissa cried.

The light struck one of the shadowy figures nearby. Ana heard a tearing sound. Clarissa and Barnaby grabbed her by the arms and half dragged, half pushed her through the cellars as Uno dashed madly ahead of them. Then they were at the Archives, diving in headfirst, and the door clicked shut behind them.

Chapter 33

THERE WAS NOT A SOUND from outside the vault—not a crash, not a muffled cry, not even a vibration through the athen floor. It was as if the attack had stopped as soon as the door closed.

"Are you sure we're safe in here?" Ana gasped, getting to her feet.

Clarissa nodded, wheezing and coughing and clutching her sides. "The walls are solid athen—six inches thick," she said.

"I thought Mr. Pound *wanted* you in the Competition, Ana," Barnaby said. He had tripped and fallen among a collection of open metal trunks, and now he was having trouble extricating himself from them.

"That's the problem with gods," Uno said, snorting dust from his nose. "Always making rules, then breaking them."

Clarissa struggled to her feet. "He wasn't after Ana," she said. "If he was, she'd be gone by now. He was after the Deceased. He feeds on them every night."

"It's not night yet. And he's not feeding," Ana said. "He takes something from them. I saw it in the park."

Clarissa shuffled to the athen table. "He's taking pieces of the Os Divinitas," she said. "He's collecting them, just like I told you. And there's something else." She shoved the piles of books on the table this way and that, searching for something. "He plans to melt them back together—in his father's forge."

"Mr. Pound has a father?" Barnaby said. He and the others gathered around the table. "I shouldn't like to meet *him*. And where is this forge?"

"On Mount Olympus, I would guess," Clarissa said. She pulled a thick book out from under four others. "When Mr. Pound came for me in the dungeons, he said a very strange thing. He said, 'The greatest forgings require the greatest heat. And the greatest heat comes from within. You will be the air upon the gods' embers.'"

She flipped the book open to a page she had marked. "I don't know what he meant. But a few days ago, I was looking through this book, and it suddenly came to me: Who was the god of forges and fires?"

She pointed with a gnarled claw at an image in the book: a squat, ugly god smithing a bolt of lightning on his anvil. His arms and shoulders were thickly muscled, his back bent. One of his legs was withered and useless. "Hephaestus. He made Zeus's lightning bolts, Athena's shield, Eros's arrows. He even made the first woman, Pandora.

"And listen to this," Clarissa said, flipping to the next page. "'His sons were Lemnian and Kabeiro, and they were known as the Kabeiroi. And all who looked upon the Kabeiroi were afraid, for their eyes carried the fire of Hephaestus's forge. One burned with the light of rubies, the other with the light of sapphires, and the heat was enough to cut a man in two.'"

Ana shuddered. "That's Mr. Pound, all right," she said. "Except I would say his eyes burn with the light of diamonds."

"All right. He's the son of Hephaestus, he likes to play with fire, and he's got nasty-looking eyes," Uno grumbled. "Does it say in there how to kill him?"

"I don't think we can," Clarissa said, shutting the book. "But if we keep him from reforging the Os Divinitas, perhaps he'll weaken or go away."

"You do that. I'm going to look for something to eat," Uno said. He began sniffing about the tiny chamber. He peered into the heavy trunks Barnaby had fallen into earlier. There were six of them altogether. Four were empty and smelled of nothing more appetizing than titanium and leather and paper, but two were filled with books and papers.

"What are these for?" he asked.

"Books," Clarissa replied. "Our ancestors put the ones that were too precious to lose in those trunks and buried them around the ghetto. But when our smiths built this room, we dug the trunks up again."

"So you haven't always known how to use athen?" Barnaby said, surprised.

Clarissa shook her head. "Only in the last hundred years or

so," she said. "And it's taken us a long time to create the tools and machines."

"I don't suppose your ancestors buried any food, or a tree?" Uno said. He was not joking. If he was not allowed out soon, he would have to relieve himself in one of their precious chests, he told Clarissa.

Clarissa did not think it was safe to go out yet, but she agreed to open the door a crack and see. Dust spilled into the athen chamber. The building above was gone, the cellar open to the sky. They could hear screams in the distance. Mr. Pound was making his way through the rest of the ghetto, it seemed.

"Go quickly," Clarissa said. Uno slipped through the crack in the door. Barnaby went with him, just to be safe.

While they were gone Ana leafed through the books on the table. They were mostly colorless histories and reference books, with a few tattered journals. One book stood out, however: a jeweled, dragon-leathered tome with the Os Divinitas stamped upon its cover. Across the spine, in heavy gold letters, the title said *Prometheus, the Fire Giver*.

"What's this?" Ana asked, flipping the volume open. It was nearly all pictures—not crude sketches or photographs, but brilliant, colorful illustrations of the gods and Prometheus, all done in a mosaic style.

"An Immortal book," Clarissa said as Ana turned to an image of Prometheus standing in chains before the Pantheon. "It got mixed up in the books we brought out of Solomon Castle. Beautiful, isn't it? Look at this one."

She flipped the pages clumsily with her thick claws, stopping at a depiction of Prometheus, bloody-faced and angry, throwing something at Zeus.

"When he shattered the Os Divinitas, the force seared his eyes," Clarissa said. "One of them turned magical; the other turned to athen. When Zeus caught him and asked him what he'd done with the Os Divinitas, Prometheus tore his athen eye out and threw it at Zeus. He missed, of course, but the eye went straight through the mountain and left a hole."

Ana remembered the hole beneath the outline of the Os Divinitas on Mount Olympus. Had that truly been from Prometheus's eye? She shuddered. And did that mean the little dot in the drawings of the Os Divinitas was not part of the relic at all?

On the last page was a depiction of Prometheus chained to the rock. Above him, floating in the clouds, was a giant image of the Os Divinitas. A caption at the bottom of the page said, *None may take me against my wish. All may break me, and they break their wish.*

"Break their wish? What does that mean?" Ana said, flipping the pages. "And where are Barnaby and Uno?"

"Whoops!" Clarissa said. She shuffled to the door, pushed the button, and as soon as the door swung open, Barnaby and Uno stumbled in.

"We've been banging on that door for fifteen minutes!" Barnaby said, red-faced. "I even tried to spotshift, and you know how much I hate that."

Clarissa snorted. "Those walls are solid athen," she said. "You can't spotshift through them, or blast them, or even curse them. You should know that."

"Solid athen?" Barnaby said. He glanced up at the walls and ceiling of the chamber. "Not a crack or slit or airhole anywhere?"

"There's a ventilation system, obviously," Clarissa said. "Why?"

"I was just thinking," Barnaby said. "What if my father were locked in something like this? Could he get out?"

"Of course not," Clarissa said.

"What about Mr. Pound?"

Clarissa frowned. "I don't know," she said. "You'd have to ask Alexander. He would know, if anyone does. But if you're thinking we can just lure Mr. Pound in here with a piece of cheese and slam the door . . ."

"Of course not. He doesn't eat cheese," Barnaby said. "But if he can't break athen, we should be able to come up with some sort of trap. Come on, Uno. Let's go find Alexander."

Uno had just crawled into one of the trunks, ready to take a long nap after his strenuous day. He was not interested in venturing outside again. But Barnaby promised to stop at the Bath first and get something to eat.

Clarissa shook her head as Barnaby and Uno vanished out the door. "I don't think it's as easy as he thinks," she said. "But we should go, too. Isak and the others will be wondering where we are. Or where you are, at least." She stooped to pick up some of the books that had fallen on the floor and suddenly let out a painful gasp.

"What? What is it?" Ana said, helping her up.

"Nothing," Clarissa said, clutching her sides. "It just—it hurts."

"Here, let me help you," Ana said. "I can't lift the curses, but I can make you feel better." She began to speak an Anesthetic Spell, but Clarissa stopped her.

"Don't," Clarissa said, digging her claws into Ana's arm. "I—I don't want it. I couldn't stand it. Please."

"It's not going to *hurt* you," Ana said.

"I don't *want* it!" Clarissa snapped. "It's magic, Ana; it sprays miracles out one end and sucks twice as many back in the other, and before you know it, there's none left for anyone. You can have magic or you can have nature, Ana, but you can't have both." She pointed to the open book in front of her. "Even poor stupid Prometheus—he thought he was doing something good. He thought he was helping humans by giving them this magical gift. But look what happened—to him, to us."

"But—"

"There is no *but*, Ana! You have to promise you won't touch me with that stuff. No matter what happens. Promise!" Clarissa was nearly frantic now, her eyes white with fear.

"All right, all right. I promise. I didn't mean to upset you,"

Ana said. She was sure Clarissa was wrong. She could help her, if Clarissa would only allow it. But Ana would not push the point right now.

"I'm sorry. I'm just—" Clarissa stopped. She was staring at *Prometheus, the Fire Giver,* her face even paler than before.

"What is it?" Ana said. She didn't see anything frightening about the illustration—just a mosaic of Hephaestus standing at a wide, black forge, putting chains on Prometheus. But Clarissa looked as if she had seen Mr. Pound himself.

"N-nothing," Clarissa said. "I think . . . I need to be alone for a little while. Go. I'll find you later."

"I can't leave you now," Ana said.

"I'll be fine," Clarissa said. "Just go. Please!"

So Ana went, promising to come find Clarissa if she did not come to the Bath soon. But, of course, Clarissa did not come back to the Bath. And when, hours later, Ana went to fetch her, the chamber was deserted. There was only the same book on the table, open to the same page, and a note:

I know where the Forge is. Find Isak.

C.

Chapter 34

HORNS WERE BLOWING in Ana's heart. A hand was touching her, shaking her.

"Ana? Wake up. It's time."

Ana sat bolt upright. She had been dreaming about Mr. Pound, and forges, and large hammers pounding down on her. But she was not in a forge. She was in the hospital, and there was her father sitting on the cot beside her, still in his UCSB coveralls.

"Where is everyone?" Ana asked, seeing the hospital was empty. "Where is Isak?" Ana had spent half the night trying to find Isak. She had finally tracked her to the firehouse, but Benjamin, standing guard outside, had told Ana that Isak was in a meeting with the Reliquum. So Ana had left Clarissa's message with him. Now she wondered if that had been the wisest choice.

"They've all gone to the tournament field," Sir Christopher said. "I'm afraid it's time for us to go, too."

Ana heard the horns again—the heralds calling the contestants to the field. Her stomach knotted. She wanted to lie down again and pull the covers over her head. But there were no covers, and the cot was not very comfortable, and, in any case, she would forfeit if she did not appear soon. However afraid she was of King Georges, she was far more afraid of losing her powers.

She pulled her boots on, tied her hair back as best she could, then followed her father out the back door of the hospital.

"Why are you bringing that?" she asked, noticing a large, cloth-covered bundle under his arm. It was nearly as long as she was tall and seemed to be weighing Sir Christopher down considerably.

"You'll see when we get to the field," Sir Christopher said.

The tournament field was empty when they arrived. Every inch of space around it, however, was filled with spectators: witches and warlocks, elves, satyrs, slothworms, hydras, naiads and dryads, hags, even a few R&D Bees. The low-net-worth Immortals stood at the rear, while those of high net worth sat at linen covered tables near the front, enjoying complimentary breakfasts and chatting amiably about the coming entertainment. Watching the cream of Immortal society blast away at each other was a spectacle no one cared to miss.

The heralds, spying Ana's approach, blared out the Royal Processional. Ana took a deep breath, her heart racing, then started the long trek across the field to the grandstand, her father following close behind.

The crowd cheered. The Queen, dressed in her finest ice-blue ensemble, a sapphire tiara on her head, clapped from the royal box atop the grandstand. She looked so delighted with the proceedings one would have thought it was *her* Competition. The King, on the other hand, standing next to the Queen, looked dour and irritated. His black business suit and black crown gave him the air of someone in mourning. And in the shadows behind the thrones, Ana saw Mr. Pound, waiting like a diamond-eyed wraith.

"Hello, darling! I knew you wouldn't disappoint me," the Queen called down to Ana.

King Georges scowled. "She never does, does she, Abigail?" he grumbled. "But there's a first time for everything." He removed his crown and handed it to a servant. "Let's get this over with."

He spotshifted down to the field. Ana, who had never seen the King except in spirit projections and holographs, was instantly sorry she had come. He was nearly twice her height, at least four times heavier, and his bald head and fleshy, moth-shaped ears gave him the look of an evil djinn. Worst of all, he had bleak, bottomless eyes. The irises kept shifting colors—from red to black to ice-blue to black again—yet every color had the same dull cast to it, as if nothing could ever satisfy them. *Hopeless eyes,* Ana thought. *Eyes capable of anything.*

Mr. Pound descended to the field for the Presenting of Champions. Ana half hoped Barnaby would appear and take his father's place, but King Georges declared himself the official champion for the House of Georges, the Queen gave her consent, and that was that. It was time for the Competition to begin.

"Darling, please get off the field," the Queen called down to Sir Christopher, who was still standing beside Ana, the bundle in his arms. "You're embarrassing everyone."

"Isak sent this," Ana's father whispered to Ana, ignoring the Queen. He unwrapped the bundle and held up a sword and shield. They were not his own. In fact, the sword was very plain, and the shield, though tall, was nothing more than a paper-thin rectangle of metal with side panels. It didn't look as if it could stop a sparrow, much less a curse.

"Take them," Sir Christopher whispered to her. "They're athen."

Ana's eyes widened. An athen sword and shield! It had never occurred to her that the mortals might make *weapons* out of athen. She took them gingerly, almost afraid the athen would bite her. They were much heavier than they looked, and stiffer.

"I wish I could do this for you," Sir Christopher whispered to Ana. "But don't worry. We're waiting in the wings, if you need us."

"Clarissa, too?" Ana said.

Sir Christopher shook his head. "I'm afraid no one's seen her," he said. He kissed her on the cheek and wished her luck, then hurried off the field.

Mr. Pound read the rules from an ancient scroll, then retreated to the judges' place at the foot of the grandstand. He raised his arm. The King and Ana raised protective shields around themselves: crackling pink Membrane Fields that sparked and shimmered around them. Then Mr. Pound dropped his arm.

The King fired first: a Curse of Submission that bounced harmlessly off the top of Ana's Membrane Field. Ana fired a Decapitation Curse at the King. It struck his protective shield and ricocheted into the crowd, taking off the heads of an unfortunate Hydra. It also left a puddle of leeches writhing in the grass. The crowd gasped. King Georges laughed.

"Ha! Fourteen years I've had to listen to your mother brag about you," he said, casting a Plasmic Dissolution Curse at Ana. "She thinks you have some special gift. Is that it—filling the park with bloodsuckers?"

Ana blushed. "I don't know what you're talking about," she said. She fired a Stochastic Parallax Disrupter at him. He deflected it easily, however, and laughed at the tangled mass of squid left behind by her curse.

"This is bad luck for both of us," King Georges said, firing a staccato stream of Melancholia Bullets at Ana. They rattled off her Membrane Field and flew into a nearby grove of maples, turning them into weeping willows. "You see, I don't much care whether I win this Competition or not. I've had my fill of mortals and Immortals and demigods and all the other rot who infect my sight every day. But to lose to an *ordinary* witch—well, I'd rather wash a mortal's clothes with my teeth. So you'd better have a special gift, Princess. I'm counting on it."

The King's ramblings confused Ana. But even his most lackadaisical curses sent ripples and cracks through her Membrane

Field. She had to keep strengthening it, and this, combined with the effort of casting curses and carrying the athen sword and shield, was already beginning to tire her.

She tried the tricks that had worked so brilliantly in the SSCCR—using illusions to divide his attention, clustering curses one inside the other. But the King guessed her every move.

"I've got a thousand years on you, girl," he said, circling around her. "There are no surprises left for me. But for you . . ." He fired a Well-Digging Spell. A bottomless hole opened at Ana's feet, and she quickly leaped back. But in that moment of distraction, the King fired a Demembranization Curse. The force tore through Ana's Membrane Field. It would have torn through *her*, too, had she not still been clutching the athen shield. Instead, the curse struck the shield, making a sound like iron striking a dragon's scales, and ricocheted into the clouds.

The King stared at Ana's shield. What kind of magic was this? He fired another curse, and another, but the result was always the same.

"Where did you get that?" he asked, his face red with exertion and anger.

"From my father. You saw him give it to me," Ana replied, gasping for breath.

"Don't be insolent with me!" King Georges said. "Where did you get those weapons?"

"From us," a voice called from the edge of the tournament

field. There was a cry of alarm from the spectators. The press of Immortals parted, and a figure in AW coveralls, bearing athen sword and shield, stepped forth.

"We gave them to her," Isak said again.

The King's great bald head turned purple at the sight of Isak. "We? Who is *we*?" he asked.

Isak motioned behind her. A wall of flashing metal rose up all around the park—hundreds of mortals bearing athen shields and spears. And from behind every tree, out of every bush, from beneath the grandstand itself, more mortals appeared, carrying swords and shields and wearing athen helmets and breastplates.

An elf fainted. Several witches and warlocks spotshifted away. The rest of the spectators raised Membrane Fields around themselves, or clutched protective amulets, or simply hid beneath the picnic tables.

But the King was not intimidated. Ana could feel the ripples of power surging through him, preparing to blast the mortals out of the park. And then, as if the tournament had not taken a strange enough turn already, someone began clapping—a sharp, mocking sound that echoed dully across the field.

Chapter 35

BARNABY AND UNO AND SIR CHRISTOPHER drew up alongside
Isak as the clapping continued. Barnaby's arms were sore from carrying the athen shield. Uno—wearing an athen helmet and vest
that Alexander had fashioned for him—looked like a bear stuck
in a stovepipe.

"This is why dogs don't wage war," he panted, already exhausted from a long trot across the park.

The clapping finally stopped. "Bravo! Bravo! Good show!"
the Queen called down from the royal box. "That was the most
entertaining Competition yet, Archibald. May I come down now
and congratulate my daughter?"

"It's not over yet!" King Georges snapped. He did not look up
at the Queen, however, but kept his eyes on Isak. And the look
on his face would have murdered stone.

"Is there nothing you don't interfere in?" he said, his lips
stretched thin, his eyes silvery and cold.

The question surprised Barnaby. *Does he know Isak?* he wondered. He kept his shield close, but Isak did not look afraid.

"Ana needed our help," she said.

"You mean *you* needed *her* help," the King replied. "Tell me, Princess," he said, without taking his eyes off of Isak, "whose idea was it to give you those athen weapons? Whose idea was it to tie your future to the mortals'? Yours? Or hers?"

The King shot a crackling stream of blue fire at Isak. She jumped. The stream dissipated against her shield, but the attack alarmed Barnaby. Suddenly he was standing in front of Isak, his shield held high.

"Leave her alone!" he shouted, the words tumbling out of him before he could stop himself.

"Are you mad?" Uno whispered behind him.

The King raised an eyebrow. "You're defending this woman, boy?" he said. "You? Have you decided to grow a spine, or are her tentacles simply stuck firmly in your back?"

"She's just a mortal, Father," Barnaby said. His voice shook and his sword arm was trembling, but he found he was not as afraid as he used to be. Then again, this King—the one breathing heavily from his exertions, the one who looked as if he had not slept in a century—was not the one who used to terrify him. This was some shadow, a darker, hollow version.

The King laughed. "Just a mortal? Tell me, boy, how is it that this *mortal* can cast spells better than my *Immortal* son can? How is it that a simple, uneducated *mortal* can get all the other mortals to do her bidding? And how does a mere *mortal* get the Queen's own *daughter* to fight for her?"

The King glanced at Isak. "You must be so pleased with yourself today, Isak," he said. "Such a victory—getting the Princess to do your bidding. Will they crown you Empress tomorrow?"

Isak stared at the King. "I kept my word, Archibald," she said.

Barnaby winced. No one addressed the King by his first name. Yet there was no defiance in Isak's eyes—only exhaustion, and something else. Pity? No, that didn't make sense.

"Then it must have been a different word than the one I remember!" King Georges said. "Because that one was very specific: You were never to see him again. *Never!*"

"I didn't know he would be there," Isak said. "He just appeared . . ."

"You want me to believe it was an accident? *Nothing* you do is an accident, Isak. But perhaps you should explain it to the boy now, since he's too dim-witted to figure it out himself."

But Barnaby had understood, finally. His shield arm suddenly went limp. He stared at Isak, and so many things made sense to him now: why she had been so shocked to see him at AW, why she had helped him and brought him back to the ghetto. She was his *mother*. The word reverberated through his head—*mother*—but it brought him no warmth or comfort or satisfaction. Why hadn't she told him? Why had she let him think she was dead all these years? Why was she just standing there, shamefaced and silent?

"Oh, it's a charming little tale," King Georges said, seeing that Isak was not going to explain. "Once upon a time, you see, there was a beautiful mortal servant who worked in a castle. The castle belonged to an evil warlock with a heart of stone, and when the servant looked at him, she felt nothing. But she knew if she could capture his heart, he would do anything for her. So she pretended to love him. The warlock fell under her spell. But then the servant decided she didn't like him much after all. So she ran away, taking a certain belly-bound child with her."

Yes; yes, it was becoming clearer now—so clear it stung Barnaby's eyes. "Why didn't you tell me?" he asked Isak.

"I couldn't, Barnaby," Isak replied, a pained look on her face.

"You couldn't or you didn't want to?" Barnaby said. He was practically shouting now. He couldn't help himself. The words felt so bitter in his mouth, so caustic. "What did he promise you? Power? Did you trade me for a handful of spells?"

"No!" Isak said. "The power was an accident. It passed into me from him, but I didn't want it, Barnaby. I just . . ."

"You just what?" Barnaby shouted.

"I made a mistake!" Isak said, tears welling in her eyes. "I was young and stupid and thought, *If this warlock loves me, he'll help me. He'll help all of us.* But I didn't know what it would be like. Every time he touched me, even just my hand or my hair, it was like being a bucket at the bottom of the ocean. I drowned in power. I got so terrified, I ran away, but he followed me. And he was going to wipe us out—all of us. But when he found out I had you, Barnaby, he wanted you more than he wanted me dead. So I had to give you up! I'm sorry, but I had to!"

She was crying now. Barnaby knew he should feel sorry for her, but he did not. She was the one who had decided his life was worth less than all the other lives around her. He understood the mathematics of it all—one for several thousand—but he could not accept it.

"You broke your word," King Georges said to Isak.

"No!" Isak said.

"You went to AW because you knew he would be there. And you thought I'd never find out."

"I was already there! Don't you understand? I'd been there for *ten years!*"

King Georges stopped, mouth agape. He suddenly looked up at the Queen, who, from her vantage point in the royal box, had been watching the row between father and son, master and mistress, with great amusement.

"This was *your* idea, wasn't it?" King Georges said to her, his nostrils quivering. "*That's* why you wanted the boy at AW. You *knew* she would be there. You knew she would see him."

"You wound me, Archibald," Queen Solomon said, her face a mask of innocence. But Barnaby remembered what she had said in her office: *I've recently discovered another way in which you might be useful. You might even benefit from it. Who knows?* She *had* known Isak was there. She had *wanted* Isak to see Barnaby. Why? To infuriate the King? To distract him?

"*Nothing* wounds you, Abigail!" King Georges bellowed. "You are the vilest, coldest, most selfish beast in the Universe."

He fired a stream of curses at the Queen. The Queen, snapping a Membrane Field around herself, fired back. Sorcery blazed back and forth, and Barnaby, cowering behind his shield, was sure they would destroy everyone and everything.

Suddenly the grandstand collapsed, burying the Queen beneath bunting, canopy, and lumber. Then the King turned on the mortals. He blasted cannonballs at them, crushed them with the sheer force of his blows against their shields. He caused the ground to explode beneath their feet, the air to spin them away.

Barnaby flung every curse he could think of at his father. But they did no good. Ana jumped into the fray now, however. She fired a Paralysis Curse at the King to draw him away from the poor mortals. The curse splattered the King's Membrane Field with a school of flying fish, but it had the desired effect.

The King turned, his eyes full of such hatred, such venom, that Ana was not sure if he was looking at her or at some phantasm floating behind her. He began to rain curses down on her. They rattled and cracked against her athen shield, ricocheted into the crowd, sending bodies—mortal and Immortal—flying everywhere.

It was all Ana could do to keep from being blasted herself. She leaped and tumbled, throwing one countercurse after another at the King, but it was no use. The barrage of sorcery followed her wherever she went, sending shock waves through her shield arm and making her shoulder ache and her teeth rattle. She could not withstand such attacks much longer, she knew.

And then a Mace Curse knocked the shield right off her arm. She went tumbling backward, sure that she had made her last mistake. But as the King aimed his coup de grâce at Ana, the earth suddenly erupted beneath his feet. It bubbled and tore and frothed, rose up in high walls, and dashed against him, smothering him from head to toe in black and white and brown foam.

Ana rose, confused. The King roared. He twisted and slapped at the foam. He ripped it off in great fistfuls and flung it from him. Only then did Ana see that it was not foam but mice—hundreds and hundreds of mice! And there, dangling from the King's ear, like a tiny pink-and-white plum, was Charles!

"Charles! Get away!" Ana shouted to him. She could feel the King's power surging. In another moment, there would be nothing left of the mice, nothing left of anyone.

Then she heard Charles's tiny voice in her head once more: *You created me!* And for the first time she realized it was true: She *had* created him. Not by magic, but by something else, something inside her. Because magic could not create anything. She knew that now. It could only preserve and pervert, twist and transport, destroy. The proof was all around her—in King Georges's face, in the broken bodies strewn across the fields, the mortals cowering under their shields.

And she knew now why Mr. Pound was so certain she would lead him to the Os Divinitas, why he had been so obsessed with

Charles's origins, why he had put poor Clarissa—*Where was she?*—in that cell. Because Clarissa *did* know where the Os Divinitas was.

The curse came to her easily then. She created it out of nothing, just as she had done in Solomon Castle. Only this one was not an accident. She knew what it was, what it would do. And she knew the King would not be able to stop it.

The King, snatching Charles from his ear and throwing him high in the air, saw the curse tearing free from Ana's lips. He saw it float like a dark and impenetrable bubble toward him. He did not try to stop it, only watched it with a sad satisfaction on his face, as if he had known all along it would come to this. And then the bubble touched him. It wrapped itself around him, collapsed into nothingness. And in that moment of implosion, in the awful dream state of destruction, a river of fire suddenly erupted inside Ana, every flame a needle in her heart.

Chapter 36

AN OLD MAN: That was the first thing Barnaby saw when the smoke and dust and noise had cleared away. A shrunken, toothless old man, with milky eyes and tendrils of pearl white hair on his head. He was sitting, legs akimbo, in the mud, and if not for the torn, red-and-black crest on his suit, Barnaby would have taken him for an addled mortal.

"Father?" he whispered.

"What is left of him. His age is revealed now that all magic has been stripped from him," Mr. Pound answered.

Barnaby started. The demigod was standing a few feet away from him, his eyes glowing with a pale light Barnaby had never seen before. But what lay at his feet alarmed Barnaby far more.

"Ana!" he cried. She was curled into a ball, her hands clutched to her chest as if she were holding a doll or blanket, and there was a ghastly, bloody light on her face. Barnaby tried to rush to her, but he could not move his legs, could not move any of his limbs, in fact—only his head.

"What did you do?" Barnaby heard Sir Christopher say behind him. "If you've harmed her . . ."

"The transfer of power has stunned her," Mr. Pound said. "But she will awaken. Then will the forging begin."

"What forging?" Sir Christopher said.

Mr. Pound flicked a finger. Ana's unconscious form rolled onto its back. Her hands fell away. Now Barnaby could see the ghastly radiance coming from inside her—a bloody light that stretched from her breastbone to her lowest ribs. And the shape was all too familiar to him:

"The Os Divinitas!" Barnaby said, gazing at the glowing form. "How—how did it get there?"

"It is not the Os Divinitas," Mr. Pound said. "It is the most important part of it, however. Half has always been inside the Princess. The other half came from your father, just now. It is the union for which I have been waiting, the union foretold by the prophecy." Even as he spoke, the crack at the top of the bone vanished.

Then suddenly the rubble behind Mr. Pound disappeared in a blast of smoke, and the Queen—much to Barnaby's surprise—stepped forth, brushing dust and bits of athen from her suit.

"That is quite enough, Mr. Pound," she said. "Please collect your fee and leave. And don't for a moment think you'll be getting a favorable recommendation. I do not forgive employees who immobilize me."

Mr. Pound did not seem surprised or bothered that the Queen had managed to throw off whatever Paralysis Spell or charm he had worked on everyone. "I will collect *everything* that is owed to me, Queen," he said. "But first, I have work to do. My father's forge awaits."

His eyes flashed again, and he vanished, taking Ana with him. In the same instant, the Paralysis Spell broke. Barnaby and the others sprawled onto the ground.

"Where is he?" Sir Christopher said, leaping up first, his sword at the ready.

"At his father's forge—wherever that is," Barnaby said. He hoped it wasn't on Mount Olympus, for he was not sure anyone could follow him there. But he seemed to recall that Hephaestus had made his forge on a volcano on Earth. There were no volcanoes left, however. They had all vanished under the oceans eons ago.

The Queen, not one to waste time, cast a Locating Spell. "He seems to have taken her to the ghetto, of all places," she said, frowning. "Some sort of spa, I would say."

"The Bath?" Isak said, surprised. "Why would he take her there?"

No one had any idea. The Queen and Sir Christopher spot-shifted away at once. Barnaby was about to attempt the same, but Isak stopped him.

"Athen won't spotshift," she said, pointing to his shield and sword, "and I think you're going to need those."

She barked orders to Benjamin and Alexander to help the wounded, then led Barnaby and Uno and the rest of the mortals into the ghetto. It was hard going, and when they finally reached the Bath, the situation was even worse than Barnaby had feared. Mr. Pound had placed some sort of Membrane Field around the Bath, and Sir Christopher and the Queen, unable to force their way through, were now attempting to resolve the situation as most frightened parents would: by shouting at each other.

"There you are," the Queen said as Isak and Barnaby and the others arrived. "I don't suppose you have any brilliant ideas."

Before Isak could reply, there was a terrific explosion. The force shook the ground and knocked everyone off their feet, and when it finally subsided, the roof and walls of the Bath were gone!

"Anatopsis!" the Queen cried, flying into the magical shield. It sparked and crackled and sent her tumbling to the ground.

Sir Christopher snatched an athen spear out of the hands of one of the mortals and threw it as hard as he could. It passed through the barrier with ease, much to everyone's amazement.

"That's it! Come on!" Sir Christopher shouted. He gripped his athen shield close to him and flew headlong into the shimmering curtain. But though the shield went through easily, Sir Christopher did not. He cried out in pain and was thrown to the ground.

"We need something that will cover us completely," he

panted, clutching at his stinging hands. "A suit of athen armor, or a box of some sort."

They had no athen suits of armor, and there were no tools handy to make a box, Isak told him. Then Barnaby thought of the fireboat.

"It's big enough for six or seven of us. It's watertight," he explained. "We could seal ourselves up in it and drive right up to the Bath on the other side."

"Go!" Isak said. "Bring the boat here. We'll try to keep Mr. Pound distracted."

"But—but I don't know anything about boats!" Barnaby protested.

"Neither does anyone else. Just follow the harbor wall, and you'll be fine," Isak said. "Go!"

Barnaby opened his mouth, but before he could protest again, Sir Christopher spotshifted him and Uno to the firehouse.

"Brilliant," Uno grumbled as he stumbled behind Barnaby to the boat. He had lost his athen vest and helmet in the spotshifting, but did not mind much, as they had been very uncomfortable. "Just sail it to the Bath. What could be easier?"

"Would you rather stay here and wait for Mr. Pound to come for us?" Barnaby grumbled.

Uno jumped aboard. Barnaby, who had also lost his athen weapons in the spotshifting, went to fetch something from the workshop. He returned with a sword and a half-finished shield and hacked through the mooring lines, pushing the boat out of the slip as hard as he could.

He leaped aboard. The boat drifted slowly out into the current, then suddenly began to pick up speed.

"I'll start the engine," Barnaby said to Uno. "You steer."

"Of course. Just a moment while I slip into my opposable thumbs," Uno replied. He was having enough difficulty keeping his footing on the athen deck, let alone steering a boat.

"Just hold the wheel in your mouth," Barnaby said.

Uno closed his jaws around the wheel and was instantly sorry. Every time the boat rolled, he slid with it, which only made the boat roll more.

Barnaby stumbled to the miniature Crucible in the stern. He pumped the lever to fill the tank with water, then pulled the second lever to open the hatch. His heart nearly stopped. They had nothing to feed the engine! They needed organic matter—paper or garbage or something! He cast about frantically, looking for a stray piece of paper or rope, but there was nothing!

The boat had reached the mouth of the Solomon River by now. The water grew more and more turbulent, and in the distance, less than half a mile away, Barnaby could see the Maelstrom, spewing its fiery breath. He tore off his rags and coveralls, stuffed everything into the Crucible, then pulled the lever to close the hatch. There was a muffled explosion, the hiss of steam. He staggered back to the wheelhouse, dressed in nothing but his boots

and underclothes, and engaged the drive. The boat surged forward. But a moment later, it sputtered to a halt again.

"What's wrong? Why isn't it going?" Uno barked.

"The uniform wasn't organic," Barnaby said. "In fact, the
only organic things on this boat are you and me."

"Well I, for one, am not going to throw myself into that mu-
tant teapot," Uno said.

The boat sped faster and faster toward the Maelstrom. A few
minutes more and they would be in the swirling mouth, and then
nothing could save them.

"What if I cut off a finger?" Barnaby said. "Don't animals do
that when they're trapped—gnaw their paws off to get away?"

"I prefer to die with all of my paws on, thank you," Uno said.
"And I don't want to watch you slice yourself into Immortal tid-
bits. Can't you just spotshift us somewhere?"

Barnaby shook his head. It was nearly impossible for him to
spotshift on land, much less from the pitching wheelhouse of a
boat. He glanced out over the water toward the Bath, saw a shaft
of ruby light rising from the center of the Bath. He felt he should
know what it was, but he didn't. And there: He could see tiny
figures—Sir Christopher and the Queen—flitting back and forth
around the sparkling shield, throwing things into the Bath.

The current was drawing the boat farther and farther away out
into the harbor, closer to the Maelstrom. Barnaby could feel its
heat, could hear the ravenous roar at its heart. If they fell in

there . . . He gripped the wheel. He was going to fail Ana. He was going to fail everyone. For the first time since escaping Georges Castle, he wished he were more like his father. Or his mother.

"Don't just stand there. Do something!" Uno said, butting him with his head.

"What?" Barnaby said, shivering. The boat was pitching and rolling like a toy in a bathtub.

"I don't know. But I don't want to fall into that thing," he said, nodding toward the Maelstrom. "And the Os Divinitas is in-side Ana, remember? How do you think Old Wax Face intends to get it out?"

Barnaby shivered again. They were so close to the Maelstrom now. He could feel it sucking away his strength, clouding his mind. If only he could get away from it. If only he could think. He spun the wheel. The boat bounced and rolled. Uno slid into him, knocking them both to the floor. And as Barnaby dug his fingers into Uno's coat, he suddenly realized they had fuel after all—lots and lots of it!

Chapter 37

FLAMES WASHED OVER ANA. A red star shone in her eyes, blowing on the flames, blowing on her heart. It hurt so much. She clutched at her chest, trying to stop the pain, but her hands seemed to sink right through.

"Your Majesty?"

"Ana?"

Something tickled Ana's chin. The flames vanished. She opened her eyes and found she was not on the tournament field anymore, but stretched out on a tile floor. *The Bath*, she thought, except it didn't look like the Bath anymore. The dome and pipes and walls were gone. She was staring up into the yellow sky. And the Crucible—it was leaning precariously over her, pushed aside by a great mound of earth and bricks that had fallen in.

"Are you all right?"

Ana glanced down. There was Charles, sitting on her shoulder, his left ear torn, his fur glowing a ghastly red color. Behind him hovered Clarissa, her cowl thrown back, her scarred face lit with the same awful light. Were they ghosts? No, she could feel Charles's weight on her shoulder, Clarissa's hand on her arm. Then why were they glowing like that?

"Ana, listen," Clarissa said. "Pound's gone to stop your mother and father. They've been pelting the Bath with pieces of athen. But he'll be back any moment."

Ana could hear the cries and shouts outside, saw the same horrible flashes of light she had seen in the cellars the night before. "How—how did you get here?" she asked.

"I'm afraid I was hiding in your pocket, Your Majesty," Charles said, jumping down.

"And I've been here since morning," Clarissa said. "Didn't you read the note?"

"You said you knew where the Forge was. You didn't say anything about . . ." She struggled to sit up. Her chest hurt terribly, as if her breastbone were cracked. She glanced down and gasped at the sight of the light shining out from her.

"Is that what it looks like?" Clarissa asked.

"I—I think so," Ana whispered, staring at the glowing shape. She knew she should not be surprised. Hadn't she already guessed that was where the Os Divinitas lay? How else could she create curses that had never existed before? How else could she bring into existence a creature so perfect and alive as Charles? Nevertheless, it frightened her to see the relic actually shining out from her—not just an idea anymore, but the thing itself.

Clarissa frowned. "Shouldn't that make you stronger than him now? Why would he bring you here?"

"I don't know," Ana said. "But we'd better get out before—"

The screams and flashes of light suddenly stopped.

"He's coming!" Charles squeaked. He scurried back into a pocket of Ana's coveralls. Clarissa scrambled up the mound of rubble and disappeared into the Crucible's open hatch.

A blast of frigid air swept across Ana's face. Mr. Pound flew down, settled with a heavy *thunk* onto the tile floor.

"Congratulations, Princess," he said, his eyes glowing like milky diamonds. "The lines of mortal and Immortal power are joined at last. The prophecy is fulfilled."

"You knew all along, didn't you?" Ana said, struggling to her feet. Her legs trembled and sweat dripped into her eyes. Why was it still so hot in the Bath, even with the walls gone?

"I knew the missing fragment would appear one day," Mr. Pound replied. "But I did not know in which family, or when. Recall the prophecy, Princess: 'In ice from a sword, flames from a shield,/Two enemies united, one bearer revealed.' It hints at a union of power between the two families. But there are only two ways to create such union: by love or by hate. That is why I needed the arrangement, why I devised the Competition.

"I set the families against each other. Yet I also insisted they be taught together. Why? To ensure love or hate would perform the necessary husbandry. Either the heirs would become enamored and produce a union via their children, or they would seek to destroy each other and meld their powers on the battlefield."

"That's what happened, isn't it?" Ana said. "But there must have been other times?"

Mr. Pound shook his head. "The two families have been perfectly matched for generations. You are the first, Princess—because of what you inherited from your father and your mother. You bear the *nexus*."

"What nexus? What are you talking about?" Ana said, confused.

"Did you think the entire Os Divinitas could rest within you? No, you hold only a fraction of it. But it is the most important fraction—the heart of the divine, as it were. It unifies the powers of the Os Divinitas, and without it, all of Kronos's gifts would remain separate and inchoate, as they are in humans. But look into the Forge. You will see what I mean."

He nodded toward the pool. Ana saw the brilliant column of light radiating out of the pool. It was the same hue as the light in her chest, but at least ten times larger and brighter. This was what Clarissa had guessed at the night before, she realized: Hephaestus's Forge was here, in the Bath. And it all made sense now—the strange mosaics, the bowl carved out of a type of rock no one had ever seen before. This was why the Bath did not match any of the other buildings in the ghetto, why it had survived all these millennia when most of the other buildings had collapsed. It wasn't a bath at all.

"My father's Forge, Princess," Mr. Pound said. "It burns with

the fire of pure magic. When its heat turns white, then will we
be ready to bind the pieces of the Os Divinitas."

Ana squinted into the light. She could see an outline on the
bottom of the forge: an indentation the size and shape of the Os
Divinitas. Each leg was filled with pieces of something. *Bones!*
she realized—thousands of bones, some no bigger than eyelashes,
others as large as her hand. Except they weren't ordinary
bones—they were wishbones, nested so tightly one into another,
floating so compactly together, that they formed the two legs of
the Os Divinitas. And the tip was there, too. But in the place
where the tip and the legs joined, there was an empty space the
exact size and shape of the fragment within Ana.

Charles suddenly stuck his head out of her pocket, gasping for
air. At the sight of the Forge and Mr. Pound, he let out a terrified
squeak and scurried up onto Ana's shoulder, hiding beneath her
hair. Then he dug his claws into her neck.

"Your Majesty!" he chirruped softly. "There's a boat—in the
harbor!"

A boat in the harbor? He must be hallucinating, Ana thought. *Nothing could survive that.* But when she turned and peered through the
bloody curtain of light, she saw it. The boat was scarcely fifty
yards away and drawing closer every moment.

Barnaby! she thought, remembering what he had said about a
fireboat. Relief flooded through her. But Mr. Pound had seen the
boat as well, she realized. He would destroy them before they
could set foot in the Bath—or worse, use them to control her.

"Do you dream of rescue, Princess?" Mr. Pound said. "Have you not learned that dreams are a sign of illness—in oneself, in the world? If all were as it should be, there would be no need for dreams, would there?"

"I don't know what you're talking about," Ana said, irritated and afraid. Why was he just standing there? What was he waiting for? She glanced about the Bath, looking for something to use against him. There were lumps of athen everywhere, and an enormous section of pipe on the far side of the Bath, but nothing she could wield easily.

"Dreams breed despair," Mr. Pound replied. "Your friend Barnaby wished for a mother, and now he has found her. But she is not what he imagined, is she? A creature who sold her son to save herself. And Clarissa: She dreamed of befriending an Immortal Princess to aid her people. But now her dream is to see that Princess suffer as much as she has."

"That's not true!" Ana said.

"Are you sure? And what about you, Princess?" Mr. Pound said. "What dreams do you cling to? It does not matter. Your mother and father and the Prince and Clarissa and Isak and all the other creatures of the world have their own dreams. And the only person whose dream ever comes true is the one who first destroys all the others."

The Forge suddenly flared. The light emanating from it shifted from the color of bloody water to a brilliant white. When Ana glanced at her chest, she saw the light within her had changed as well.

"The Forge is ready," Mr. Pound said. "Now we begin."

There was no warning. His eyes flashed, and the next thing Ana knew, she was flying over the Forge. A terrible shredding sensation flooded through her, as if every cell in her body were tearing free. She twisted and turned, praying she would not land in the Forge. She cast curses blindly all around her. And then the tearing sensation suddenly vanished.

She raised her head, dizzy, confused. She was not in the Forge, but sprawled on her back on the other side. Yet Mr. Pound had meant to knock her into the Forge. How had she ended up here? She saw a dozen trees in a tight clump between herself and Mr. Pound, not saplings but giant oaks. Two of them had been blasted to stumps. *Did I make those?* she wondered, struggling to her feet. *I must have.*

But in the next moment, the trees vanished.

"Creation and Destruction are joined in you now, Princess," Mr. Pound said. "You are more powerful than any Immortal before you. But you are not a god. Nor will you ever be one."

He fired another blast of light at her. Ana dove behind an enormous athen pipe. No, she was not a god—she could see that. She was not even a match for a demigod.

She aimed the curse she had used against King Georges at him. The bubble floated across the Bath and broke, but it made no more mark on Mr. Pound than if it had been made of soap. And in the curse's wake, thousands of fat green frogs suddenly appeared, hopping across the floor.

Why is this happening? Ana thought, almost weeping with frustration. What good was all this power if she couldn't control it? She heard a *thunk* behind her. The boat had reached the Bath! She couldn't let Barnaby and Uno come up here. Mr. Pound would use them against her, the way he had used Clarissa.

"Charles!" she whispered, rolling onto her side. There was no answer. She patted the pockets of her coveralls. Had he been crushed? No, there he was—crouched inside the pipe.

"Charles—listen!" she said. "Go to the boat. Tell Barnaby and Uno they must not come out. All of you. You must stay in there no matter what happens!"

"What about you, Your Majesty?" Charles said, gripping his tail.

Ana had no chance to answer. Mr. Pound cast a Rift Curse. A chasm opened beneath the pipe, and Charles only just managed to leap to safety before the pipe tumbled away.

Ana took to the air, rolling and spinning and firing curses no one had ever dreamed of before. But it was no use. Nothing seemed to harm Mr. Pound.

"You are wasting your energies, Princess," Mr. Pound said, following her with his eyes the way a cat would follow a fly. He did not even bother to dodge Ana's curses, but let them wash over him. "You will go into the Forge. It is your destiny—and mine."

She gave up trying to hurt him. Instead, she flooded the Bath with every form of life she could think of: frogs and fish, snakes, trees, vines, locusts. They flapped and flipped toward Mr. Pound; they wrapped themselves around him. Trees pushed up beneath him. Packs of rats and wolverines bit at him. A unicorn even tried to gore him. But it was no use. As soon as he touched them, they shattered into dust.

A movement from the Crucible caught Ana's eye—the hatch slowly opening, the tip of a sword peeking out. *No!* Ana thought, but she had no chance to do anything. For suddenly a shaft of light pierced her body. It held her pinned and wriggling for a moment, like a fish on a spear, then drove her straight down into the Forge.

Chapter 38

THE LIGHT JUMBLED EVERYTHING inside Ana. Her muscles turned rigid. Her bones flexed. Every thought and impulse seemed to swirl inexorably toward a hole at the center of her sight.

You must not resist, Princess, Mr. Pound said, his voice emanating from the empty point. But Ana could not help resisting. Her hair was burning—she could smell it. The heat of the Forge was searing her face and hands.

There will be pain, Mr. Pound said. *But afterward, peace.*

Something stabbed into Ana's chest, a fiery knife cutting her open. She could feel the bone cracking, icy fingers prying at her. Suddenly her heart was open to the withering heat, and she could feel her life spurting out—not blood, but her self, the part that was Ana, that would never be anyone but Ana. She cried out, trying to break free, but every movement only made the pain worse.

Do you still cling to life, Princess? Why? It is a pitiful one. See what it could be. See what it will be, once I have the Os Divinitas.

The black hole beneath Ana swirled and spread. Water filled

it. It became a lake—the lake where she had camped with her father. Only it was infinitely clearer and purer, infinitely more inviting than any lake Ana had ever seen. Fish swam lazily under the surface. An enormous turtle poked its head up. The sun caught at the waves, teasing them into golden ripples.

And there, splashing and laughing and barking, were Barnaby and Clarissa and Uno. Except not as Ana had ever seen them before. They were happy, perfect, no worry in Uno's eyes, no clouds of gloom or loneliness on Barnaby's face. And Clarissa—she was whole again, her hair brilliant and fiery, her skin soft and untouched by magic or fire. They waved to Ana, calling to her to join them, and Ana wanted nothing more than to dive into that lake, to escape the terrible fire eating away at her . . .

I could release you, Princess. I could allow you to take your proper place in the Immortal world, as your mother intended. But you would do nothing but watch your dreams die, one by one. Your friend Clarissa would perish first—from her wounds. Then the dog—of old age or magic or both. Then Barnaby, blasted out of existence by an irritated witch or warlock. Your father and mother would be cursed by vengeful Immortals. And you—you would live forever, scarred and alone, your heart hardening until you were nothing but a stony image of yourself.

Hope without end is the best your kind can aspire to, Princess. But I offer you happiness without end. You have only to surrender what is inside you.

Yes, Ana thought, staring down into the lake. What Mr. Pound said was true. Mortals and Immortals could never rise beyond their imperfections. All they could do was wish and hope. And when all was said and done, wasn't that the source of misery? For whatever they wished for—love or health or happiness, wealth, friendship—would never come true, not in the way they envisioned. Yet they wished and wished and wished until everyone died of broken wishes.

But this . . . To dive into a perfect world, to live with her friends forever—unburdened by endless conflict, by mortals and Immortals, nature and magic. Ana could not imagine a better fate than that. Why was he tormenting her, then? Why didn't he just push her down into the Forge and be done with it?

The answer came to her suddenly, unexpectedly: *None may take me against my wish. All may break me, and they break their wish.*

He can't! she realized. *Not unless I want him to.* And she remembered, then, the faces of the victims in the dungeons, how one half had always borne a look of peace, the other a look of despair. She knew why he had always sought out the despairing, why he had preyed on the Deceased and the prisoners and the mortals. Because every piece had to be surrendered willingly. Every fragment, no matter how small, had to be offered without struggle.

The vision before her was nothing but a dream, she realized. And what was a dream to Mr. Pound? Bait for his traps.

Ana screamed. She twisted and writhed. The lake vanished, and there was nothing but fire and heat and the twin rivers of bone beneath her. And then, suddenly, miraculously, she was free!

She shot out of the Forge, elated, bewildered. Why had he let her go? Was she too strong for him? Where was he?

She looked down. There were Barnaby and Uno and Charles behind the Crucible. Why hadn't they stayed in the boat? And there was Mr. Pound, standing at the foot of the Forge. But there was something odd about him—a long gash stretching from his shoulder to his hips. Ana could see a swirling gray emptiness inside him, as if he were made of smoke, and through the smoke, a sword—Clarissa's sword!

Silence hung over the Bath. Clarissa let go of the sword and stepped away from Mr. Pound, looking more shocked than exultant, as if she had not expected her blow to do more than distract him.

For a moment, it looked as if Mr. Pound had met his fate. A simple athen blade had defeated him. Then the sword clattered to the floor. The wound vanished. And Mr. Pound turned.

"No!" Ana shouted, firing a curse.

Too late. The light from Mr. Pound's eyes struck Clarissa's shield and sent her flying high into the air. She crashed against the peak of the Crucible, rolled across the top, and landed with an awful *thud* below Ana.

"Clarissa!" Ana cried, dropping to the floor. Blood was pouring from Clarissa's mouth. Her shield arm was crushed, her legs bent at an unnatural angle.

"You have other friends here, Princess," Mr. Pound said. "Your family is outside, frozen and waiting. I can destroy them all. I can hang them on death's door and let them writhe for centuries on end. Or I can save them, and you as well. It is your choice, Princess."

Clarissa moaned, gripped Ana's sleeve. "Break it," she said, the words gurgling from her throat.

"Don't talk! You're hurt!" Ana said, tears blinding her. She started to speak a Healing Spell, but Clarissa stopped her, digging her claws into Ana's arm.

"You promised. No magic. Please. Just break it," Clarissa said.

"Break what?" Ana said, heartbroken, frustrated.

"Your friend understands better than you do, Princess," Mr. Pound called to her. "But her hope lies in me, not you. I am the gatherer of paths, the end of all struggle. I am the Unity of all things, and only through me can mortal and Immortal, magic and nature, life and death be joined."

Broken. United. Break it! Joined. None may break it, except it is your wish. My wish, Ana thought. And she understood then. She knew what it was Clarissa wanted, what Mr. Pound was afraid of, why the fragment had to be surrendered willingly. She knew why it had taken him so long to gather the pieces.

She rose slowly. The Crucible made an awful creaking sound, and when she glanced up, she saw Barnaby and Uno pushing at it with all their might. It would do no good, she knew, even if it toppled straight down on Mr. Pound. There was only one thing that would stop him. But how did one break a wish?

She stooped and picked up a fist-sized piece of athen.

"Will you throw that at me, Princess?" Mr. Pound said. "I am not Zeus, and you are not Prometheus."

No, Ana would not throw it. She clutched it tightly to her chest. She hugged it to her, letting its chill spread to her heart, and walked to the edge of the Forge. She heard the terrible groan of the Crucible, saw Mr. Pound start toward her, his eyes flashing. And then she dove into the Forge.

She felt only pain, at first, and sadness—the athen pressing into her heart, crushing into her, into the Forge, splitting what burned within and what burned without. She could destroy the Os Divinitas or it could destroy her; she could join it or it could join her—the possibilities were endless, each full of glories and horrors, riches and losses. But no matter what she chose, sorrow would follow. She knew that now.

She made her choice. Or perhaps it was a wish. She was not sure. She simply thought of all the people she loved: Clarissa and Barnaby and Uno; Charles; her father. She thought of the places she did not want to live without—the lake; the park; the oceans— and the places she never wanted to see again: Solomon Castle; the city; the ghetto. She thought of all she hated, all that had kept her bound and tormented these fourteen years, and all she had discovered in her few days of freedom.

She felt a crack, heard a great crashing sound above her. An enormous shadow bore down on her, but she slipped away. She was not in the Forge anymore. She was exploding upward and outward, her self swelling and stretching, rising high above everything. She was a medusa enveloping the world, a starfish cracking open clouds and oceans, wreaking havoc below her. It frightened her. Yet there was beauty, too: snow and rain and glittering ice following in her wake, burning sand, a sun so bright it hurt Ana's eyes.

And then it was over. She was soaring high above the earth. Everything below was blue, the most beautiful blue she had ever seen. She did not know what it was or how it had come there, but she would know soon enough, for she was falling toward it. Down and down she went, into the blue, into the greens and browns and gray. She could see the island, the city, the Bath, growing larger as she fell.

Then she saw people—her father and mother, Isak, Barnaby, Alexander, and Uno—and, in the middle of the Bath, where the Forge had been, a bright, shining egg. But no one seemed to be paying attention to the egg, and Ana thought that was very strange, for it was enormous, the size of a house, and she thought if something like that had appeared near her, she would be very curious about it. But they were all gathering around a lifeless figure Uno had tugged from the Forge, and Ana wished they would move, for she was falling fast.

Chapter 39

ANA AWOKE WITH A START. The Bath was gone. The Forge, the Crucible, the strange, silvery egg—all gone. She was on a cot in a large green tent, and she could hear voices outside, whispering.

She tried to sit up, but she could not. Her right arm was in a cast, she found. Her hands were wrapped in thick bandages, and her face smeared with some sort of medicine. Worst of all, there was a horrible ache in her chest, as if she had been kicked by a centaur.

She pushed the blankets aside. Someone had put her in an old collared shirt. There was nothing glowing beneath it. But when she unbuttoned the shirt, she found a fat, purple scar the shape of a wishbone running from her chest to her ribs. She cried out, jerking the blankets to her chin, and began to shake and weep.

"Ana! You're awake!" her father said, rushing in. At least, Ana *thought* it was her father. But through her tears, he looked strangely old, his skin mottled and papery, his neck wattled like a turkey's.

He put his arms around, saying "It's all right. Everything's go-

ing to be all right." But Ana did not think everything was going to be all right. She pressed her face into his chest and cried and cried until she could cry no more, then collapsed back onto her pillow, aching and exhausted.

Dr. Azhkima entered, no longer clumping noisily on crutches, but walking with the aid of a cane. Had someone healed his legs? *Perhaps the UCSB,* Ana thought. He was wearing one of their uniforms. Isak appeared behind him, also dressed in a UCSB uniform. She looked exhausted, as did Dr. Azhkima, but neither of them had aged the way her father had. Why was that?

"Four days," Dr. Azhkima said, setting his cane down. "I think that's a long enough nap for anyone." He began to check Ana's injuries. She had burns on her hands and face, a broken arm, a concussion, and a cracked sternum, he told her. She should not expect to get out of bed for at least another day or two.

"Where—where's Mr. Pound?" she asked as Dr. Azhkima smeared salve on her face.

"Oh, don't worry about him," her father said. "He's sealed up quite nicely, thanks to you."

"Sealed up?" Ana said.

"In the Crucible. Don't you remember? You melted it into a giant athen egg—with an ugly godling inside."

"Godling? Egg? What are you talking about?" Ana said, bewildered. She did not remember melting the Crucible. She only remembered diving into the Forge, and the pain in her chest, and the awful groaning noise above her. But wait—she had seen an egg in her dream, when she was falling. *But that couldn't have been real,* she thought.

Sir Christopher told her how Barnaby and Uno and Charles had pushed the Crucible over onto Mr. Pound just as he was trying to stop Ana. "When you broke the Os Divinitas, every piece of athen on the planet turned to soup. Pound literally got poured into his own Forge."

"But then he's not gone," Ana said, her panic returning. "He'll get out. He's got the Os Divinitas in there with him."

"He doesn't have anything," Isak said, approaching the bed. She smiled, but Ana thought there was as much pity as reassurance in her eyes. "You *broke* the Os Divinitas. Remember? Without it, Mr. Pound can't get out, because athen can only be worked by a living hand—and the one thing he is definitely not is alive."

"Lord, can't we go one day without someone mentioning that ghoul?" a familiar voice grumbled. The tent flaps parted, and in walked two figures who vaguely resembled Barnaby and Uno. Except the boy, in UCSB coveralls two sizes too big for him, looked as if someone had hacked the hair from his head with an ax, and the dog looked more like a bristly, piebald pig.

"What happened to you?" Ana said, laughing and grimacing from the pain in her chest.

Uno rolled his eyes toward Barnaby. "Ask Sir Hacks-a-Lot," he growled.

Barnaby blushed. He recounted their adventures in the boat and how they had almost fallen into the Maelstrom. "But when I grabbed on to Uno, I realized we had all the organic matter we needed: hair!" he said.

"And a nice dull sword to cut it with," Uno grumbled.

"Then we got to the Bath, and Charles told us to stay in the boat. But Mr. Pound had you in the Forge, and Clarissa was sneaking out of the Crucible, and when I saw how far the Crucible was leaning, I thought perhaps we could—"

"Clarissa!" Ana said, suddenly remembering Mr. Pound's attack. "Where is she?"

No one answered. "She's hurt, isn't she?" Ana said. "Why didn't you tell me?" She kicked the blankets aside and tried to get out of bed, but nearly fainted from the pain.

"There's nothing you can do," Isak said, pushing her back gently.

"Of course there is," Ana said. "Where is she?"

The silence turned painful. Ana saw the look on Isak's face, and on her father's, and Barnaby's, and she suddenly felt very hollow inside.

"She's gone, Ana," Isak said, tears welling in her eyes. "I'm sorry."

Ana sank slowly back onto her pillow. *It's not possible,* she thought. People didn't die. Friends, especially, didn't die. Only the characters in those books Clarissa had read died—and then only if the Prince did not arrive in time, or the spell did not work, or the sword failed, or they were betrayed by friends or family. And why should that happen when there was always magic, always miracles?

And suddenly, Ana realized she had never understood those stories before. It wasn't death that terrified mortals. It wasn't even death that killed them. It was this feeling. She did not know what to call it, yet it tore at her from the inside, and she thought she would be crippled forever by its sharpness.

"Clarissa," she whispered. And that became its name, the name of unending sorrow, the name for eternal loss.

Ana slept. When she was not sleeping, her father or Isak or Barnaby and Uno would visit her, chattering about the goings-on outside her tent: the USCB's Disaster Relief Team, the mortals and Immortals working together. But she could not follow what they were saying and did not want to.

At last, her father decided she had been in bed long enough. "You need some fresh air and exercise," he said, and he made her put on a robe and boots, and led her out of the tent.

All the stories and all the whispered conversations Ana had heard could not prepare her for what she found outside. The city was gone—every building, every street, every stone and pane of glass. The castles and towers and moats on both sides of the island were gone. The park was nothing but a muddy camp with row upon row of tents and hundreds of people—mortals, witches, warlocks, elves, dwarves—all bustling about.

Everyone wore the same green UCSB coveralls, Ana noticed, and they were all working. Some were at the cooking fires, some watering the trees and grass, some digging or carting dirt from one place to another. But most were loading pieces of athen into carts and hauling them away. For the stuff was everywhere.

"Where did all this athen come from?" Ana asked, stepping gingerly over grains and lumps and pieces the size of boulders.

"You," Sir Christopher replied.

"Me? I don't understand," Ana said.

"Neither does anyone else. But there's not a speck of magic left on the planet, and there is a lot of athen," Sir Christopher said. "So I think when you broke the Os Divinitas, you somehow converted all of the one into the other."

"You mean the Os Divinitas did," Ana said.

Sir Christopher shrugged. They walked down the slope in silence and passed into the ghetto—or what was once the ghetto. Most of the buildings had collapsed or burned to the ground, but because their materials were not magical, they had not vanished the way the Immortals' materials had. Mounds of brick and wood and rusted iron lay everywhere. In the cracks between them, Ana saw grass and tiny seedlings sprouting, mice scurrying about.

They came to the ruins of the Bath. Ana stepped to the edge of the wall, glanced down, and saw a gleaming egg below, nested in what had once been the Forge. It looked as if a giant athen bird had laid the egg and flown away, and Ana shivered at the thought of what was inside. This egg would hatch someday, she was sure. Mr. Pound would find a way. Beings like him always did.

She turned away, feeling light-headed, and remembered what her father had said earlier. "Is there no magic left at all?" she asked.

Sir Christopher shook his head. "I don't think so. At least, not here," he said. "I haven't been able to cast a single spell since you broke the Os Divinitas. And neither can you, I suspect, or anyone else who was here at the time."

"But how do you know it's really broken?" Ana said.

"Because Mr. Pound would have it, otherwise," Sir Christopher said. "That's why he tormented you so, Ana. He needed you to feel trapped and hopeless. That's why he had Barnaby sent away, and poor Clarissa put in that cell. So you would think you had no other choice but to surrender your piece of the Os Divinitas, that he was the only hope left to you."

"Then why did breaking it destroy all the magic?" Ana said, confused.

"It didn't. *You* did," Sir Christopher said. "It seems you can't break the Os Divinitas without making a choice. When Prometheus did it, he chose to put the fate of mankind above that of the gods. He gave us freedom and self-determination—and doomed himself. When you broke it . . . Well, I think you decided there were more important things than magic."

You can have magic or you can have nature, but you can't have both, Clarissa had said. *She must have been right,* Ana thought. Yet now

Ana felt as if all fire had left the world. What was her future without magic? What were all her dreams of travel and knight-errantry and planetary engineering when she could not so much as lift herself off the ground, let alone create a mussel or a mouse? And her father and mother—what would become of them? She remembered the caption in the book: *All may break me, and they break their wish*. It was true. Her wish was broken.

Chapter 40

THEY BURIED CLARISSA in a little mound overlooking the harbor. The seawall was gone. There was no grass or trees or flowers, only dirt and a path of athen stones Alexander had laid around the mound. Ana thought Clarissa would like it, however. She could look out over the blue water, see the things she had never seen before: wind and tides and clouds and rain, fish and birds. She could watch the Maelstrom spin and churn and spray its misty white breath into the air, and know that she had won. There was no monster anymore.

At dinner that night, Ana joined her father and Isak and the others around the main campfire. Her father talked about ferns and mosses and whatever else the UCSB had scheduled to be planted that day. Isak discussed plans for a mortal–Immortal council. On the other side of Ana, the Queen and King Georges were chatting happily about their favorite foods. The Queen kept batting away her few remaining hairs and wiping the King's chin with her napkin, and now and then she would lay a knobby hand on Ana's knee and say how much Ana reminded her of her daughter. She was lost in the fog of old age, Ana knew, and it made her sad. But her mother seemed happier now.

Uno appeared, carrying a bone in his mouth, and lay down beside Ana. His coat was already starting to grow in. As he gnawed his bone, Ana curled her fingers into his short, soft fur and closed her eyes, basking in the warmth of the fire. Snatches of conversation dashed against her and broke, like tiny waves.

"Then how did Barnaby get him?" she heard her father asking at one point.

"From me, of course," Isak replied. "He couldn't survive in the ghetto. And I couldn't bear the thought of Barnaby growing up all alone. So I had Alexander bring him to Georges Castle."

Uno? Are they talking about Uno? Ana thought. Suddenly there was a sharp chittering noise in her ear. She opened her eyes to find Charles sitting on the log beside her, and another white mouse—its pink nose twitching nervously—crouched behind him.

"Your Majesty, I'd like you to meet my fiancée, Eleanor," Charles said.

Ana recognized the mouse she had made at her father's campsite. "But—but how did she get here?" she asked.

"Do you know each other?" Charles said, surprised. "Eleanor just arrived yesterday, in a tent the UCSB brought in."

Eleanor stood on her hind legs and whispered something in Charles's ears. His little pink eyes opened wide. "Why, this is marvelous! We have even more in common than I thought, darling," he said.

"Imagine that," Uno muttered from his place below the mice.

"In any case, we're going to be married, Your Majesty," Charles said, "and we would like to name our first daughter after you."

"Oh, joy. Would that be 'Princess Rodent' or 'Anatopsis Cat-snack'?" Uno growled, irritated by all the mouse chatter. He much preferred the old-fashioned kind that ran at the sight of him.

Later, when Charles and Eleanor had left and Uno had gone off to find a quieter spot for his bone gnawing, Ana went to talk to Barnaby. He was engrossed in a conversation with Alexander, however, drawing plans in the dirt for some new invention—another dirt mover or well digger or other such device that the UCSB would not let him build. He did not seem to notice her, and finally she left, feeling very much alone.

She walked to the harbor and sat down at the water's edge, near Clarissa's grave. A few dandelions had begun to sprout here and there, but it was still mostly barren earth and rocks and bits of athen. She dangled her feet over the water and threw athen pebbles at the waves.

"I'm alive. I'm free. I should be happy, shouldn't I?" she said. There was no answer from anyone, and Ana had not expected one. The silence made her heart ache more, though. She missed Clarissa. She missed her more than she could bear.

The scar beneath Ana's clothes began to throb again. She

pressed her palm against it, wondering, for the hundredth time, what was inside her. If her portion of the Os Divinitas was broken, where were the pieces? Had they fallen out? Had they vanished? What did breaking it even mean?

Her father had told her everyone had fragments of the Os Divinitas inside them. The original pieces had been reproduced so many times, however, through the generations, that one could conceivably construct a thousand Os Divinitas, if one could retrieve all the fragments. "It's the combinations that are unique," he had told her. The mix of mortal and Immortal, love and hate, craft and imagination, the thousand and one traits bestowed by the Os Divinitas—those were always different. And it was the juncture of those traits, the nexus where they touched and acted as one, that was rarest of all.

Barnaby suddenly appeared out of the darkness. "There you are," he said, sitting down beside Ana. He smelled of smoke and dirt, and there were bits of leaf in his hair. "Why did you run off? I was just sketching my idea for rolling Mr. Pound into the Maelstrom."

"You're not serious?" Ana said, alarmed at the thought of anyone touching the egg.

"Of course I am. Sooner or later some idiot's going to try to let him out. Whereas if he's at the bottom of the sea . . ."

"What if it cracks open? What if it falls into an undersea volcano and melts?"

"It's athen," Barnaby said.

"That doesn't mean a thing," Ana said, remembering all the athen she had cracked.

They sat in silence for a while, Ana staring up at the night sky as Barnaby tossed pebbles into the water. There were so many stars, peppery and luminous, but it was the blackness behind them that amazed Ana: a gargantuan sheet of glass, clean and thick and black. It seemed to hold the stars in, keep them from spinning off into oblivion, and she wished she could fly up and touch it.

"Have you decided what you're going to do?" Barnaby asked, tossing a lump of athen into the water. "I mean, once you're healed and everything? Are you still going to be a knight-errant?"

Ana looked at him, amazed. "I can't cast a spell to put my socks on, Barnaby, much less spotshift to another planet or fight a dragon," she said. "How can I be a knight-errant?"

Barnaby shrugged. "You don't need magic," he said. "Look at Charles. He didn't have a thing, not even a sword, but he traipsed all through Solomon Castle and took those mice through miles of sewers. He even attacked my father."

"He had five thousand other mice helping him."

"Well, you have people to help you—"

"Stop it, Barnaby!" Ana said. "I don't have anything now. I destroyed every ounce of magic on this planet. I lost the greatest gift anyone could possibly have. I can't even dig a trench or boil a pot of water. All I can do is sit about feeling useless and afraid."

"Afraid? Afraid of what?" Barnaby said, surprised. He had never thought of Ana being afraid of anything.

"Of Mr. Pound, of course! Of what's going to happen to me. Look at me, Barnaby! I'm nothing but a scarred, stupid witch with the magic torn out of me. I'm going to spend the rest of my life wishing I could flick my fingers and make things change, wishing that some little sprout of magic is left inside me and it will grow bigger and bigger until I'm finally the way I used to be, and Clarissa is alive again, and we'll all live happily ever after—when you and I both know that is never, ever going to happen!"

She hid her face in her hands and sobbed. "I thought you of all people would understand," she said.

Barnaby opened his mouth to say something, but nothing came out. He knew what it was to be afraid all the time. But he was not afraid now. This world without magic, this world in which people grew old and there was starvation and sickness and death and where an object behaved the same way no matter what words you spoke—this was his world, the one he had wished for nearly every minute of every day. He thought it was the most wonderful thing that had ever happened to him, and he was only afraid of one thing now: that Ana would be as miserable in this world as he had been in the other.

"How do you know you destroyed *all* the magic?" he said. "I mean, Uno still talks, doesn't he? And Charles, and that other mouse you made—they still talk. So perhaps . . ."

"I don't know," Ana said, sniffing. "I just wish—"

"Wait—don't!" Barnaby said, reaching into one of his breast pockets. "I almost forgot. I saved this for you." He pulled out a wishbone.

Ana wiped her eyes. "You're not serious?" she said.

"Why not? It's just a wishbone," Barnaby said. "Nothing mythological about it. But it might bring you luck."

Ana scowled. "No one ever got luck from one of those things," she said. "Most people don't even know how to use one. First, you've got to split it exactly down the middle: one wish for each, or no wishes at all. And it won't even give you whatever you ask for. It only grants your heart's desire. How many people do you know who have gotten their heart's desire?"

"Me," Barnaby said. "Well, not exactly. I mean, I certainly didn't want all these awful things to happen. But you know, the night before Father sent me to Solomon Castle—I made Uno break one with me. It split straight down the middle, and I thought, *That's it, then,* because I didn't know how it was supposed to work, you see. I mean, I had a lot of tutors, but they called it 'kitchen magic,' and no one told me it was supposed to split right in half. But look at me, Ana. I'm not afraid anymore. I'm—I'm happy. I mean, I miss Clarissa, and I wish Mr. Pound had never come to Solomon Castle. But part of my wish came true, at least . . ."

"It's not going to grant my heart's desire," Ana said.

"How do you know?" Barnaby said. "I mean, have you ever

truly wished for anything? I don't think you have, Ana, not really." He thrust the wishbone at her. "Come on. What have you got to lose?"

"All right, all right," Ana said, wiping her nose. "Promise you won't go on and I'll do it. But just this once. And if something bad happens . . ."

"How can it be bad if it's your heart's desire?" Barnaby said, grabbing hold of one leg of the wishbone.

Of course it could be bad, Ana thought, wrapping her fingers around the other leg. Look where Clarissa's heart's desire had led. Look where the Queen's had led. And Mr. Pound's; he had no heart at all, yet his desire had nearly destroyed everything.

She closed her eyes and pulled, praying nothing would happen. But even before she heard the crack, before she felt her wishes spilling out of her—thousands and thousands of them, more than she had ever imagined—she thought she had never wanted anything more than this: to pull and be pulled, to split and join and split again.